Prais

"A perfect addition to the Snow Globe Shop Mysteries. Endearing and gutsy characters, a unique mystery, along with a surprising conclusion will keep readers enthralled and reading late into the night." ~ Julie Seedorf, Author of the Fuchsia, Brilliant, and Whistle Stop, Minnesota Cozy Mystery Series.

"There's plenty of action in Ms. Husom's novel *Cold Way to Go*, fourth in the Snow Globe Mysteries series, with newly elected Brooks Landing Mayor Camryn Brooks hot on the trail of another killer in her town." ~ Marlene Chabot, Mystery author of the Mary Malone and Matt Malone Series.

"Christine Husom brings her wealth of police procedural knowledge to the page. Intriguing characters, mystery, and suspense—it's all here. Another well-written winner to delight readers." ~ Cathlene Buchholz, Contributing Author, Minnesota Not So Nice, Cooked to Death: Lying on a Plate, Festival of Crime.

"I'm so glad the Snow Globe Shop Series is back. This cozy is a must read, especially in the winter. I love the characters and the story is very unpredictable with great twists." ~ Rhonda Gilliland, Author and Editor of the Cooked To Death Series.

"Christine Husom's latest cozy, *Cold Way to Go*, is a delightful read, complete with intrigue and a rich sense of the community you find in small towns. Cami Brooks, newly-minted mayor of Brooks Landing and proprietor of Curio Finds, has the misfortune of witnessing the local police chief's last moments. Armed with her intrepid curiosity, she uncovers layers of his secret past that reveal answers, but spark even more questions not only about his death, but about his life that even his fellow officers never knew. *Cold Way to Go* is like a mug of hot peppermint cocoa with a dollop of twisty mystery that kept me guessing until the end!" ~ Julie Holmes, Author, *Murder in Plane Sight*, Camel Press.

Also by Christine Husom

Winnebago County Mystery Series:

Murder in Winnebago County, 2008

Buried in Wolf Lake, 2009

An Altar by the River, 2010

The Noding Field Mystery, 2012

A Death in Lionel's Woods, 2013

Secret in Whitetail Lake, 2015

Firesetter in Blackwood Township, 2017

Remains in Coyote Bog, 2019

Snow Globe Shop Mystery Series:

Snow Way Out, 2015

The Iced Princess, 2015

Frosty the Dead Man, 2016

COLD
WAY
TO GO

CHRISTINE HUSOM

Copyright © 2022 by Christine Husom

All rights reserved, including the reproduction in whole or part in any format without permission, except in brief quotations used in news articles and reviews.

This book is a work of fiction.

Names, characters, locations and events are fictitious, or used fictitiously. Any resemblance to an event, locale or person, living or dead, is purely coincidental.

The wRight Press edition published November, 2022.

Cover photo from Canva. Full cover design by Precision Prints, Buffalo, MN

The wRight Press
46 Aladdin Circle NW
Buffalo, Minnesota, 55313

Printed in the United States of America

ISBN 978-1-948068-15-4

Dedication

To all my readers who have patiently waited for Cami and her friends' next adventure!

Acknowledgments

I am grateful to everyone who helped bring this book to fruition. My humble thanks to my faithful beta/proofreaders and editors who gave their time, careful reading, and sound advice: Catherine Anderson, Arlene Asfeld, Cathlene Buchholz, Barbara DeVries, Rhonda Gilliland, Elizabeth Husom, Edie Peterson and Ken Hausladen who also came up with the book's title. Also, thank you to all the respected authors who read the manuscript and wrote a review. I appreciate each one of you.

And with deep gratitude to my husband and the rest of my family for their patience and understanding when I was stowed away for hours on end, researching and writing.

Thank you all from the bottom of my heart.

1

Alice "Pinky" Nelson flapped her arms like she was ready for takeoff. "Cami Brooks, you might have known something like this would happen after you got roped into taking over as the Brooks Landing mayor."

"Pinky, really. How could I? First off, Mayor Frost asked me to take the vacant seat on the city council and died before I gave him my answer."

"I know. You felt guilted into it after poor Frosty passed the way he did."

"I admit that was part of it. You know how dumbfounded I was when the council voted me in as their new mayor. Word is Harley Creighton had his eye on the mayor's seat."

"That's what a lot of people thought all right," she said.

"Then they delegated me to talk to the police chief about his frequent and extended absences. It's not like I'm seasoned in service to the city, not like the rest of them."

"That's why. They're scared if you ask me. You don't know Chief Newel or how intimidating he can be. He probably makes every council member shiver in their boots."

I put my hand on my heart. "Reminding me how he scares people is not a good way to boost my confidence."

"Sorry, but I need to give my best friend an honest opinion, that's all. And think about it. You worked in Washington, D.C. for a senator who's not a nice person, so you have experience with difficult people in power. That awful woman fired you over something her philandering husband did. And would not even listen to your side of it."

"I'd rather not take a trip down that particular memory lane. But you bring up a good point. If Senator Zimmer wouldn't listen to me after all our years together, why should Chief Newel? Especially since I haven't even met him yet," I said.

"Hmm. Maybe you should take Erin with you. Her students listen to her, she makes sure of that. And we do too." Erin Vickerman was a fourth-grade teacher at the local elementary school and our third musketeer.

I smiled and nodded. "Yes, everyone listens to Erin. Pint-sized though she be."

"Yeah. She's scared me a time or two when she thought I was out of line." Pinky snapped the dishtowel in her hand. "Back to the police chief. Maybe you should take his next-in-command with you." Clinton Lonsbury, assistant police chief, and the man I dated.

"Ah, no. Chief Newel is Clint's boss, so no way would that work. And it crosses more than one ethical line."

"I suppose. What does Clint think about him, anyway?" Pinky asked.

"He's pretty quiet on the subject, keeps whatever opinion he has of Chief Newel to himself."

She narrowed her eyebrows. "You think he's afraid he'll lose his job if he blabs out something Newel doesn't like?"

I shrugged. "Maybe he likes the guy. From what I hear, Newel was a great chief, a top-notch guy, trusted city employee. Until about six months ago, that is."

"When he turned into a man of mysterious absences."

"Yep. The main reason I haven't met him yet. He's been absent."

She held up two fingers. "And you've been mayor two whole weeks now."

"Word is he was in Mexico over Christmas. Who knows? I'm bound and determined to get his explanation and take it from there."

"When you go in for the big showdown, you want me to hang out in the hallway as your backup?" She raised her eyebrows, stepped forward in what looked like a karate move, and snapped the towel again.

I stifled a laugh. "You have quite the weapon. I guess it'd be a good defense tactic if the dish you're drying decides to attack you. Or a pan gets out of line."

She waved the towel in a circle above her head. "Very funny, Cami."

"Got any advice on how to approach Chief Newel, what to say?"

She puffed out her chest. "Besides show up for work or turn in your badge?"

"Besides that, yes. Not to mention, the bulk of work fell on Clint's shoulders when he was gone."

"That's for darn sure and not fair at all. Clint works hard enough the way it is."

"That he does. One thing I've wondered, maybe Newel has an illness he's kept secret. Some people are proud that way," I said.

3

"Could be. Or he's leading a double life like a lotta folks suspect."

I raised one eyebrow. "The good old rumor mill."

"When people don't have facts, they make stuff up."

I chuckled. "True. What surprises me is why our now deceased mayor and the city council didn't call out Chief Newel on his behavior months ago."

"He can terrify the best of them. Like I said, he makes a lot of folks shake in their boots."

"Keep talking and you'll have me shaking in *my* boots." I feigned a quiver.

"At least your feet will be warm, given the thermal ones we need this time of year."

The doorbell on Pinky's shop, Brew Ha-Ha dinged, and two young women blew in from the frigid outdoors in puffy parkas. They stomped their boots on the welcome mat in Minnesota fashion to release any snow caught in the ridges. Both released loud exhales.

"Uff da! The wind chill dropped to twenty below zero," one said.

"Downright nippy," the other added.

Pinky pointed to the list of daily specials on the whiteboard behind the service counter. "Come in and warm yourselves with a hot cup of your favorite beverage."

The women stepped up for a closer look. "Mmm, I'll have the Kona Mocha Latte," the first one said.

"Ooh. That sounds delish. But I *have* to go with the Creamy Caramel Mocha," the second one said, and looked around. "This is like our favorite place. It's so retro, like a soda fountain where my grandparents would've hung out."

4

Pinky smiled and nodded. "That's why I kept as much of the original shop as possible. The counter and stools were in good shape, except for the padded tops, that is. And the black and white tiled floor polished up well. I hit the jackpot when I came across the gray metal chairs and found someone to make pads for the seats." She waved at the furniture.

The chairs sat around gray Formica-topped square tables with metal pedestal bases. Pinky had integrated her favorite color of pink into the décor but didn't overdo it. She wanted men to feel at home in the shop, so half the metal chairs had black vinyl padded seats and the other half had pink. Same with the counter stools. People enjoyed the pink Betty Boop "Boop-Oop-a-Doop" clock on the wall behind the counter, the Lucy and Ethel character pictures, and the other memorabilia from the 1950s.

An open archway separated Brew Ha-Ha and my shop, Curio Finds. I slipped back in there while Pinky whipped up coffee drinks for the pair.

She joined me a while later. "It's nice to have customers venture out in the cold. After the usual mid-afternoon rush, the coffee shop's been kinda dead."

"In here too. Not unusual in January after the bustle of the Christmas season."

Pinky pointed at the three boxes by the door. "Some orders came in, huh?"

"Yeah, I found some neat snow globes from a few different vendors. Christmas sales about emptied the shelves."

"People love giving snow globes for gifts," she said.

"It helps keep us in business."

My parents had opened Curio Finds, a shop that specialized in snow globes and other unique items from around the world, some years before. I found myself back in Brooks Landing, Minnesota after Senator Ramona Zimmer fired me from my director of legislative affairs position. She thought I was guilty of something I wasn't.

My parents had asked me to manage their shop and it helped me through a rough time. Plus it was good to be back with my family and friends again. The mayor thing was unplanned and unexpected. I'd agreed to take a vacant seat on the city council, and at my first meeting the other four council members voted to appoint me mayor.

They cited all my experience working in our nation's capitol. I countered that I was a researcher, not an elected official who had to navigate the political side of things. To no avail. They thought I was qualified enough. Qualified *enough?* I reluctantly agreed to do my best. They next gave me the "talk to the police chief" assignment for all the weeks he'd missed work. Lucky me.

I had set up a meet and greet with Chief Newel and pumped myself up to anticipate any curve balls he might throw me. I told myself there was no reason to feel intimidated. Newel had failed to meet the minimum expectations of his position. Police departments needed strong leaders who showed up and took care of business. A chief who citizens respected and knew they could count on.

Assistant Chief Lonsbury had filled that role far too many times.

I picked up one of the delivered packages, carried it to the counter, found a cutter, and sliced through the shipping tape. I removed a snow globe with a winter wonderland scene, shook it, and smiled. It featured kids on a skating rink that could be anywhere in Minnesota or Wisconsin or other northern region.

As I unpacked the box, I mulled over what approach to take

with Chief Newel. Kill him with kindness or sock it to him with my best shot? I decided a direct, firm, and respectful approach was best. After all, I had no idea what he might be going through on a personal level.

Maybe he had an illness and sought alternate medical treatments in places like Mexico. A desperate person often tried alternative methods in a quest for a cure, things that seemed iffy to me, but who was I to judge?

I set the empty box on the floor and picked up a pen from the counter. I hovered it over a writing pad a moment as I thought, then jotted down:

I'd like to discuss your absences from work. In the last six months you've been gone about half the time. I understand you haven't given reasons most of the time. The city council needs an explanation so we can determine the next course of action. They have been more than patient, and I can't believe they haven't fired you.

I crossed out the last sentence and dropped the pen. What Newel told me would determine how I responded. It would be prudent to record the conversation and avoid any "he said, she said" misunderstandings and potential questions down the line. I'd once been wrongly accused of an indiscretion with Senator Zimmer's husband and wished a camera or recorder had captured the actual incident.

One scenario I considered: what if our talk went south and the chief filed a lawsuit against the city? Councilor Wendell Lyon was a former attorney and conducted himself with dignity and decorum. He should've been the one to confront Newel.

Gail Spindler was another good choice. She maintained a calm presence under pressure and helped others settle down when they blew up. On the other hand, the chief might bulldoze her over.

That was not true of either Harley Creighton or Rosalie "Stormin" Gorman. By all accounts, they both had low boiling points and erupted when stressed. I'd witnessed Harley's anger displayed in a heated debate with Mayor Frost. He had threatened to quit the council over a controversial issue.

Stormin' was not afraid to butt heads with anyone. But word had it she defended Newel and made excuses for his behavior. Not the best person for a showdown with Chief Newel.

They'd decided to send in the rookie.

All had years of history with Chief Newel yet it seemed not one, with the possible exception of Rosalie Gorman, had a comfortable relationship with him. That didn't assure me the meeting would go well. On the other hand, Chief Newel might like me at first sight. *Right.*

I set the unpacked merchandise on a shelf to price in the morning. The clock on the credit card machine told me it was almost show time. If I was late, it would be the first strike against me. I slipped into boots, thermal coat, wool cap and mittens, then poked my head in Pinky's shop. "Would you rather I locked up now?"

"No reason to. Murphy's Law says if you lock the door early, you'll be sure to get a customer before closing time. Leave it unlocked, I'll be on the lookout. And hurry back 'cause I can't wait to hear what Chief Newel has to say for himself." Pinky made fists and squeezed them into her chest in an excited move. "Bye. Oh, and fingers crossed. Break a leg. Lotsa luck."

"Thanks." I smiled and headed into the dark and frosty late

afternoon air. It was two blocks to Brooks Landing City Hall and the police department that adjoined it. I'd dealt with a lot of high-powered people in Washington and survived. How bad could Chief Newel be? Compared to Senator Ramona Zimmer, for example?

My face, the only exposed flesh on my body, was half frostbitten by the time I arrived. It was after business hours for city hall, but the police department was open to the public until 5:00 p.m. I stepped into the spacious atrium entry area at 4:42 and opened the door on the right to the police station. Margaret—the receptionist I'd scared the beejeebers out of after I'd found Mayor Frost's body and had run to the station for help—was not at her post.

The door to the inner office sanctum required key card access. Chief Newel expected me but I didn't see him, or anyone else. I leaned on the front counter and called out, "Chief Newel? Anyone back there?" No answer.

"Chief Newel?" I yelled louder.

He stepped from his back office. "I'll push the button to release the lock," he said and disappeared inside. A few seconds later I heard a click, pulled the door open, and headed to his office. When I reached the door's threshold, Chief was at his desk. He looked at me as he finished licking an envelope. He frowned and stuck his tongue out partway, maybe to get rid of the taste. I hated envelope glue myself.

His eyes and mouth both opened wide, like he'd seen an apparition. The unsealed envelope fell from his hands as he clutched his neck. He stood, gasped for breath, and collapsed back down on his desk chair.

Was this real or had my stress level caused a hallucination? My body went into autopilot action. I tried to yell, "Chief Newel!"

but no sound escaped my lips. I rushed into the room, around his desk, put my hand on his shoulder, and shook it. Had he suffered a sudden heart attack? Did he have a serious health issue after all? Instincts made me search for his pulse, but I couldn't find one. I put my hand on his chest and checked for breathing. Nothing.

I struggled to get my phone from my coat pocket and dialed 911.

A woman with a raspy voice answered. "Buffalo County Dispatch. Is this an emergency?"

"A major one. Chief Newel needs help *now*. In his office. Not breathing, no pulse."

"My partner is dispatching EMS. Who are you?"

"Camryn Brooks. The, umm, mayor."

She slowed her speech. "Mayor Brooks, can you do CPR?"

Newel was huge. No way could I get him to the ground for chest compressions. "If he was on the floor, but he's in a chair."

"Have you been trained to use an AED, an automated external defibrillator? There's one at the PD."

"No." In my current state, would I be capable even if I was trained?

"EMS will arrive in under four minutes. Not to worry. I'll stay on the line with you until they arrive." Four minutes. How long had it been since the chief had stopped breathing, besides forever ago? I'd heard getting a heart started soon after it stopped was critical. The sooner the better.

Newel's open eyes appeared to be fixed on my forehead. I turned away from him and stopped myself from running away, from screaming at the top of my lungs.

"Mayor are you still with me?" the dispatcher said.

"Umm, yeah."

10

"Are you doing all right?"

"Umm, not the best."

"EMS just announced they've arrived at the PD's back door. Can you let them in?"

"Yes." I beelined to the exit.

Two EMTs I knew as Chad and Bill climbed from their rig with equipment in tow. Neither wore a jacket yet didn't shake from the cold. I pushed the door open and held it for them. Once inside, the door automatically closed.

"Lead the way," Chad told me.

We covered the short distance in seconds. Sweat beaded on my brow so I unzipped my coat and dropped it along with my cap and gloves on the floor against the wall, a few feet past the chief's office door. I stood to the right of Chief Newel's door jamb and braved a look at him in his desk chair as the EMTs rushed into his office. They wasted no time. Each slid an arm under Newel's, lifted him from the chair with some effort, and laid him on the floor.

Bill opened the AED case and turned it on. A recorded voice from inside gave them instructions. Chad pulled scissors from his case and cut through Newel's uniform and tee shirts. It took me aback, but desperate times called for desperate measures. He started chest compressions while Bill gathered two pads from the AED case and attached them to the chief's chest without interrupting Chad's CPR efforts. When the pads were attached, Chad stopped compressions.

The voice from the AED said it was analyzing, then preparing to shock. "Stand back, and do not touch the patient." The pair complied. The AED delivered the shock then said to continue CPR. Minutes later it was ready to deliver another shock. Then more compressions and one last shock. My own heart pounded through

11

the entire operation. I had never witnessed an AED used before.

I heard a door close and glanced down the hallway. Clinton Lonsbury ran toward me, his face drawn and flushed. "I heard the radio call as I got out of the shower. What in tarnation?"

When I faced Clint, tears I'd held too long flowed from their ducts. I shook my head and pointed at the chief and the men at work to save his life. Clint moved in beside me and we stood in silence, staring at the surreal scene.

"No heart rhythm," Bill said.

Chad looked at his watch. "Time of death is seventeen hundred hours, on the dot."

"He's *dead?*" Clint's voice sounded quiet and loud at the same time.

Both EMTs looked at him and stood up.

Bill gave a nod. "We sure didn't expect this. Chief Newel wasn't that old, struck me as healthy."

Chad's face was flushed. "Unreal."

"Any idea what happened?" Clint said.

They both shook their heads and Bill said, "When we got here, Chief wasn't breathing, no pulse. We started CPR and attached the AED pads. The machine detected v-tach, ventricular tachycardia, that usually responds well to defib. It delivered a series of three shocks until it didn't detect a rhythm," Bill said.

Clint sniffed a few times. "My brain's not processing this right now. All I can think is he died with his boots on. What a crass thought."

I put my hand on his arm. "Clint, it's okay."

He squeezed the bridge of his nose. "We need to call in an outside agency. The PD can't investigate our boss's death. I'll, um, get a hold of Buffalo County." Clint wrestled his phone from its case and dialed. "Mary, Clinton Lonsbury. We need the coroner, the county's on-call investigator, and their major crimes unit at the PD, ASAP. . . . This is not for public consumption yet—Chief Newel is deceased. . . . A *terrible* shock, all right. . . . Detective Garrison? Thanks."

He disconnected and turned his attention to Chad and Bill. "The detective will need to talk to you guys, but there's no need to hang around now. I'll take photos of you with the . . . victim. Chief Newel."

The phone was still in his hand, and he pushed the camera icon and shot photos of the scene with the EMTs and the chief's body.

Clint stuck his phone back in its case. "Team, you said when you got here Chief Newel wasn't breathing, didn't have a pulse, but he had a heart rhythm. What does that tell you?" Clint asked.

"Ventricular tachycardia's caused by any number of things, like heart disease that could be congenital, an inherited condition, or electrolyte disturbances, or medications, drugs," Chad explained.

"Chief never mentioned a heart condition, and we have yearly physicals. He's not on any meds that I know of. As for other drugs? No," Clint said.

"His autopsy should give us the answer," Bill said.

The EMTs gathered their equipment, offered kind words of comfort, and headed out.

2

Clint sniffed a few times and turned to me. "You found him, Camryn. Tell me what happened, what you were doing here."

I swiped at tears with the cuff of my sweater. "Umm, I was supposed to meet with him. When I got here, no one was around so I called his name. He stepped out of his office, said he'd buzz me in. then went back inside. I heard the door lock click and let myself in. When I got to his office I saw him sitting at his desk, licking an envelope—"

Clint interrupted. "Licking an envelope?"

I nodded. "I guess he wanted to finish what he was doing before we talked."

"Go on."

"Out of nowhere he got this terrified look on his face, his eyes and mouth opened wide. He dropped the envelope, grabbed his neck." I demonstrated. "He jumped up quick-like and moved his mouth like he was trying to catch a breath. Then he sunk down on his chair and didn't move after that.

"I checked for a pulse but couldn't find one. He wasn't breathing, I called nine-one-one." A quick, involuntary breath escaped from deep inside me and came out my mouth as a sucked in a "huh" sound.

"Did you touch anything besides his neck and chest?"

I thought a moment. "I guess I gave his shoulder a shake."

"Anything else?"

Had I leaned on the desk or the arm of the chair for support? I wracked my brain. "No, nothing inside the office," I said.

"Not even his phone when you called nine-one-one?"

I shook my head. "I used mine."

"You said Chief stepped into the outer office when you called to him. How did he look?"

Like a giant. "Fine, I guess. It was the first time I'd seen him in person. Sounded fine too."

Clint's eyebrows drew together. "He looked fine and sounded fine. Then he licked an envelope and stopped breathing. You didn't touch the envelope?"

"No."

"If my instincts are right, I'd say something on that envelope, or maybe on his desk, caused his death. Did you notice any powdery-like substance on his uniform?"

"No, but things went a little blurry for a bit. Plus I was zeroed in on the chief's face." I cringed at the thought.

Clint squeezed my elbow. "Understandable. Dire circumstances. Buffalo County will process the scene, get to the bottom of what happened."

"He's been your boss a long time. How are you feeling?"

His shoulder lifted. "Right now? Numb. It'll take a while for me to believe he's gone. We were colleagues for ten years. I respected him, considered him a friend, but we weren't close. It bothered me, but that's the way it was. Chief did things by the book and expected the same from his officers. Didn't give out kudos much. I think that's why we lost some officers along the way. The rest of us would've liked more attaboys, but knew that's the way he rolled."

The door lock from the reception area clicked and startled me. Clint and I both turned on a dime. The door opened and a small, dark-eyed, and dark-haired, thirty-something woman entered. She held a bucket in one hand and the other one flew to her heart when she saw us.

"Oh, Assistant Chief Lonsbury, you startled me."

"Gina." Clint acknowledged her in a low tone.

The intense way she stared at me made me question the reason. "I'm here to do the cleaning and didn't expect anyone would still be around." She directed that comment at me.

I raised my forearm. "We haven't met. I'm Camryn Brooks."

"The new mayor," Clint said.

"Yes, um hi, um Mayor." Did I make her nervous? Why? Gina cleared her throat. "You both look upset. What's the matter? Is something wrong?"

"Something's very, very wrong. Chief Newel passed away in his office this afternoon."

Gina leaned against the counter's half wall and hugged herself. The pail clunked against the wood paneling. "What do you mean? No, *no*. I don't believe it. How could he just *die*?"

"We don't have that answer yet. We're waiting for authorities to come and help us, so no cleaning here tonight. I need you to keep this quiet until we can notify his next of kin and prepare a statement for our staff, city officials, the public. You'll do that?" Clint's eyebrows lifted as if to coax an agreement from her.

She nodded. "Oh. Okay."

16

"It's best if you leave now."

"Okay." But she didn't budge.

"Gina?" Clint said.

She looked confused, bewildered when she answered. "What?"

"Do you need help getting to your car? Should I call someone to pick you up?" Clint offered.

"Um, no. I can drive. But I don't understand why Aaron died." *Aaron*. She was the first person I'd heard call him by his first name. Everyone called him Chief.

Clint shook his head. "No, but we intend to find out. We'll be in touch, Gina."

She glanced around us, toward Chief Newel's office. "Okay." After a drawn-out moment, she turned and let herself out.

Clint walked to the front counter, watched Gina leave via the front door, and returned with his eyebrows raised. "Her reaction seemed kinda personal to me."

"I thought the same thing. Think she had a crush on him?" I said.

"Could be. I know she's married."

"A married person can have a crush on someone other than their spouse. It doesn't have to be romantic. You can have a crush on a celebrity, someone you admire, someone you like being with."

Clint lifted his shoulders. "Never thought much about it."

His phone rang. "Clinton Lonsbury. . . . Back entrance? I'll meet you there." He pushed the end button. "The Buffalo County detective and major crimes deputies are here."

I followed Clint as far as Chief Newel's office and planted myself in the same spot as before.

The Buffalo County deputies stopped at the end of the

hallway and removed their outerwear. They wore black cargo pants with pockets in the front, back, and sides of the legs. Their black polo shirts had a sheriff's star and their first initial and last name embroidered above their hearts. T Garrison, E Holden, and G Thompson. Garrison had Detective under his name and the other two had Crime Scene Team.

I'd met Tim Garrison on another case before he made detective. He was seasoned, serious, and straightforward. His gravelly voice paired well with the deep lines that crisscrossed his cheeks and forehead.

Emily Holden and Greg Thompson were the same team that had responded to City Hall the infamous night poor Frosty died. Both were in their thirties, the same height, around 5'10, and had clean cut looks. Holden wore an ever-present single frown line like she was a deep thinker. Thompson had sparkly brown eyes that had no doubt drawn in lots of people over the years.

We greeted one another with mumbled words and nods. The three pulled on shoe coverings and vinyl gloves. Thompson carried an equipment bag and set it down outside Chief Newel's door.

Clint tipped his head in my direction. "Camryn here witnessed the chief's death."

They all raised their eyebrows and looked at me. I could only imagine what they thought. The previous month I'd happened upon Mayor Frost's body, and now had the misfortune of being with Chief Newel when he died. I figured none of them would invite me over for dinner anytime soon.

Garrison pulled a memo pad and pen from a side pocket. "Mayor Brooks, can you tell me what happened? Walk me through the event starting from when you arrived here. You never know what might prove to be useful."

"I had a meeting scheduled with Chief Newel."

"So he was expecting you?"

"Yes."

"What was the purpose of the meeting?" Garrison said.

"Chief Newel had missed a lot of work the last months. The council wanted me to talk to him, find out what was going on. The fact is, his job was on the line."

Garrison looked up from his pad. "I see. Did Chief Newel know that?"

"He must have guessed it. I'd never met him in person. He was out again yesterday. When I called this morning, I half expected him not to answer. I introduced myself, asked to meet with him. He was not friendly. In fact, he was gruff and pretty much ordered me to report to his office at four-forty-five today."

"He didn't ask what the meeting was about?" Garrison said.

I shook my head. "No."

"Hmm. He gave you a specific time. He likely knew he was at the end of his grace period and didn't want others in the office to witness a probable showdown."

"Maybe." I shrugged.

Garrison narrowed his eyes. "From what I've heard, he missed a lot of the monthly meetings the sheriff has with the state patrol and police chiefs in the county. With only three PDs, and Brooks Landing being the largest, it's been mentioned. More than once."

"That's true. I'm the one who filled in for him when he wasn't around," Clint said.

"Yep, heard that too." Garrison turned back to me. "Anyone else know about the meeting?"

"Besides the city council members—who didn't know when

we were meeting—I confided in my friend Pinky, ah, Alice Nelson. Her coffee shop adjoins mine and we watch each other's shops when we need to. No idea if the chief told anyone."

Clint lifted his hand. "He didn't tell me. Maybe because of my relationship with Camryn."

"Oh?" Garrison said.

"We started dating last month, before she got appointed mayor and became one of my bosses. And the chief's too. As they like to say, it's complicated."

"I didn't tell Clint because Newel was his boss, and it would've put us all in an unethical and awkward position," I offered.

Garrison cleared his throat. "Camryn, getting back to your friend Alice. She have any connection to Chief Newel?"

"No connection I know of." My phone rang, and I looked at its face. Pinky. As if her sixth sense had alerted her. "Detective, is it okay if I answer? My friend Pinky must be wondering what's taking me so long. She worries about me." With good reason at times.

He nodded. "Go ahead."

The officers watched as I pushed the talk button. "Hi, Pinky."

"Cami, thank God you're alive. You've been gone so long my nerves are tied up in knots. Where are you anyway?"

"Still at the police station. I got delayed here."

"After your meeting? You should have called, you know I was worried about the whole thing because of who you'd be with," she said.

"I know, and I'm sorry. Chief Newel couldn't meet with me after all. I'm here with Clint and it will be a while yet. It's past closing time, so head on home. I'll catch up with you later."

"All righty then. Since you got nothing to report, and you're safe with Clint, I'll let you go. See you tomorrow, Cami."

Nothing to report. Not nothing, it's a really big *something*. "Bye, Pink." I pushed the end button and slipped the phone in my pocket.

Garrison wiggled his pen. "Got a little sidetracked. Mayor Brooks, continue with your account."

I spelled out every detail and Clint nodded a couple times, like he was mentally confirming what I'd told him earlier.

"Chief Newel licked an envelope, seemed to have a bad reaction to it, and then died?" Garrison summed up.

"I don't know if it had anything to do with the envelope, or if he had a sudden heart attack, or what," I said.

He raised his eyebrows. "You're right. The envelope may have nothing to do with his death. But it's possible something was on it, or inside it, or on his desk, that caused it."

"The scenario I surmised," Clint repeated what the EMTs said about the chief's heart rhythm, possible reasons his heart had stopped. "Chief never mentioned a problem, but a person can die not knowing something was wrong with their heart."

"Happens fairly often. Especially sad when it's a young athlete." Garrison dropped his pad and pen in a pocket. "Team, let's get started processing. Doctor Long will be here any time now." Trudy Long was the county coroner.

Emily Holden pulled a camera from the bag. She and Greg Thompson visually scanned the office and its contents before they stepped inside. Detective Garrison pulled on gloves and hung back until Holden finished photographing the scene. All three put on N-95 face masks, then spent time checking the few items on Chief Newel's desk. He was a bigger neat freak than me.

Garrison withdrew a flashlight from his belt, turned it on, and shined it on the desk. "I don't see any powdery substance on, or around, the envelope. Let's turn it over, see who it's addressed to."

Thompson used a long scissor handle tweezers and flipped the envelope. "Fresh Start Rehabilitation. It's west of town, Chatsworth Township. Lots of our arrestees are court ordered to treatment there, mostly for alcohol, but some for drug addiction too."

Holden snapped a photo of the envelope.

Garrison singled out Clint. "You think Newel had an addiction problem?"

"I have no reason to think that, no. We didn't hang out socially, but I've been at his house a number of times, and odd hours. Never noticed he'd been consuming alcohol, much less that he had a problem with it. No clue about other chemicals, but his behavior didn't indicate he did," Clint said.

"Some people are good at keeping it hidden. At least for a while," Garrison said.

Clint shrugged, shook his head. "The chief was good at keeping a lot of things hidden, so it's a possibility."

"Maybe the reason he was absent from work so much?" I said.

"I considered that a number of times. Just never saw evidence of it," Clint said.

"Let's see what's inside the envelope," Garrison said.

Thompson turned it with the tweezers and pulled out a personal check. "Hmm, a check Newel wrote to Fresh Start for five hundred dollars."

"Wow," slipped out of my mouth.

"That's a hefty amount, all right. I'll look into it, see if he got treatment there, or if someone he cares about did," Garrison said.

"Or it might be one of the organizations he supports," Holden said.

Thompson pointed at the desk. "Envelope is from Fresh Start Rehab, has their logo on it. Someone went to the trouble of hand addressing it to Newel. A personal touch. Looks like there might be a note underneath, partially sticking out."

He lifted the envelope with the tweezers. "Handwritten too. It says, 'Thank you for your generous support. All my best, Matt.' Ha, I know Matt, Matthew Anderle. He serves as both the CEO and CFO at Fresh Start. Newel might've been a regular contributor," Thompson said.

"Probably why he got a personal note," Holden said.

"I'll head over to the center during business hours tomorrow, get some answers," Garrison said. "In the meantime, let's get these papers bagged and tagged. The crime lab can test 'em for chemicals, see if anything turns up. Not many papers on the desk and we'll collect 'em all."

3

Buffalo County Coroner Dr. Trudy Long arrived as the crime team marked and sealed evidence bags. Clint let her in the back door. She was around forty with a golden-brown pixie bob that framed her comely, small face, and presented a kind demeanor. She'd given me sage advice when I first met her at a death scene and it had established a sense of kinship with her from then on.

When they came down the hall, Long's eyes landed on me. She frowned, nodded, and went into Chief Newel's office. The Buffalo County deputies gathered their evidence bags together and packed them up.

Garrison gestured at Thompson and Holden. "Our team is ready to take off. It'll give you room to do your exam. I'll stay around until Chief Newel is transported."

"Thanks, Detective. Will you apprise me of anything you know regarding his death?" she said.

Garrison lifted his hand toward me. "Mayor Brooks witnessed it, as it turns out. Mayor?"

Dr. Long's eyes implored me to spell out the details.

"Yes." I told her everything. After I finished, my body started to shake. The floodgates opened and a hundred tears poured from their ducts. Clint found a box of tissues for me. I took a few and dabbed my face.

Dr. Long stepped in close to me. "Camryn, this traumatic event has caught up with you and it's good to let your emotions loose like that. Why don't you go home, have a warm drink to help soothe you, calm your nerves. Assistant Chief Lonsbury, will you see to that?"

"Of course," Clint said.

"Good. Camryn, I think the sheriff's office will arrange a debriefing session for you and the others who were involved in this. Probably sometime tomorrow. Is that right, Detective Garrison?" Dr. Long asked.

He nodded. "Sure. We'll take care of that."

My tears would not stop no matter how many times I blinked. Nor could I squeeze a single word out of my mouth. I managed a few nods instead.

Clint picked up my coat from the floor, held it for me, and guided me into it. He pulled gloves and a cap from my pocket, fitted the cap on my head and slipped the gloves on my outstretched hands. Between the waterworks and needing help to get dressed, I had turned into an oversized baby.

"If you leave before I get back, the back door is on auto lock. Just make sure it latches, sometimes it catches in the cold," Clint said.

"Okay," Garrison said.

Clint guided me down the hallway. Officer Jake Dooley came through the door and frowned as he looked from me to Clint. "What's going on here? Buffalo County and the coroner? Was it Margaret?"

25

"No, it was our . . . chief."

Jake jerked like he'd been tapped with a stun gun. "Our chief, Chief Newel, that chief?"

"Yes, Newel. His heart stopped and EMS couldn't get it started again."

"*No.* He was always the strongest man in the room. He's not even fifty yet," Jake said.

"I don't get it either," Clint said.

Jake touched my shoulder. "What are you doing here, Cami?"

I shook my head unable to utter a word.

"She had a meeting with Newel, and he died before they even got started."

"*No.* You poor thing. In the wrong place at the wrong time. Again." Jake said the last word under his breath, but I heard it.

"I'm taking Camryn home. When I get back, we'll notify the other officers and the rest of our staff. And his next of kin. I only know of his ex-wife and the one brother," Clint said.

Jake gave a nod. "They're the only ones I know of. Sorry, Cami. Big time bummer for you. I would've gotten here earlier but I was out on a welfare check. A guy's wife was frantic when she couldn't reach him. He was in a fish house halfway across the lake, and I was on my way out when I heard EMS get paged to the PD.

"I was able to make contact with the guy. He'd left his phone in the car and was none the wiser. Then I got called to a domestic right after and just cleared from it. Had no clue what was going on here. The calls to the county and the coroner didn't go out on the radio?"

Clint shook his head. "No reason to get everyone riled up and have media folks outside in the freezing cold waiting for the scoop."

"No. Well, take Cami home. I'll see if the others need anything. I'll stay here till they're done if I don't get another call."

"Thanks, buddy." Clint took my arm, pushed open the door, helped me into his police car, and slid behind the wheel. "You want someone with you till I get back? I can make that call."

Maybe? "I don't know. I need to process the whole thing first, that Chief Newel actually died."

"I get that. I can contact Pinky and Erin. They'd be happy to keep you company. You can tell them about Chief's death without getting into details. Word will be out soon enough."

"Let me get home and I'll think about it." My decision-making ability was bound to kick in anytime.

"Is your car parked at your shop?"

I had that answer. "Yeah."

"Okay. We'll drive it over later tonight. Jake will help me with that."

Thankfully, we rode in silence until Clint pulled into the alley that led to my backyard. The alley divided the properties on either side of it. Most houses in the 1960s era neighborhood had detached garages that abutted the alley, as did mine. He pulled into the short drive, parked, and left his vehicle running.

"Let's get you inside." He offered his hand and helped me out. The frigid air took my breath away as we walked to the back door. Clint held out his hand. "Keys?"

I pulled off my glove, fumbled in my pocket until I found them, and handed them over. I was relieved Clint was with me when we stepped inside the dark brick Tudor-style house. "It can't be sixty degrees in here," he said and laid the keys on the kitchen counter.

"I turn it down to save on fuel when I'm gone."

"So do I." He flipped on lights and made his way to the thermostat. "What should I set it at?"

I needed warmth. "Um, seventy is good."

He adjusted the dial then turned to me. "Let me take your coat."

"I'll wait till it warms up in here." But I slipped off my boots and kicked them into the back closet off the kitchen.

Clint brushed my face with the back of his hand. "Doctor Long said you should have a hot drink."

"I'll make some tea in a bit."

"I wish I didn't have to leave you alone."

I put my hand on his. "Not to worry. I'll call someone if I need to. Or wait for you to come back."

He took me into his arms and held on tight a long moment. "It could be a while." When I nodded, he pulled back, looked at me, and kissed my forehead. "Almost forgot. I'll need your car keys."

"They're on the ring with the house keys."

"I guess I knew that. Don't forget to lock up after me." He picked up the keyring and left.

Keeping my doors locked was his constant reminder, and I had to admit, in light of the evening's events, I appreciated that. Not that I feared boogey men, but at that point my own shadow would have spooked me. *Get a hold of yourself*, I chided.

With some effort, I headed to the living room and dropped down on the couch. I studied the ceramic bowl of pennies on the coffee table then closed my eyes and brought cheerful memories of my birth parents to mind. They had died in an automobile crash when I was five. I believed when I found a penny, in random places at opportune times, they were heaven-sent. More specifically, they were sent from heaven by my birth mother, Berta.

When I was sad or scared or lonely, the pennies appeared seemingly out of nowhere and gave me assurance. Other times, it seemed they were warning signs. I needed to be on the lookout for something about to happen. I'd kept my penny belief on the downlow because a lot of people thought it was hooey. If I wasn't the one with unusual or unexplained experiences who received penny gifts from heaven, I might have been in that camp myself.

It's not like I found pennies every day, but it was often enough to fill the ceramic bowl every year or so. I'd cashed in the last batch at the bank days before Christmas. It was a modest amount but helped pay for a young mother's groceries. She was in line behind me with three children. I slipped away while she dug in her purse for bills before she discovered what had happened. I caught her look of joy when I peeked in the store's front window and my heart sang for the rest of the night. It was a secret I sent up to my mother.

I lived in the house that had belonged to Sandra, my mother's best friend. I felt close to both of them there. Sandra's children had left most of her furnishings and that suited me fine. It'd made the move easier. When I returned to Brooks Landing, I wasn't sure how long I'd stay. I was accustomed to my high-octane job in Washington, D.C. and felt impatient at the slower pace at first. It took me a while to adjust, and a year later I was still there.

Not much drama the first months back in Brooks Landing. Then I found a body in the park, another in our shop's restroom, still another in the former mayor's office. Shouldn't three strikes mean you're out? No more bodies? Yet I'd stood in Chief Newel's doorway and watched him collapse. The only words we'd exchanged were, "Chief Newel!" and, "I'll push the button to release the lock."

I was overheated in my thermal coat, shrugged it off, and carried it to the kitchen. My arms were weak when I slipped it on a hanger and hung it on the pole. I realized three things: I had expended every bit of stored up emotional energy in my body's reserves; it had been a long time since lunch; and I'd spent time with a dead man. I needed a shower, food, drink, and time to reflect on the bizarre chain of events.

I spotted a penny on the kitchen counter by its lonesome and figured either Clint dropped it when he picked up my keys or my mother was nearby. I looked heavenward and sighed on my way to the bathroom. I undressed, climbed in the shower, and let the hot water work its magic on my shoulder muscles for a good five minutes. I was all soaped up when the word 'poison' popped in my mind and triggered a peculiar thought. What if Chief Newel had swallowed a dose of poison after he let me in? He must have figured I was there to give him an ultimatum. Had he determined he couldn't face the future after that?

Maybe his time was short due to an illness and he'd reached the end of the line. As Clint had said, "he died with his boots on." Was it by choice? It was strange Newel had let me in and went back to his desk without waiting for me. Maybe he wanted to seal the contribution envelope to Fresh Start Rehabilitation before he died, but didn't quite make it. I rinsed off the suds, intent to banish the crazy poison idea from my brain.

Chief Newel's death investigation was in good hands with Buffalo County, and his autopsy would reveal what had caused his death. Still, an ominous sense of dread made me tremble. I needed to find out if he'd been ill or involved in something illicit he didn't want his employer to know about. Did his friends or his brother or anyone else know what circumstances Aaron Newel faced, and why he kept it secret from the City of Brooks Landing?

4

It was a little after 7:00 p.m., but seemed hours later. In mid-January, less than a month after the shortest day of the year, the sun set before 5:00, about the time I'd planned to meet with Chief Newel. Too much had happened since then. Unbelievable things. Newel's sudden death, the EMS team who tried to save him. Clint. Gina. Detective Garrison. The Buffalo County crime scene team. Dr. Long. Jake.

The darkness coupled with the intense emotional event made me long for an early bedtime, a long winter's nap. I put on flannel pajamas, a soft robe, and the pink bunny slippers Pinky had given me. She was excited when she presented her gift, and I honestly hadn't known if I'd ever wear them. Pinky's style, not mine. But they were warm and fluffy, and the realistic eyes looked outward instead of inward, so all was good.

It surprised me when my stomach growled. How could it even think of food on such an evening? On the other hand, if I had any chance of slumber tonight, something in my stomach would help. Comfort food. I looked in the refrigerator and decided an omelet would be easy and quick. I pulled out the needed ingredients: eggs, milk, shredded cheddar, baby peppers, and bacon bits. I chopped the peppers, stirred everything together, added oregano and basil, and poured the mix into a pan on medium high heat. When it was fluffy and cooked, I put a piece of cranberry almond bread in the toaster and a chamomile tea bag in a mug of hot water, then dished up my plate.

The kitchen smelled friendly and soothing, but it felt lonely. Instead of eating in there, I carried my meal to the living room and balanced the plate on my lap. I had planned to eat for sustenance, not enjoyment, but the omelet, toast with honey, and calming tea hit the spot. As my belly filled, my contentment grew. I was first to admit I appreciated good food. And yes, it showed with the extra fifteen or twenty pounds I carried.

I'd planned to start an exercise program many times over the years, but aside from a fair amount of walking, I hadn't found a program I stuck with. My schedule was partially to blame, especially in D.C., and life had been plenty busy since I'd returned to Brooks Landing. And more recently, my new role as mayor added another layer of busyness. Excuses, true. But legitimate ones, right?

I finished eating, carried the dishes to the sink, and filled it with hot soapy water. I was exhausted and keyed up at the same time, about the worst combination. Why did Chief Newel have to up and die like that? My thoughts in the shower about Newel circled back.

If Newel suspected I was about to have a serious talk with him, deliver an ultimatum, would he have done something to himself on purpose? And why? Had Clint's "boots on" comment held special significance? Was Chief Newel the kind of guy who would never quit or get himself into a position where he'd get fired?

I knew taking one's own life was not a rational act. I didn't know Newel personally but found it hard to believe he would've done something that drastic in front of me. Or anyone else. I regretted I'd never have a conversation with him or learn the reasons for his frequent absences.

My phone buzzed and I plucked it from my robe pocket. Clint. "Hello."

"Camryn. First off, I wanted to see how you are."

"Still on the stunned side, but okay."

"Hang in there. I also wanted to give you a heads up. I believe you can expect some visitors this evening," he said.

I straightened my spine. "What do you mean? Who?"

"Someone, I think it was the nosy local reporter, let one of the city council members know the coroner's van was at the PD. Rosalie Gorman showed up here first, followed by the other three in short order. I kept them outside. I wanted to notify Chief's brother and his ex before all of Brooks Landing knew, but councilors figured it was either the chief's—or your body—they were putting in the van."

"Oh, my."

"I asked them to give me an hour or so to make notifications and they agreed, but said they needed to talk to you ASAP. If they show up at your house, it's okay to tell them what you witnessed. Hope that helps keep the facts straight so we don't end up with a game of telephone, made-up stuff getting weaved in with the truth. Don't go into specific details about what the EMTs or county guys or the coroner said. Or the investigation thus far," he said.

I was not privy to the "investigation thus far."

"I'll keep it high level. I can say the EMTs worked to save him?" I said.

"Sure. Just no speculation about why he died, other than his heart stopped. Don't mention the envelope since we have no evidence it had anything to do with his death."

"I won't. Maybe it's a weird coincidence. In any case, the council will need to meet to discuss next steps. Maybe call an emergency meeting tomorrow. I'll run it by Gary Lunden." The city administrator.

"Speaking of Gary, I called his cell after the councilors left and caught him at the conference in Minneapolis. I hated to inform him over the phone, but not much choice. He was shocked, of course. He'd planned to stay overnight, then wondered if he should head for home. I assured him there was nothing he could do here tonight," he said.

"You had to tell him. If Rosalie Gorman knows, she'll be hard pressed not to tell whomever, no offense to her. How about Mark, any word from him yet?" Mark Weston, a Brooks Landing Police Officer, and another best friend, was on a three-day ice fishing trip with a buddy in northern Minnesota.

"No cell phone service where he's at. Earlier today, he drove to an establishment in town with wi-fi and called to check on things. Before all this went down. I'm counting on him to do the same tomorrow."

"I hope so." I pinched the back of my neck. "Everything feels upside down. How are *you* doing, Clint?"

"Doing. Too busy to process. The truth is bound to hit me like a lead balloon anytime now."

"You know how sorry I am, for you, other officers, and staff. And Margaret, especially."

He sniffed. "Thanks. Better get back to it, tell Chief's brother and his ex-wife the sad news. Find out if there are others to contact."

"You have their phone numbers?"

"Yeah, we found a memo book in his desk with their names and numbers. Garrison took Chief's work cell to see who he's talked to in the last months. Turns out the only people in his contacts are the city staff and councilors," he said.

"That's odd."

"Tell me about it."

"No personal cell phone?" I asked.

"Not that we found. Gotta go. We'll talk later."

"Bye." I disconnected.

I'd reeled from the shock of Chief Newel's scary death, and hadn't thought of what needed to be done, who needed to be contacted. They'd found Chief's work cell phone, but where was his personal one?

The front doorbell rang on my way to change into clothes. My heart jumped into my throat. The motion detection light turned on, and as I reached the front door, I saw a group huddled on the front stoop. All four councilors. Clint had warned me. I opened the door and they piled in, nearly knocking each other down in the process. The cold air from both the great outdoors and their persons dropped the room temperature several degrees in seconds.

"Camryn Brooks, oh my God!" Rosalie "Stormin" Gorman's green eyes flashed and her red hair stuck out in all directions when she pulled off her wool cap: an emotional whirlwind made more so by the tragic news.

"Come in." I stepped back so they could get further inside and closed the door behind them.

They shed boots and outerwear. "There's room in the closet for your coats." I pulled the door open and moved to give them space. All were silent. Now that we were together, it seemed the unspoken consensus was we needed a minute to collect our thoughts before I launched into my account about the meeting with Chief Newel. That hadn't happened after all. It seemed we also recognized the need to set aside any personal or professional differences we had to deal with issues that arose from Newel's death.

"Let's sit down." I waved at the couch and chairs, and that's when I remembered I hadn't changed out of my pajamas, robe, and bunny slippers. I might have felt embarrassed under other circumstances, or if any of them had given me the once over.

As they took seats, Harley Creighton fixed his beady brown eyes on me, his blond comb over mussed. Gail Spindler waited with an almost serene look that helped calm me, her shoulder-length hair somehow perfect. The twinkle was missing from Wendell Lyon's eyes. He smoothed out his gray beard while he waited.

"What happened?" Stormin' said, her voice at a volume high up on the decibel scale. It grated on my overly sensitized nerves.

It didn't seem possible I could tell the story again but managed to all the same. I spoke slowly to let the councilors absorb the words, words I had trouble believing myself. I started by recapping the little speech I'd intended to deliver to Chief Newel and finished with Dr. Long's arrival. Their rapt attention was on me and no one, not even Stormin' interrupted my story from beginning to end. I brushed away a tear that had found its way down my cheek. "So I never got the chance to find out what was going on. Why he missed so much work."

"I can't imagine how terrified you must have been," Gail offered.

"I think I would have had a heart attack myself. On the spot," Stormin' said. I imagined that was possible, all right.

"I'm thinkin' he might've had a heart problem he didn't want us to know about," Harley said.

"If he had a heart problem, he might not have even known about it himself," Wendell said. Clint had suggested the same thing.

Stormin' shook her head. "I just can't believe it really happened. That he just died like that. He was always bigger than life. It seems like he could come through the door and tell us it was all a big joke—"

The bird cut her off when it popped out of the clock and shouted, "Cuckoo!" A collective gasp sounded as we all jerked and our shoulders lifted. I thought I was used to the little guy cuckooing twenty-four times a day, but the thick tension in the room and the others' reactions did me in.

The bird shouted "cuckoo" six more times.

Stormin' clutched her breast. "My dear God, my heart. I thought I was a goner for a minute. Why do you have that . . . thing?"

I shrugged. "It came with the house. And I'm mostly used to him by now."

"It's loud enough to scare any burglars away, I can say that much," Gail said and smiled.

"A bird on her wall and bunnies on her feet," Harley said. "Did you ever notice how those bunny eyes seem real, Camryn?"

"You think so?"

"Yes. They're looking straight at me," Stormin' said.

38

I don't know what got into me, but I lifted my feet, put them on the coffee table, and crossed my ankles so the bunnies' faces pointed toward all four councilors. "Is that better, Rosalie?"

Stormin' covered her eyes. "No, it's not. I think you should put them away. Hide them somewhere."

Harley waved his hand and changed the subject. "What are we going to do about filling Chief Newel's seat?"

I tucked the bunnies under the couch. "We can't talk about that tonight. This is not an authorized meeting."

"The mayor's right. It would be in violation of the open meeting law," Wendell, our resident attorney, said. "We can call an emergency meeting in the next day or two. We'll need to get it posted. In the meantime, protocol says that in the absence of the chief, the assistant chief is the acting chief."

"He's been filling that role a lot already," Stormin' mumbled.

Time to end the conversation before it took a wrong turn. "I know it's only a little after seven, but I'm pretty beat," I said.

"You sure you don't want one of us to stay with you?" Gail offered.

I shook my head. "But thanks." Plus, I'd hoped Clint would be by soon. His strong character and down to earth demeanor helped calm me. Unless he was upset with something I'd done, of course.

The four council members donned their warm outerwear again and headed out the door, and said, "take care" and "get some rest" and "call if you need anything."

"Thanks, I'm glad you came by." I closed and locked the door. I glanced first at the cuckoo clock with its closed doors and then at the bunnies on my feet. "You guys shook up the poor councilors. What a night. They didn't argue, they didn't call each other names, or use cross words. Despite the awful circumstances, I have to admit it was kind of nice having them here." I bopped my arm with the other fist. *Cami, are you talking to yourself or inanimate objects?* When you live alone, does it matter?

My phone buzzed and Clint's name on the display made me smile. "Hi, Clint. The troops just left."

"The troops?"

"All the city council members. Turns out it was actually a good thing. We needed to talk about Chief Newel, and they're in disbelief, like I am."

"Of course. They've known him a lot of years. And so you know, Jake and I will be by with your car in ten or fifteen minutes," he said.

I smiled. "Okay."

"I was able to contact Chief's brother and ex-wife. His brother lives in South Dakota and the two haven't had much contact for years. He was shocked about Aaron's death, felt bad they'd drifted apart. I asked about a family medical history, any known heart conditions. He said none that he knew of. Their parents both died fairly young. Mother from cancer, father from blood poisoning—septicemia—of all things, after a surgery. The dad had gone home, got sick, didn't go back to the hospital like he should have."

"That's sad."

"Yeah. I learned more about Chief's family history from his brother in a few minutes than he told me in our ten years working together," he said.

"It's no secret he was secretive."

Clint made a "haw" sound. "Right. And his ex's reaction was strange. All she said was, 'Thanks for letting me know.'"

40

I wandered into the kitchen and glanced at the dishes soaking in the sink. "Really? That *is* strange. Where does she live?"

"Here in Brooks Landing. She's a nurse at a metro hospital."

"Hmm." Maybe I'd look her up in a day or two.

"Have you told your parents or Pinky and Erin about Chief's death?" Clint said.

"No. I should call the girls, let 'em know. My parents can wait until tomorrow. If they get upsetting news this late in the day, they won't sleep tonight. And they'd have to tell my sisters and brothers. I don't think I can handle a bunch of phone calls or a big family gathering if they all stopped by."

"I can understand that. See you in a bit."

I pushed the off button and called Pinky. "Cami, I've been wondering what in the heck happened. Was Chief Newel a no show? Again?"

"Not quite. Brace yourself: he died before we could meet."

A clattering noise meant Pinky had dropped the phone. A few seconds later she yelled, "No *way.*"

"Believe it or not. And the extra bad part, I was with him when he died."

"No *way.* What *happened?*" She sounded breathless.

"Think you can come over so we can talk in person?" It came out as a whine.

"I'll be there in two shakes of a lamb's tail."

"Maybe see if Erin can come too, and I'll tell you what happened at the same time."

"I'll pick her up on the way."

"Thanks, Pink."

A warm sensation ran through me as I hung up. My best forever friends were always there for me.

5

Pinky and Erin arrived ahead of Clint and Jake. I unlocked the back door and they almost fell into the kitchen together. Like the councilors had.

At 5'10, Pinky was almost a foot taller than Erin's 5' even. They were a study in opposites. Pinky had round hazel eyes, prominent cheekbones, a narrow straight nose, and a chin on the pointed side. With her animated movements, she was all arms and legs at times. Or so it seemed.

Erin was of Vietnamese-Caucasian descent, a classic beauty with a high forehead, almond-shaped dark brown eyes, small nose, straight black hair, nearly flawless skin, full lips, and perfect teeth. She had the astounding ability to quiet a room with one stern look.

I was between the two of them in height and had a rounder body with more curves. My mother called me "shapely." Neither of them carried any extra weight. I had Scandinavian English heritage and kept my wavy dishwater blonde hair shoulder length. I straightened it when I wanted to look more professional.

"We can't stand it anymore! Tell us what happened." Pinky tossed her coat on a chair and put her hands on my cheeks.

Erin leaned on Pinky's arm. "Pinky, Cami needs some space. Let's go into the other room."

They each grabbed one of my arms, pulled me into the living room, sat me down on the couch, and plopped down on either side of me. I'd lost count of the times I recounted the chief's strange and sudden demise. Unlike the councilors, Pinky interrupted me a few times and made me repeat or clarify what I'd said. As instructed, I didn't disclose details about the envelope.

After I'd finished, Erin rested her head on my shoulder and looped her arm around mine. "That is one of the scariest things I've ever heard. I'm so sorry you were with him when it happened."

Pinky reached her long arm across me and rested her hand on Erin's arm. "Agreed. We've had scary things happen. In the last year, for sure. But this sounds like the scariest. Especially being all alone with him, nobody else in the building. After dark."

A cold chill zipped through me. "I won't argue about that. As terrified as I was when I found the other victims, I wasn't with them when they died."

"Hopefully, he suffered a fatal heart attack. Without any dirty pool from anyone else," Pinky said.

"Dirty pool?" I asked.

"You know, someone did something to him somehow."

I'd wondered if he'd done something to himself, but hadn't considered that. "Somehow, like how?"

Pinky shook her head. "I don't know. Bad guys find ways."

"If that's the case, we all know what will happen. Right, Cami? You'll feel driven to dig around until you get to the bottom of it, find out who did whatever it was to Chief Newel," Erin said.

I lifted my shoulders as high as possible, trapped in their arm holds. "If it turns out there was any 'dirty pool' and I was the one with him when he passed on, don't you think it gives me a certain level of responsibility to help uncover the truth?"

Erin elbowed me. "I can see why you think so because you can't seem to help yourself. But no, it doesn't. That's what the police and investigators do. It's their job. You've had some close calls with bad guys when you were hell bent on solving murders."

"Not that this was a murder," I said and mentally crossed my fingers since my arms were pinned against my body.

"No, but just saying if it was," Pinky replied.

Another chill ran through me.

A four-tap knock sounded at the back door and the girls released me from our group hug.

"Hello? It's Jake and me," Clint called from the kitchen. We rose from the couch and met them halfway. Jake's eyes fell on Pinky and they exchanged small smiles. Pinky had found romance at last, after a brief, unhappy marriage years before. Erin and I were thrilled for her.

As far as Erin's absent love life was concerned, Pinky and I had secretly hoped Cupid would shoot a golden arrow at her one day and she'd give Mark Weston another chance. He'd carried a torch for her since they'd dated in high school, but hadn't been able to ignite another flame after college separated them.

Erin had confessed she was afraid something bad would happen to Mark in the line of duty as a police officer and couldn't face that worry every time he went to work. I told her anything could happen to anyone at any given time. All those years later, she hadn't lost what I considered a somewhat irrational fear.

Clint handed me the car keys. "I put your car in the garage."

"Thanks." I laid them on the counter and turned to the group. Each one had varying degrees of somber looks and I stopped myself before I said, "Who died?"

Jake gave me a hug. "Sorry, Cami."

I nodded when he released me. "Thanks."

Clint looked from Pinky to Erin. "It's a school and work night, if you two have things to take care of." Then he turned to me. "Camryn, I'll stay as long as you need me."

"As it turns out, I have some work to do on my lesson plans tonight," Erin said.

"And more baking awaits me at home," Pinky said.

Jake raised his eyebrows. "Your muffins and scones are famous in these parts. All right if I help you for a while, Pinky?"

She smiled. "You bet."

Erin, Pinky, and Jake gave me parting hugs, got into their gear, and left.

Clint drew me in his arms and held me for a long moment. When he pulled away, he took my hand and led me to the living room couch. We sat so we faced each other. "You must be exhausted," he said.

"It's hard to describe, and I am. Chief's death was a total shock. The EMTs did their best and it was the first time I saw an AED used. But I couldn't watch when it delivered those shocks to Chief Newel."

He squeezed my hand. "That's a tough thing for all of us."

"I was impressed with Detective Garrison and his team. Man, they were very thorough. And Doctor Long. You can tell how much she cares about the living and the dead."

"Between the evidence and the autopsy, they'll find out what caused Chief's death."

"They will." I thought a moment. "Clint, did the chief have any enemies you knew about?"

He shrugged. "You mean someone who'd harm him? No. I think he would've said if he'd ever been threatened. A lot of us officers get what I'd call 'idle threats,' like when we arrest a person under the influence."

I tucked my ankle under my knee. "What do you mean?"

"Things like, 'Wait till I talk to my lawyer, he'll get you fired.' Or 'I know where you live.' Stuff like that."

"Things bad guys say in cop movies," I said.

"Yeah. Aaron Newel was hired about ten years ago when our old chief retired. He was chief at another city prior: Ironwood. When he came to Brooks Landing, I got the impression he'd left Ironwood because something had happened. But no red flags came up in his background check, or with his references."

"Makes you wonder."

Clint nodded. "It seemed like Chief was married to his job, didn't like to talk about life outside of work, was protective of it. But in the past six, seven months he turned into a clam. And he looked more haggard, distracted at times, like he was under a lot of stress. I don't think it was work that caused it and suspected problems with a love interest. When I asked him about it, he told me he was fine. Whatever secrets he had he took to the grave."

The expression "took to the grave" made me gulp. Clint squeezed my hand again. "You okay?"

I nodded. "I wish I'd had a chance to talk to him. He may not have told me anything either, but you never know. People often reach the point where they need to spill the beans, and it's sometimes easier with someone you don't know."

"You could be right."

"My thoughts keep going back to Gina. Something was definitely up with the way she reacted. Probably the shock of it all,

46

but it struck me as more personal than professional. And she called the chief 'Aaron'—nobody else does."

"I'm sure I have at times over the years. But you're right, not many do. I agree it's curious Gina was on a first name basis with him," he said.

"She called you Assistant Chief Lonsbury."

"She always does."

"Hmm."

When I yawned Clint pulled the quilt from the back of the couch, stretched it over me, and pulled my body against his. "Why don't you close your eyes, think about something happy, relaxing. How about imagine lying on a beach in the warm sun?" He'd spoken the words softly and slowly and the last thing I remembered was the imagined sun's rays on my face.

I woke up on the couch Wednesday morning with a start, a pillow tucked under my head and my body wrapped in the comfy quilt. As I grew aware of my surroundings, I saw a note from Clint on the coffee table. *You looked like an angel. I hope you slept all night. We'll talk later.*

Angel? A sweet, unexpected sentiment. I sent Clint a text message, *Thanks for lulling me to sleep. I just woke up* and added a smiley face. He wrote back seconds later, *Good to hear. Later then.*

I noticed eleven missed calls and would return them at some point. Reality set in as I watched coffee drip from the brewer into a cup. I took a sip then carried it to the kitchen table and sank on to a chair. Images of Chief Newel dead in his chair and the chain of events that followed filled my mind. The EMTs, Clint, Detective Garrison, the crime scene team, Jake.

One thing that grabbed my attention was how dumbstruck Gina was when she heard the news. I wondered if she had information on Newel, what she knew about his personal life. The way she'd reacted to his death it was a given their relationship was not strictly professional.

As mayor, I could get an employee's address and phone number from the city. Problem solved. I dialed the office.

"City of Brooks Landing," Receptionist Lila answered.

"Lila, it's Camryn."

Her voice went up an octave. "Mayor Brooks, oh my goodness gracious. What an awful thing you went through last night. Worse than awful."

As per usual, news traveled at lightning speed in our small town. Hence all the attempted calls on my phone. "Thanks, Lila. A big shocker, but I'm okay. We'll talk later, all right? The reason I'm calling is I need our cleaning lady's—Gina's—address and phone number. I have something to talk to her about and she's not around during business hours."

"Oh. Well, I hope it's nothing serious, like something the city administrator should be aware of, like a performance issue."

Not that I would or could tell you if it was. "Nothing like that."

"Okay. I'll look it up." She rattled off the info a moment later. "I suppose the council will have a special meeting about the chief and all. Since your next regular meeting isn't for two weeks."

"Yes, we'll need to take care of that. Thanks, Lila."

"Anytime. See you later then?"

"I'll stop in to check on things sometime today. Is Gary in?"

"Not yet. He's driving in from Minneapolis this morning," she said.

"That's right. I'll catch up with him later. Thanks," I said and disconnected.

The mayor and city council positions were part time, and none of us held regular office hours. Some weeks were slow, others were crazy busy—like this one had shaped up to be.

Pinky was grinding coffee beans and didn't hear me when I walked through the archway into her shop. I tried to get her attention without creeping up from behind. When I was within six feet, before I made a wide swing to her left, some internal alarm woke her, and she turned on a dime. And sucked in an "A" sound, followed by, "Cami!"

I touched her shoulder. "I think you go into some kind of meditative state when you work with those beans."

"Too darn loud for that."

"I suppose."

Pinky gave me a hug. "You look rested. Not what I expected. I thought you'd be more worn out after, um, everything." She noticed my downturned lips. "That wasn't nice of me. I didn't mean to make you feel bad."

I shrugged. "It's okay. Yesterday's trauma wiped me out and I didn't think I'd sleep. But I went out like a light last night and woke up rested. The answer to prayers and a very nice surprise, no question about that."

"Maybe a little part of you was relieved you didn't need to have that talk with Chief Newel."

"Pinky—"

"Not that you wanted him to die. But you were pretty worked up about the whole thing," she said.

"I was, but the meeting would've been way easier than what happened instead." My phone interrupted us and I pushed the

49

accept button. "Camryn Brooks."

"Mayor Brooks, it's Detective Garrison."

"Oh, hello Detective." I glanced at Pinky and watched her eyebrows rise.

"We've arranged a debrief for everyone involved with last night's incident. I'm hoping noon today works for you."

I glanced at the clock. 8:35. "Um, yes, I can make arrangements to be there."

"Good. Go to the front desk at the sheriff's office and they'll direct you to the room," he said.

"Okay, thanks."

I hung up and Pinky threw her arms up. "What?"

"Detective Garrison wants me to come in for a debriefing at noon. Along with everyone else who was with Chief Newel last night."

"Wow, oh wow. How come you didn't have to do that before? With the last victims you found?"

"Not sure, maybe it's because I witnessed his death. I actually feel worse for the EMTs who worked on him, tried to save his life. The county guys, Clint, Jake, it was hard for all of them," I said.

"It had to have been."

"With the other victims I found, no question it was awful. So I was advised to talk to a professional. Which I did, of course."

"Yeah. I know it helped you a lot," she said.

I smiled. "And so did my friends."

She returned the smile. A text message came in from Clint. *See you at the debrief?*

I'll be there, I wrote. He sent back a thumbs up symbol.

"Clint and the others will be there too," I told Pinky.

"I didn't think to ask Clint last night how he was doing.

50

Losing his chief like that."

"He'll be okay."

"Jake and I talked, but he didn't say much. Mostly that he couldn't believe Chief Newel was gone."

"It'll take a while," I said.

Pinky's eyes opened wide. "Oh my gosh, it just hit me. We'll need a new police chief."

6

I left Pinky to her coffee beans and settled in my shop office to make some phone calls. One to my parents to break the latest news, one to Emmy, our some-time helper, and one to Gina, the city office building cleaner.

My mother had recovered well after months of cancer treatments, but I liked to keep her stress level as low as possible. She picked up after a few rings. "Hi, Mom. How's everything?"

"It's all good here. What's up?" She knew me well. More times than not, I didn't call without a reason.

There was no easy way to say it. "I wondered if you'd heard Chief Newel died yesterday?"

She gasped. "Oh, no. No, we hadn't heard. We haven't had the local radio station on yet today. What happened? He was young, at least not very old."

"No, I guess late forties. They don't know why his heart stopped, but it was sudden. And, as it turns out, I was at the police station when he died." I kept my voice as relaxed as possible.

"Oh, Cami. Oh, no. The wrong place at the wrong time." She didn't add "again" like Jake had.

"I know, I won't pretend it wasn't awful. The EMTs came and couldn't bring him back. County detectives are looking into it, and he'll have an autopsy to find out why he died."

"What a shock for everyone at the police station and city hall. I'm just sick you were there when it happened. Are you okay, Cami? You know Dad and I are here for you."

"Thanks, Mom. We have a debriefing today, so that will help a lot."

"I'm relieved to hear that, dear," Mom said.

"I'm going to call Emmy, see if she can watch the shop while I'm gone."

"We don't have any plans and we'd be happy do that. It'll give us a reason to get out of the house. What time do you need us?"

"Okay, thanks, Mom. How about eleven?" I said.

"We'll be there."

My parents enjoyed working in the shop from time to time. Especially after my mother had regained her health and most of her strength. I didn't need to call Emmy after all, so I pulled the paper with Gina's number from my pants pocket and stared at it. Would it be better to phone or pay her an impromptu visit? I hoped she'd help piece together the last six months of Chief Newel's life, enlighten me on things he'd kept secret.

I decided on a phone call followed by a meeting.

Gina answered as I was about to disconnect. "Hello?" Her voice held uncertainty.

"Hi, Gina. It's Camryn Brooks."

"Oh, ah, hello, ah, Mayor." More uncertainty, hesitancy.

"I wanted to check in, see how you're doing after yesterday."

"It hasn't sunk in yet," she admitted.

"I'm with you on that one. Forgive me if I'm out of line, but it seems like you got along well with Chief Newel. I'd hoped to get to know him but didn't have the chance. I'm wondering if I could stop by, talk to you for a bit?"

"Why?"

"I have a few questions and I'd rather talk in person," I said.

It took her a few seconds to answer. "What kind of questions?"

"About Chief Newel, what he was like."

"Oh. I didn't know him super well, but I guess that'd be okay," she said.

"Thanks. What's your schedule like? Do you have time later this morning?"

"That should work. My cleaning jobs are mostly in the evening, like at city hall."

"How does a little after eleven look for you?" I asked.

"It's fine, I guess."

"Good. I have your address and will see you then. Thanks."

I hung up and wondered, given her reluctance, what she'd be willing to tell me. But at least she agreed to see me. I took that as a positive sign.

My parents arrived at 10:47. After they'd shed their outerwear, they gave me warm hugs. Dad's was more like a bear's.

"My goodness, Cami. Who'd have thought you'd have more dreadful things happen to you in sleepy Brooks Landing, Minnesota than in Washington, D.C.?" Mom asked.

Dreadful was an apt way to put it. The lights in our shop flickered.

Dad glanced up at the ceiling. "Still having a problem with

the lights here? The electrician said it all checked out a-okay. Said the wiring looked good."

"Yes he did, and he was very thorough. A fluke of some kind, I guess." I had reason to believe it was the ghost of our very short-term employee, Molly, who played with the lights from time to time. No reason to mention that to my parents.

Pinky was the first to believe it was Molly's active spirit. I was reluctant to go down that path, but it seemed probable. The lights sometimes flickered, and on occasion, turned off when certain things were said, or when danger was imminent.

One notable time, I was saved from serious injury, possible death. I hadn't been able to save Molly's life, but I believe she saved mine. The lights went out in the nick of time when I was under attack.

I waved goodbye to my parents. "Thanks for helping me out. I should be back by three or so." I put on my cold weather gear and popped into Brew Ha-Ha. "See you later."

Pinky wore a slight frown when she looked up from the plate she was piling muffins on. "I'll hold good thoughts for all you debriefing people."

"Thanks." I hadn't told her about the meet up with Gina. She was over-the-top curious what the debriefing session would hold. I'd had more briefings and debriefings in my job as director of legislative affairs than I could count, but none because I'd witnessed a bizarre death.

I climbed into my frigid vehicle, let it idle and warm up a few minutes, then drove to Gina's on the northeast side of town, about a mile from our shop. I'd stopped shivering about the time I pulled to a stop in front of her house. It was the same era as mine, but a different style. Her house was a brown, one-level ranch in a neighborhood of similar homes in a range of colors.

A wave of anxiety hit me as I walked up the steps to her house. Why? Maybe it was the strange way she acted when we first met at the police station. Maybe it was anticipation of what she'd tell me.

Gina opened the front door before I rang the bell. She'd been watching for me. I smiled, but she didn't smile back. She frowned instead. *Off to a tense start.*

"Come in, Mayor."

I stepped into the small entryway, pulled off my boots, and set them on a shoe tray opposite the closet.

Gina extended her arm. "Can I take your coat?"

"Thanks." I stuck my gloves and cap in the pockets and slipped it off. When Gina hung it up it gave me hope we'd have more than a two-minute visit.

Her house was homey; the living room walls a caramel color, the overstuffed chairs had a tasteful paisley pattern, the leather couch a soft brown shade. Gina pointed in the general direction of the furniture, and I chose a chair that was cushier than it looked. I sank down a foot and hoped I'd get out again without much struggle. Gina sat in another chair, a good eight feet away from me.

She eyed me with the same frown. "Tell me what you were wondering about."

I took a quick breath. "Sure. Chief Newel was private about his life and activities. And I respect that. I don't want to pry into anything he wanted kept secret, but I feel bad that I never got to talk to him. We had a meeting scheduled and he died before we had that chance."

She nodded. "Aaron was worried about that, about what you had to say." *He talked to her about our meeting.*

56

Some of my tension lifted. "Why was that?"

"Because you were the mayor and he thought you were going to fire him," she said.

I leaned forward. "Really, he told you that?"

"Yes."

"You must've been good friends." *Or more?*

She shrugged. "I guess."

"No, I was not planning to fire him."

"Oh."

"Gina, it sounds like you knew Chief pretty well, so I hope you can help me out. You know he missed a lot of work the last months," I said.

She looked at her hands. "Yes."

"That's what I wanted to talk to him about. To find out what was going on in his life, if we could do something to help in any way."

"He did have things he was dealing with, but I can't tell you what. But nothing you could've done to help. He was handling things on his own. Now he's dead." She blinked away the tears in her eyes.

"Were you part of those things, since you were friends?" I asked.

"I can't really say we were friends, like good friends, I mean. I felt sorry for him and kind of respected him for what he was doing, or trying to do, about those things."

Those things. "So you didn't hang out together, socialize?" I asked.

Her eyebrows shot up. "I'm married and even if I wasn't, he's not my type. He confided in me for reasons I can't share because of the people involved."

I lowered my voice. "Something illegal?"

"No, nothing like that. He was the police chief, after all. He followed the law."

"You knew he had a brother and an ex-wife?"

She nodded. "He wasn't close to his brother, I know that much. His ex-wife hated him. And Aaron admitted she had good reason to."

"Do you happen to know the reason?"

She shrugged. "You'll have to ask her. That was between them." In other words, she knew the reason all right.

I drove back to city hall while all kinds of scenarios circled around in my head. After our conversation, Gina's account had left me far more curious than before. She and the chief seemed like two clams who'd lived in the same closed shell. She admitted Newel had secrets she was privy to. And his ex-wife had good reason to hate him. According to Gina, Newel hadn't been involved in illegal activities. But had she known him well enough to know for sure?

I was frustrated what she'd shared told me nothing of real importance about Chief Newel, or his struggles. I felt compelled to find out, but why? I would never get to know him or work with him on city police issues.

I entered the city building, took off my gloves and cap, unzipped my coat, and entered the police station. Margaret took one look at me and tears filled her eyes. "It's a sad, sad day around here. None of us expected this," she said.

"Of course not. Can I come in for a hug?" I laid my things on a visitor chair.

She nodded and pushed the button to unlock the door. Icy fingers crawled up my spine as I stepped into the inner office area.

Less than twenty hours had passed since Chief Newel buzzed me in the same door. A minute later his life ended, and mine changed forever. I put my arms around Margaret for a gentle embrace and she held on for dear life in one of the longest, tightest hugs ever.

When she loosened her grip, I stepped a comfortable distance back. "It can't be easy for you being at work today," I said.

Margaret pulled a tissue from the top of her sweater and dabbed her eyes and nose. "I had to be here, but it's not the same knowing Chief Newel will never come back. He was gone plenty the last months, but I figured things would get back to normal after he took care of whatever it was."

"That's why I was here to talk to him yesterday. To see if we could help him in any way."

Margaret nodded. "That would've been nice. I'd asked him about it too."

A new source for information. "What'd he say?"

"That he was working on some things and it was taking longer than he'd figured."

"A health issue, you think?" I asked.

"He didn't say, but now I wonder if it was, after he died like that."

"I know." I paused a moment. "He ever talk about his ex-wife, or his brother?"

"I met Elissa—that's his ex—back when they were first married. That was six years ago, and I don't think they made it three months," she said.

"Really? What in the world happened?"

"I have no idea, and it surely got me to wondering. They'd seemed pretty lovey-dovey if you ask me. Elissa stopped by to see Chief lots of times. Then one day she came up to the front counter here, instead of in the back door like she usually did. Didn't even say 'hello.' Just told me she was there for a garage door opener and house key. She asked me to get them from her 'estranged husband.' That's how she put it. I thought it was a joke but didn't dare smile when I saw how serious she looked."

I shook my head. "That is strange. So you got them for her?"

"Yes. I went back to Chief's office and when I said, 'Elissa is here,' he picked up the two items from his desk and handed them over. He didn't say a word, and when I gave them to Elissa, she didn't say anything more either. Not a 'goodbye' or a 'thank you.' Just left. Of course, I was as curious as could be. I figured they had a big fight and things would work out. But the next day, he asked me to change his address back to his old one," she said.

"So, he had a house, and moved in with Elissa, and then moved back?"

She nodded. "He'd just put his house on the market, and as it turned out, I guess it was lucky for him it hadn't sold."

"Where's his house?" I asked.

"A few blocks from here," she said and gave me the address.

"Hmm. What did Chief Newel say about the whole thing with Elissa?"

"Not much at all. Just that they had an issue they couldn't resolve. That's all he would say," she said.

"Margaret, you worked for the chief the whole time he was here, right?"

"Yes, I did."

"Did he ever talk about what he had planned on his days off, or other things about his life in general? Hobbies, activities?" I asked.

She had shaken her head after each question then said, "No,

he didn't. And he never asked about my life, either. When he was in the office, it was all about work."

I'd known people like that in my career. Some people kept their work and personal lives separated, but almost everyone had at least one friend they brought into their personal loop. In Washington, not everyone I'd worked with was trustworthy. Maybe Chief Newel had a similar experience and it'd soured him. Someone he'd confided in who hadn't kept his secret.

Margaret cleared her throat. "I will add one thing. Chief Newel was always guarded, but it seemed like the last half year or so he was carrying a bigger burden, and got even more secretive."

"Really. And no idea why?"

She shook her head.

"Thank you, Margaret. I appreciate you talking to me, letting me know a little bit about our chief. I'm sorry he had to leave us so soon." I gave her a quick parting hug. "Take care."

She sniffed a few times as I collected my things. I fought back tears and headed to the administration office. I'd meant to ask Margaret about the chief's brother, but that could wait.

Lila was at her front desk post and jumped up when she saw me. Like Margaret, she was in her mid-fifties, and both had spent their adult lives working for the city. Reliable, faithful employees.

"Mayor." Lila took my hands in hers. "Are you okay, after being with Chief Newel when he died like that?"

"I'll be fine, with help from my friends and fine professionals."

She tightened her grip. "It's good to have friends, and you can count on me if you need someone to talk to, you know that, right?"

"I appreciate that, Lila. I'm looking for Administrator Lunden. Is he in?"

She used her thumb to point at the corridor behind her. "At his desk. He tried to contact you earlier, so he'll be glad you're here." His phone call was one of the many I had missed. I'd texted him, let him know I'd meet with him that morning.

"Thanks." Gary Lunden, another longtime employee, had served the city for decades. I arrived at his office and popped my head inside. "Hi Gary, okay to come in?"

He waved me in, pushed his lithe body from his chair with ease, and met me with a one-arm hug. "What an ordeal."

"A major one. Sorry it took me a while to get here."

He shook his hand back and forth. "No, no, no. Don't apologize. Have a seat." He returned to his office chair, and I took one of the visitors' chairs.

"We are all reeling from Newel's death, and to think you were with him. As terrible as it must've been for you, I have to tell you it gives me great comfort Aaron Newel didn't die alone, that you were with him." He squeezed his eyes together.

Lunden's sentiment gave me a new perspective. "It was bad all right, but he wasn't alone."

"And I understand the emergency responders got there right away."

"After I called nine-one-one, they arrived in minutes and did everything they could," I said.

"I got the report from Clint this morning." He paused and cleared his throat. "I'm sure you're aware we'll need to call a special city council meeting, discuss next steps. The first decision you'll have to make is to appoint an acting chief. Clinton Lonsbury is the obvious choice. My opinion."

I nodded. "He has filled in as chief many times. I have a feeling the council will agree with you. I do too, of course, but will have to recuse myself given that Clint and I started dating last month."

"Yes, that throws a monkey wrench in the works, no question about that. We should take care of this ASAP. I suggest you call an emergency meeting for this afternoon or evening, and I'll get it posted for the public."

"Oh. Okay, I can arrange to be here just about any time, but after five o'clock is better," I said.

He jotted a note on his pad. "I'll have Lila get in touch with the other councilors, see if we can get a quorum together at, shall we say five thirty?"

"That'll work. Lila will call or text me when it's arranged?"

"Yes," Gary confirmed.

"I have a debriefing at noon, along with the others who were involved with the chief's incident last night."

"Good to hear. It's an important exercise to go through after something tragic like that happens." He looked at his watch. "It's a quarter of, now."

I nodded. "Better be on my way."

"Take care of yourself, Mayor."

7

The Buffalo County Sheriff's Office was a block away, so it was an easy walk and my fleece coat kept me warm. I was either blessed or cursed to have a strong curiosity and was determined to find somebody who'd share something prophetic about Chief Aaron Newel. It seemed he'd kept his life and activities private forever, but the last six months his behavior had changed enough for people to notice. That included his employer, the City of Brooks Landing, Minnesota.

I went in the north door of the historic courthouse. The original structure was a two-story brick building with a mansard roof and a domed tower in French Second Empire style. An addition, attached to the south side of the building, was built twenty years earlier. The atrium from the original structure had been extended and joined the two buildings. The county attorneys and court services offices occupied the west side, the sheriff's office was in the center, and the jail wing was on the east side. It was designed to blend in and not distract from the original century old courthouse.

I walked through the wide center atrium past the expansive

staircases—one on each side—that led to the second-floor offices. Elevators had been installed some years back. The east and west corridors on the first level led to service offices on one side and courtrooms on the other. The addition had afforded more space to move and expand the departments' needs. I entered the newer section, and the sheriff's office was straight ahead. A front desk receptionist sat behind glass in the front entry. There was a six-inch pass-through area between the glass and the base.

The young receptionist looked up at me. "May I help you?"

"Yes. Hi, I'm Camryn Brooks and I'm here to meet with Detective Garrison and some others."

She stood and walked to the door. "Oh, sure, Mayor Brooks. Yes, come on in, and I'll take you to the conference room."

The lock clicked, so I opened the door and stepped inside.

She fell in beside me. "I'm Tammy. It's good to meet you."

"Likewise," I said.

Tammy lifted her hand and pointed at the open path between desks as we made our way through the maze. Six people, four women and two men, sat at computers. Buffalo County had over eighty deputies who patrolled the roads and responded to calls. Along with a long list of other duties, it kept office staff busy. People nodded as we passed.

I spotted the sheriff's office in the corner, the chief deputy's office straight ahead, and a captain's office to the right when we turned that direction. "We'll take the next left down that hallway, the conference room is the last door on the right."

When we stopped at the open door, I saw Detective Tim Garrison, Deputies Emily Holden and Greg Thompson, Clint, Jake, and the two EMTs, Chad and Bill. They stood in small groups around the table.

Garrison smiled at me. "Mayor, come right in."

"Thanks, and call me Camryn."

"Sure. Before we get started, just checking to be sure we all know each other," he said.

We looked around and nodded. Clint's smile warmed my heart. As people found seats, Clint pulled a chair out for me then took one himself. Jake sat on his other side.

Detective Garrison stood in front of the whiteboard on a wall. "Let's go ahead and get started. Our session today will be informal. I'll take notes and may or may not use the whiteboard." He waved his hand behind him. "There are notepads and pens on the table. Feel free to use them if you'd like. Consider this a safe environment. And a comfortable one. You can say whatever you think or feel without criticism from others. That's the one rule. Do you all agree to that?"

Most nodded, and I heard a few affirmations.

Garrison continued, "Law enforcement officers don't always want the world to see their touchy-feely side. I know the same is true for a lot of EMTs and paramedics. It's a culture thing. We witness all kinds of tragedies and put on a brave face more than we should.

"There's evidence that first responders and others who witness traumatic events often don't realize at the time how much they're impacted. A month or even a year later they start having panic attacks or other delayed reactions and symptoms. Health-related issues. If we bottle up our emotions, try to pretend we aren't negatively affected by a bad event, those responses can happen to any of us. We're doing debriefs more and more for that very reason. We can lay our cards on the table, so to speak, to help us heal and move on."

Deputy Emily said, "Yep. They've helped me a lot after critical incidents."

Garrison nodded. "Same here. Terrible events are hard to forget. Some we never will. They play over and over and over in our brains. A few times in my career, after a bad one, I made the mistake of drinking *way* too much to try to forget. It didn't work, and I ended up with splitting headaches that made it all the worse. Don't do that."

I heard a few quiet comments.

Garrison went on. "For your own peace of mind and good mental and physical health, you need to stop that replay, move it to a different place in your memory bank. Put it into perspective. The best way to do that is to confront it, talk about it, work through it."

Some audible comments.

Garrison cleared his throat to quiet the room, get our attention. "We were all involved in Chief Newel's case. Camryn, you witnessed his death. Chad and Bill, you worked to save his life. Clint and Jake, Newel was your boss. Emily and Greg, you processed the scene, collected evidence.

"It helps to verbalize what happened. But if you're not comfortable doing that, we'll respect that. We each process things in our own way. And that might be by listening to what others have to say." He paused and glanced around the room. "Whoever wants to start, go ahead."

Chad raised his hand. "I'll go. Me and Bill did a mini debrief last night, talked about it for a while. Chief Newel's death was really tough for us. We figured the AED would bring him back, and when it didn't, it was hard to accept."

"Yeah, we kept asking ourselves why. Did we do all we could? Did we get there too late? We know we did what we were trained to do and need to accept the times when we lose a patient, not dwell on it too much. Easier said than done," Bill said.

I was not cut out to respond to life-or-death situations, be responsible to save—or try to save—someone's life. When Chad and Bill relayed their experience and how they felt, my insides started to tremble. I had a greater admiration for them and the work they did. I'd seen emergency workers in action many times and realized I thought of them more as professionals than as individuals with human emotions who had to come to grips with traumatic incidents.

Emily went next. "Death scenes are always tough. You feel bad for the ones who died, and then you want to make sure you don't screw anything up, evidence-wise. I laid in bed last night going through every step we took. When we were there, I tried not to focus on Newel's body and concentrate on processing the scene instead."

"What Emily said," Greg added.

I didn't know if Clint or Jake would speak, so I decided to go next. I raised my hand. "It was the first time I was actually with someone when they died. It scared me half to death. I was set to meet the chief for the first time, and just got a short glimpse of him before he died. I'll never forget the expression on his face when his heart must've stopped beating."

"It was a traumatic experience for you, no question about it, Camryn. Is it helping to talk about it with others who were there?" Garrison said.

I nodded. "It does. Seeing what all of you did last night, trying to save the chief, and then making sure everything was done right after he died, helped me a lot. You know what our city administrator, Gary Lunden, told me this morning? He was glad

68

Chief Newel wasn't alone when he died. Thinking about that gave me some peace."

The group smiled and nodded at that.

Garrison glanced at Clint and Jake. "Anyone else?"

Clint hitched up a shoulder. "It was a big shocker all right. I think when we find out what caused his death, I'll be able to work through the process better."

"Yeah, we're in limbo right now," Jake said.

"That's a valid way to feel. We all want an answer, a good explanation to help us move on." Garrison's phone vibrated. He pulled it from his pocket and looked at its face. "Excuse me and hang tight, I need to take this." He left the room and we sat in silence a minute, then Emily looked at me. "It sounds like you're gonna be okay."

I attempted a smile. "I'm glad Garrison arranged this debriefing. I had a lot of briefings, some debriefings, when I worked for a senator. Now I see I could've used a lot more debriefings."

That got a few chuckles from the group. "What exactly did you do?" Emily said.

"I was Senator Zimmer's director of legislative affairs. In a nutshell, I worked with planning and legislative policies. It involved a lot of research and developing good working relationships with members of congress. Probably the phrase that best describes the whole scope of the job is, 'other duties as assigned.'"

"Wow. I don't know how you managed a high-pressure job like that." She wrapped her ponytail around her finger.

"I didn't think of it that way when I was in the thick of things because I loved what I was doing. It was a big adjustment when I moved back to Brooks Landing, but I miss Washington less and less every month that passes."

"No wonder the city council folks wanted you as mayor, having that background and experience," Emily said.

"It's a whole different ball game. I found out from the get-go that a mayor has a long list of duties. Presiding over the city council meetings, following Robert's Rules. It's a steep learning curve. All the local ordinances, like zoning as one example," I said.

"Nothing I'd want to do," Jake said.

From their mutterings, I gathered it was a job not one of them had their eyes set on.

"Will the city council hire a new chief, or how does that work?" Chad asked.

"Yes, we'll work with the city administrator on that." I couldn't say anything specific, especially with Clint and Jake at the table.

The seven of us chatted for a few more minutes until Detective Garrison returned with a deep crease between his eyebrows and a paper in his hand. He took his position at the head of the table. Grim was the best way to describe his expression. It seemed like an hour passed before he said, "This is Chief Aaron Newel's preliminary autopsy report. It shows he had a lethal level of fentanyl in his system."

"*What*?" Clint and Jake said at the same time as they both stood and moved to either side of Garrison.

Garrison passed the paper to Clint and said, "Plus, there were traces of fentanyl on the envelope glue and on the chief's lips and tongue."

My heart dropped into my stomach. Oh, my dear Lord, it wasn't a weird coincidence that he died after licking the envelope, as I'd hoped. He died because he'd ingested a lethal drug from the envelope. Had my random "poison" thought been some sort of premonition? Someone had deliberately killed Chief Newel. *I had witnessed a murder.*

"It says here only Newel's fingerprints were on the envelope. We know that if Chief had taken fentanyl, he wouldn't put it on the glue of an envelope, one that had a check he'd written in it," Clint said.

"Which means the killer wore gloves," Garrison said.

"What an awful thing. Who would think up something like that?" Emily said.

"No kidding. Not to mention how risky it was. What if he'd had his secretary send the check for him?" Greg said.

We would have lost poor Margaret instead. The thought made me shudder.

"I can't think of a crime we've investigated quite like this one," Garrison said.

Clint finished reading the report and passed it to Jake.

Jake shook his head. ""I thought we'd find out Chief Newel had a bad heart. Now come to find out he had an enemy who hated him enough to kill him."

"We know people kill for any number of reasons, and I intend to uncover what the killer's was," Garrison said.

"A homicide sends us down a whole different path, Detective," Clint said.

"From a suspected medical to probable murder. The first thing that comes to mind is the killer must've been convinced Chief Newel would send in a contribution, would lick that envelope himself instead of having his secretary do it, as Thompson suggested," Garrison said.

"I'm with you on that. So someone from Fresh Start Rehabilitation who knew him well enough? It's where the thank you note and fateful contribution envelope came from," Clint said.

"That'll be the first place to start." Garrison rested his hand on Clint's shoulder. "We'll get right on it. Give it the time it deserves. I'll ask the captain to reassign my other case to another detective."

Clint nodded. "Thanks."

Bill read over the report. "Two milligrams, that's less than half a teaspoon, is fatal. With the high level in his system, we know why the AED didn't revive him, why we couldn't bring him back."

"And the drug traces on his lips and tongue supports one of the reasons they got away from mouth-to-mouth resuscitation back when. For unexpected risks like that," Chad added.

Bill homed in on me. "Plus when Good Samaritans came upon someone unconscious and not breathing, not all of them liked putting their mouths on a stranger's. Experts discovered chest compressions alone were about as effective. But if someone I know stops breathing, I'll do both. I keep a shield in my pocket all the time."

"So do I," Chad said.

The report had gone from one to the next as each read it. When it got to me, my eyes filled with tears and the words on the report got blurry. I blinked them away and focused on what it said. It was my first experience reading an official medical examiner's report. And for a man I'd seen die, besides. The look on Newel's face as he died popped into my mind and sent shivers up my spine and down my arms.

"Chief Newel needed help and there was no way to save him," I summed up.

Clint walked over, put his hands on my shoulders, and gently squeezed. "With the high level of fentanyl in his system, even if we had known he'd ingested an overdose, an opioid antagonist wouldn't have brought him back."

"Clint's right. But it serves as a good reminder for us to use the naloxone spray when we don't know what caused someone to stop breathing. And we have used it, plenty of times over the years," Chad said.

"It is contraindicated for someone with known heart problems unless you know it's an overdose. Then you have to use it anyway," Bill said.

"Camryn, Chief's autopsy results add another stressor. That aside, I agree with Gary Lunden, what he told you. I'm glad you were with our chief when he died, that he wasn't alone," Clint said.

"Thanks." I used the top of my sweater to soak up the tears on my cheeks.

Garrison took the report from me. "That phone call from the ME's office interrupted our debrief. If we'd known Chief's cause of death before we started, it might've coaxed different responses. That being said, do you have anything you'd like to say, anything to add?"

I didn't know what else I'd be able to share and shook my head. Others did too.

"No one?" Garrison handed me a business card. "Here you go, Camryn. I forgot to give you this last night. The rest of you have my contact information, right? Feel free to get a hold of me for any reason. We can always do a second debrief if needed. And if you want a one on one that's fine too."

"Thanks, we'll see how the investigation goes," Clint said.

"Sure. In the meantime, you probably know the newspapers

and local radio station contacted both the city and the county, asking for a statement about Newel's death. I'll work with the chief deputy, get one out this afternoon that says we're looking into his unexpected death and leave it at that for today.

"We don't want details leaked at this point, although the killer likely has figured out by now his deadly scheme worked. Chief Newel was a high-profile individual and it would be appropriate to schedule a short press conference in council chambers at Brooks Landing City Hall over the noon hour tomorrow. By then we can tell the public we're investigating the death as a homicide. Camryn, can you make those arrangements with your administrator?" Garrison asked.

"Sure," I said.

8

I felt better after I'd voiced my thoughts and feelings at the debriefing. But after the bombshell news that Newel had been murdered, my emotions went from better to worse to worst in the blink of an eye.

I had an even greater need to unveil the reasons Aaron Newel kept his personal life under lock and key. What had changed in his life that posed a threat to his job, his longtime career? He had an enemy, one who'd killed him. Was that person responsible, at least in part, for Newel's closed lips?

It was no secret he had intimidated the council members. And I had yet to ask them point blank why. Pinky mentioned he'd frightened others, as well. His mammoth stature, serious demeanor, or a combination of the two could've been the reason. He'd ruffled someone's feathers enough that it led them to commit murder.

Since Newel was no longer his boss, Clint might provide candid insights. The same could be said for Mark and Jake. I'd checked into Newel's work history with the city before our scheduled meeting and found not a single written complaint filed against him by community members or his staff.

The reason he'd left his former post hovered in the background. It would be unethical and probably illegal for me to access his personnel records to learn where he worked prior to Brooks Landing and the reason he'd left. No red flags when the city did Newel's background check, or they wouldn't have awarded him the position.

After Newel's first few months of absences, some "Where's Waldo?" comments had circulated among the councilors and staff members. That's when the city administrator and council gave it more serious attention. Newel had sick and vacation time to burn and managed to use up most of it. He'd need to revert to unpaid time off after that. Why?

When I got back to the city office building, I stopped to see Margaret before checking in with the administrator. She stood and attempted a smile when I walked through the door. "Hi, Mayor."

I unzipped my coat. "Call me Camryn, really. That is, unless you come to one of our council meetings to talk about an issue."

She raised her eyebrows. "Like that will ever happen."

The look on her face made me smile. "Margaret, I meant to ask you this earlier but forgot. What do you know about Chief Newel's brother?"

"What do you mean? Is there something I should know?"

"Not specifically. What I meant was, did the chief ever talk about his brother, growing up, things like that?"

She shook her head. "No. Like I told you before, he didn't discuss his personal life with me."

"I thought he might have dropped a casual comment about him and his brother when they were kids. Like some fun things they did, or trouble they got into."

Margaret shook her head again. "Nothing like that. He was a good boss when you consider he was fair and never yelled, even when a police officer did a dumb thing. I did my job as good as I could, and he noticed it too. Every so often he thanked me for that. I was curious about some things in his life, like his five-minute marriage, but didn't pry, and we got along fine," she said.

I lifted my hand and gently waved it. "So why were people scared of him?"

"They were? No one here was, that I know of. Maybe it was because he didn't back down when he thought he was right. A fight to the finish kind of guy."

He'd tried to fight against his finish too.

I wanted to ask Margaret if she knew about Newel's connection to Fresh Start Rehabilitation, but that had to wait. I figured Garrison would question her about it soon enough. "Okay, well thanks. I'll let you get back to it."

I left with the sad realization Margaret and other staff—along with the whole city—were in for a bolt from the blue when Garrison held his press conference the next day. A police press conference in our small town was rare. It was warranted, of course. A police chief's murder was big news, and would be reported around the state, maybe beyond. The grievous part for our city: it had happened in Brooks Landing.

Gary Lunden was on the phone when I stuck my head in his office. I held my hand up to indicate I'd check back later, but he waved me in and ended the call soon after. "I'm interested how your session at the sheriff's office went," he said.

"The first part was good. We all got a chance to voice what we'd experienced with Chief Newel's death, how we felt. The second part, not good at all. Not after we got the report of what caused his death." I stopped. It was difficult to say the words out loud.

Gary leaned over his desk, his eyebrows drawn together. "You have a strange look on your face, Camryn. What was it? What caused it?"

I got up and shut his office door then released a deep breath. "You need to keep this quiet until tomorrow. Promise?"

He raised his right hand. "Of course."

"Chief Aaron Newel was murdered."

Gary sprung up like a jack-in-the-box. His chair rolled backward with force, enough to send it to the bookshelf on the wall behind him. It started my heart pounding for the umpteenth time that day. He shook his head as if to clear it. "What do you mean? How is that possible?"

When I told him about the envelope with the lethal drug on it, his face drained of its natural beige color. "How could someone get that envelope into the police station?"

My shoulders lifted. "It was mailed to him, as far as I know."

"This is the second worst thing that's happened in all my years with the city. After Frosty." Mayor Lewis Frost, and Gary's close friend, had died the previous month.

"It's beyond horrid. Detective Garrison plans to release a statement to the public this afternoon saying they're looking into Newel's death, without referencing it as a murder. He wants to hold a press conference in council chambers tomorrow at noon, let the public know at that time Chief's death is being investigated as a homicide."

"This is ghastly." Gary started to pace back and forth in obvious distress. "We lost our mayor last month, now our police chief. What is going on here?" Lunden was on vacation when Mayor Frost had been killed, returned a week later. He was in the early stages of grief over the sad loss.

"As awful as what happened to Frosty was, it wasn't intentional. Poor Frosty bought a snow globe filled with diamonds bad guys wanted. If he hadn't been in his office when the bad guy came looking for it, he'd still be alive. I'd sold him the globe, so that will always haunt me. On the other hand, Newel's murder was premeditated. What haunts me about his death is, if Chief'd thrown the envelope away, he'd still be alive."

"What a tragic deal. Both their deaths will forever haunt me as well."

We fell silent a moment. "Gary, back to our earlier conversation, were you able to contact the other council members about the special meeting?"

He rubbed his face and it helped bring back some color. "As a matter of fact, when you got here, I was on a call with the last councilor. Everyone will be here for the emergency meeting at five thirty. It's a closed session, so no one besides the seven of us are allowed in."

It was my first closed meeting as mayor. "Seven of us?"

"The city attorney, Micah Stanley."

Legal counsel. "Of course."

"I'll have Lila get it posted on the front door right away," Gary said.

"I wish we could tell the councilors about Chief Newel, but I'm not sure they'd be able to keep it secret. Okay, I admit I'm thinking of one in particular."

He nodded. "Yes."

I reached my arms around Gary's neck for a quick comfort

hug.

"I'll be in my office checking emails and phone messages before I head back to the shop. Anything else I should do here?" I asked.

He shook his head. "Not that I can think of. Not that I'm able to think all that clearly right now. We'll get through this, Camryn."

"We will, and the investigators will find the guy who killed Chief. I'm sure of it." At least 99% sure.

I had a string of new emails, and most were matters unrelated to Chief Newel's death. That gave me some relief, but questions from citizens needed to be answered and issues addressed.

The eight phone messages told a different story. Six were from Sandy Gibbons, long-time local newspaper reporter, still employed at seventy something. She was tenacious in her pursuit of newsworthy scoops. It wasn't enough that she'd tried my cell phone a hundred times. Or so it seemed. I prayed for strength, lifted my desk phone receiver, selected her number, and hit redial.

Sandy answered partway through the first ring, like she held her phone with her eyes on its face. She was notably spry. "Cami! When you didn't call me back, I was worried something had happened to you. Like . . . well, I didn't know what to think."

"Sorry, Sandy. I'm fine, just very busy."

"Of course, of course. First off, I want you to know how sorry I am about Chief Newel. And I heard *you* were with him when he died. I can't imagine how awful that was."

"I was, and it was. But I'm working through it."

She laid her cards on the table. "Can I get a quote for the paper?"

"Sandy, I really don't want to make any personal comments

80

about how I feel, so that leaves me with nothing to say for now. I understand the sheriff's office will release a statement this afternoon. They also plan to hold a press conference at city hall tomorrow at noon, after they know more about Newel. You'll be invited, I'm sure."

"Oh! Okay. Thanks for letting me know. The city council will need to appoint a new chief, right? Like how they appointed you, after Frosty died."

"Yes, we'll be meeting in closed session to discuss that," I said.

"So you'll let me know what happens?"

"Sandy, I can't share our discussion with you, but if we pick a candidate and that candidate accepts, we'll make it official at our next council meeting."

"Really, you'll make me wait a whole two weeks?" she whined.

"There's a reason the session is closed, but we should be able to share the council's recommendation before that."

"I would hope so. I mean how can you keep that secret?"

I smiled at her comment. Someone had leaked Chief's death the night before and I suspected the council member who had Sandy's number on speed dial. Stormin' Gorman. I had kept more secrets for people than I could remember, as far back as my childhood. Sandy was a champion at pulling out information, confidential or not, and I was on guard when we spoke, weighing what would be okay to go into the public realm, and what needed to stay private.

Time to end the conversation. "Take care, Sandy, I need to run."

"Okay, but don't forget about me."

81

As if I could. I hung up and stared at the watercolor on my office wall. It was a still calm lake with nearby trees that stood on its bank and reflected from its surface. After an attempt to lose myself in the tranquil scene, my mind flipped back to Chief Newel and his cause of death. Someone had come up with an original scheme to kill him. And at great risk. What if someone other than the intended victim died instead? Like Margaret. The thought sent a shudder through my body.

I planned to talk to Gina again, after Detective Garrison held the press conference. What he told the public would help me figure out what to say to her. She would ask me why Garrison thought it was a homicide, but I couldn't tell her about the poisoned envelope from Fresh Start Rehabilitation. I wondered how Garrison and Clint would frame questions when they interviewed people.

It appeared someone connected to Fresh Start was guilty of the crime, but that seemed too obvious. What made the most sense was the bad guy used the treatment center's envelope to either frame them, or as a distraction to send investigators down the wrong path. But who wrote the personal note, posed as the center's CEO? It had to be someone with inside knowledge.

I was deep in thought until Clint gave a knock on the door and stepped into my office. "You look like you're in a faraway place, Ms. Mayor."

I blinked a few times. "I guess. Lots to think about."

He closed the door behind him. "It's going to be a tough investigation."

I stood and pointed at the wingback chairs by the side wall. "Let's sit there." After we took our seats, I said, "Clint, you never wanted to say much about Newel, but now that we have proof someone killed him, can you think of a reason they'd want him dead?"

"None that I know of. I've been wracking my brain since we got the report." He blew out a big breath.

"Margaret said he was a fair boss. Didn't yell when officers screwed up."

"That's true. Newel mostly stayed out of our way, let us do our jobs."

"Where did he work before he came here?" I asked.

"Ironwood, up north. Smaller town than Brooks Landing."

"You think something happened to make him leave?"

"I'll let you in on what one of my buddies from the next town over from Ironwood told me. Newel got involved with women he shouldn't have. One in particular, namely the city administrator's wife. That sealed his fate in Ironwood," he said.

My eyebrows lifted. "And Brooks Landing didn't consider that a red flag?"

"I doubt they knew about it. According to my source, Ironwood asked for Newel's resignation with the understanding they'd give him a recommendation to his next employer in exchange. Happened that we had an opening and he jumped on it. I heard about that arrangement after he'd been here a couple months."

"Could Ironwood's city administrator be considered a suspect?" I asked.

"Newel left their town ten years ago, so not likely."

"You said Newel got involved with women he shouldn't have. Meaning there were others?"

"That's what my reliable source told me," he said.

I narrowed my eyes. "Was the chief some sort of Casanova?"

"I don't know if he always initiated the affairs. Believe it or not, some females throw themselves at men in uniform."

I smiled. "I can easily believe they'd throw themselves at guys like you. And I guess Newel was a good-looking man in uniform, if that's what attracted the females you're talking about."

"I saw him put on the charm over the years," he said.

"Really? So why were people intimidated by him, like city council members?"

"Chief didn't back down. He considered himself as the one with the most authority in the city, which wasn't true. He wouldn't let anyone—like the city council—tell him how to run his department. If they tried, he convinced them otherwise. He did that plenty of times over the years."

"You're saying Newel was a bully and the councilors let him get away with it?"

"I wouldn't say that. He never yelled or threatened anyone. When he thought he was right, he insisted on his own way and got it." Margaret had alluded to the same thing.

"Wow. But no suspects among the councilors, in your mind?" I asked.

He frowned. "Can't imagine it. Even if we discovered one of 'em had a compelling motive."

"What about Rosalie Stormin' Gorman? You think she ever had a personal relationship with Newel?"

His eyebrows lifted. "Why do you ask?"

"She defended him and had the biggest emotional reaction to his death."

"Gorman is an expressive person, any way you look at it. Besides, why would she want him dead?"

"Maybe he done her wrong?" I said.

"Hmm. She'll be questioned, along with everyone else.

9

Clint left me to my thoughts. Newel was involved with women—plural—he shouldn't have been. Had an inappropriate relationship led to his death? Had someone from Ironwood, or elsewhere, carried a grudge against Newel and acted on it? In that case, they would've known about his connection to Fresh Start Rehabilitation. Probable? Maybe not. Impossible? No. Some people let old wounds fester for years before they took action.

If the city administrator was still with Ironwood, it'd be easy to learn his name and if he was married. I added that to my mental list of things to check out. Clint's comments about Aaron Newel had opened new possibilities to dig into. Was the reason for his "five-minute marriage," as Margaret had dubbed it, because he had an iron in a fire outside his own home?

I'd track down his ex-wife and hoped she'd talk to me. What Garrison revealed the next day should be a game changer for her and others. People reacted in a variety of ways to unexpected news. But the bottom-line question was, would they be more likely, or less likely, to talk to investigators?

I'd witnessed the way fear brought out either reaction. People withheld information to protect themselves and their loved ones. Because they'd done something bad, or because they'd been threatened. Fear also caused people to come forward with information. They knew the truth would come out eventually, and it saved everyone's time.

Fear wasn't the only motivator, of course. Some people could not withhold the truth whether their life depended on it or not. A good and honorable thing in my book. On the flip side, some guilty parties had no problem lying, even when the evidence and eyewitnesses proved they were. They would not admit to wrongdoing to the bitter end: "Not guilty."

I realized I'd gone down a rabbit hole and rubbed my temples to clear my thoughts.

Gary Lunden popped his head in my office. "Detective Garrison just issued the statement about Chief Newel's death and announced they'll hold a press conference tomorrow when they have more information. That should hold the wolf hounds at bay." Beads of sweat appeared on his brow and above his collar.

"The timing seems good in one way and not in another. The public deserves the truth, but Garrison needs time to follow up on any early leads he's gotten."

"I tend to agree, but it's their call."

I mustered some confidence when I said, "Gary, they'll find Newel's killer. Rest assured about that."

He pulled a hankie from his pocket, wiped the sweat from his forehead and neck, and left without another word. The poor guy was downright distressed. The city had lost their mayor and police chief. We needed the city administrator to stay healthy.

My parents had held down the Curio Finds fort for a few hours. I made my way down the city hall corridor, told Lila I'd see her later, and left the building. The brisk, cold air felt good. It refreshed me, cleared my mind to help plan the next steps. If there was time before the closed session, I'd do some online research on Ironwood, its city administrator, and the former police chief from a decade ago.

Pinky spotted me from behind her counter and swept into my shop. No one was in Curio Finds, including my parents. She waved her hand toward Brew Ha-Ha. "Cami! Your folks are having coffee. Hang up your coat and join us so we can hear all about your debriefing and everything else you've been up to the last few hours."

"Everything else" I'd been up to made it seem like the debrief was the day before. "Okie doke." *Not that I can tell you everything.* I dropped my things off in the office then joined the others next door.

Pinky went to the other side of her counter. "What can I get you to drink and eat, Cami?"

I glanced up at her whiteboard, but couldn't decide. "I guess I missed lunch, so any kind of muffin and your featured coffee is great." I'd had the same thing for breakfast, but what the heck.

She had them ready in a flash. "Go join your folks. I'll bring these over."

"Thank you, my friend."

My parents put on smiles when I sat down. Pinky set the goodies on the table and snaked an arm around my shoulder. "Okay, take a bite and then spill the beans."

The blueberries in the moist muffin tasted fresh. "Where to start. People at city hall and the PD are having a hard time, of course. I talked to Margaret and Lila and Gary Lunden. And Sandy

Gibbons—"

"*Sandy*? She's more of a gossip than I am," Pinky said.

I lifted a hand. "I didn't have a lot to say to her. On a related subject, Detective Garrison released a statement a while ago about Chief Newel's death."

My mother leaned forward. "What did he say?"

"I didn't hear it. Gary told me. It sounds like they'll have a press conference noon tomorrow at city hall."

"Really? That's kind of unusual," Pinky said. She was perceptive.

I sipped my coffee. "It's not every day a youngish police chief dies in office. I guess Garrison wants to inform the public; give the media a chance to ask questions."

Her eyebrows lifted. "I suppose."

"It'll be on the local radio station, I imagine," Dad said.

I gave him a nod. "I'm sure."

Pinky pushed at my hand. "Okay, you're done with your muffin. Now tell us about the debriefing."

I gave them an overview, from the time I arrived at the sheriff's office to what Garrison said about the importance of addressing our thoughts and feelings. But I didn't get into the specifics of what people said, or share the news bomb from the medical examiner's report.

Mom reached for my hands and squeezed. "It sounds like a good exercise to do, after all you've gone through."

Dad wore a slight smile when he said, "That's a good way to put it, Beth. Cami, you have gotten caught up in unexpected circumstances, and we're glad you have resources available to help you."

"Me, too," I said.

"Me, three," Pinky added.

I shook my head at the familiar joke. "The city council will meet in closed session at five thirty today to appoint an interim police chief," I said.

"Can't Clint just keep doing what he's been doing for months?" Pinky said.

"We need to make it official, whoever the council decides to appoint. I'll need to recuse myself, given my relationship with Clint."

They all agreed.

"You've had an emotional twenty some hours. We surely can stay in the shop for the rest of the day so you can go home, have more time to debrief," Mom said.

"Thanks, but I'd just as soon stay here until the council meeting. You know, keep busy," I said.

Mom's smile looked sentimental. The corners of her mouth lifted, but her eyes looked sad. "Cami, you get that keep busy trait from Berta. Along with other things, like your natural curiosity, your need to figure things out, solve problems." She blinked away tears. "It's like having my sister still here with me." She'd told me similar things over the years, and it usually caused us both to tear up.

Dad put his hand on Mom's forearm. "We've been blessed to have Cami. What do you say, Beth, should we head for home?"

"Yes, but I'd like to stop at the grocery store on the way. In case we get that snow they're predicting."

"We can do that," Dad said.

After my parents left, Pinky straightened the chairs. "When your mom talks about your birth mother, it chokes me up every time."

I stacked the cups and plates. "It's happy and sad at the same time. Mom's words play through my brain the times I look in the mirror and see my birth mother."

"The older I get, more and more I see my mother staring at me from my own mirror. It's a little eerie." Pinky laughed and broke the moment.

I carried dishes to the sink behind the counter, washed them in the soapy water, and dropped them in the sanitizing rinse water. "Not a lot going on in the shops today, huh?"

"Not too much. Your folks had a few customers, and my afternoon coffee rush should start any minute. Might not be the same as it'd be on a nicer day."

"You never know. Hot beverages hit the spot when it's freezing out there. I'll be in my office if you need me. Text me if you get busy," I said.

"Will do."

I went to the office, turned on the computer, and connected to the internet. I searched the City of Ironwood website. It was a town about two hours north, population 5,250, a few thousand people smaller than Brooks Landing. I learned Lowell Fischer had been the city administrator for sixteen years. That meant Fischer was the one Newel had wronged, so to speak, when he took up with his wife.

I looked up Lowell Fischer on social media and located his professional profile on one site, and his personal one on another. He looked to be in his mid-forties, had 1,621 friends, listed the high school and college he attended, his occupation and employer, and his status as married. Fischer had photos of himself with a woman and teenage kids at social and sporting events. He'd tagged Jeni Fischer, and she had tagged him, in family and social photo posts.

I looked at Jeni's profile next, and a recent post showed Lowell and Jeni on their wedding day with a "Happy 20th Anniversary to my husband and best friend," in the description. The snarky comment that came to my mind was, *so why did you get involved with your city's police chief?*

Their family looked happy and cohesive, given the photos from present days to years past. Whatever the reason for Newel's and Jeni's fling, it did my heart good to know it hadn't ended the Fischer's marriage. And to give them the benefit of the doubt, they may have ended whatever brewed between them before it went too far. I'd been told by others who went through rough patches in their marriages they'd been tempted by greener pastures, but had stopped "in the nick of time."

The City of Ironwood was right to ask for Newel's resignation, given the personal and professional conflicts and the lines he'd crossed. Whether their affair had ended by the time Newel got his ultimatum or not. After my brief search, it didn't seem Lowell Fischer had a reason to kill Newel for something he'd done ten years before.

On the other hand, if Newel was involved with another woman along the way that had led to a broken marriage, it was another matter. I'd ask Clint to check with his buddy, see if he knew of other affairs or threats Newel had gotten when he worked for Ironwood.

Had Chief Newel's own marriage ended over an affair? Gina wouldn't say, and Margaret didn't know. I planned to talk to his ex-wife, realized I didn't have her name, and phoned Margaret.

"Brooks Landing Police," she answered.

"Hello. Sorry to bother you again, but when you mentioned Chief Newel's ex-wife, I forgot to ask her name. In case I know her," I added.

"Oh. Her name was Elissa Warne and I doubt she kept Newel as her last name after the divorce."

"I wouldn't think so. I may know Elissa by face if she's been in our shop, but not by name. Thanks, Margaret. I'll let you go, bye." I hung up so she wouldn't question me further.

I searched Elissa Warne's name on a social media site. Her profile and photo—an attractive brunette with sparking eyes— popped up. Her marital status wasn't listed, but the college she attended and her occupation as a nurse were.

I ran her name on another search engine and learned she lived about two blocks from me. Small world. If we weren't in the middle of a deep freeze, I'd walk by her house, and if she happened to be outside, I'd strike up a casual conversation, gain her trust. But warm spring weather was three months away. Too long to wait.

I decided to contact her after Detective Garrison made his big announcement about what had caused Newel's death. That might coax a deeper emotional response than her brief and odd reply, "Thanks for letting me know," when Clint delivered his death notice. When I considered how Newel died, I wondered, had she hated him enough to kill him? As a nurse, she'd know about medications and doses and what levels would be fatal. But given the way prescriptions were regulated and closely guarded, how would she manage to steal any?

And how would she get a hold of envelopes from Fresh Start Rehabilitation? She might have a personal or professional connection there. I knew cell phone and computer use was limited or restricted in some programs. It was possible the facility had a stack of stationery and envelopes available for clients to write letters to people in their lives. In that case, visitors would also have access to them.

I guessed Elissa Warne would be among the first people Garrison questioned, so I needed to stay out of his way and wait my turn. If he got word I was conducting a separate investigation, it might poke the bear. I'd gotten in hot water with law enforcement in past investigations. But I was in a different position, and as mayor of Brooks Landing, it seemed I had some responsibility to help find the person who'd killed our police chief.

I was lost in my thoughts when Clint phoned. "Camryn, Detective Garrison released the planned statement via Kip Jones at the radio station, so it aired, and they'll include it in their news reports throughout the day and evening. Garrison made a point to say the sheriff's office should know more before the press conference tomorrow."

"Okay. People will have to sit tight until then. And then the floodgates will open. Any idea who Garrison's interviewed so far?" I asked.

"No, but Fresh Start was at the top of his list."

"Clint, I know next to nothing about Fresh Start's program. What do you think about it?"

"Only heard good things, high success rate helping people get clean and healthy again. And if Chief Newel was about to send them five hundred big ones, he had good reason. Chief kept his personal life private. That said, it seems he would've mentioned the program. Unless he had a personal reason not to."

"You gotta wonder, all right. What doesn't make sense is that someone from there would kill the chief with a toxic chemical," I said.

"No, it does not."

"So how do you think it happened, the drug on the envelope

from Fresh Start, I mean?"

"It looks like a set up to me. Someone got a hold of a Fresh Start envelope and thought it was the perfect alibi," he said.

"It'd have to be someone who knew Chief Newel sent them contributions, right?"

"Right."

"You've known him a lot of years and he never mentioned Fresh Start to you," I said.

"No, he did not."

"So it stands to reason very few people would know Fresh Start was an organization he supported."

"No idea if he told anyone or not. But people talk, say things they shouldn't," he said.

"Huh. You mean like a Fresh Start staff tells his spouse about how generous Chief Aaron Newel is, and she tells a friend who happens to be Chief's enemy."

"Could be something along those lines."

"But that doesn't explain the personal note to Chief from Fresh Start's CEO," I said.

"No, it doesn't. And I don't doubt it's one of the first questions Garrison asked Matthew Anderle. Did he write the note, send him the donation request?"

"Yes. Clint—"

He cut me off. "Wait. Sorry, I need to go, finally got Mark calling back."

"Okay, bye."

Poor Mark was in for a shock when he got the news about Chief. I'd seen him die, witnessed the EMTs' efforts, watched the deputies at work, met the coroner when she arrived, and went through the debrief. Yet a part of me didn't believe he was gone.

10

As nosy as local reporter Sandy Gibbons was, I hadn't expected her in the waiting area outside Brooks Landing City Council Chambers when I arrived for the meeting with the council, city administrator, and city attorney.

"Cami, hi!" she called to me.

"Sandy, what's up?"

"I thought I'd hang around, see if any of you wanted to make a comment after your closed session meeting."

I chuckled and shook my head. "I can give you mine now. No comment."

"The meeting notice says that if council makes a decision in closed session, and the candidate agrees to accept the job and is available to be sworn in, you will open the meeting to the public as soon as possible, probably tonight."

I put my hand on her shoulder. "We'll see how it plays out."

"You should get the new chief sworn in as soon as possible, the sooner the better. Remember how you got sworn in as mayor at your first council meeting?"

I would never forget. "See you later, Sandy."

"You bet. I'll be here when you finish your secret meeting. As long as it takes."

Secret meeting. On a cold, dark winter night, when a relaxed evening at home seemed like a better option, I had to admire Sandy's tenacity. She was willing to hang around city hall, holding on to the possibility she'd be the first media person to get the name of the interim police chief she no doubt believed would be Clint.

I opened the chambers door at 5:20 p.m. and felt like I was late to the party when I spotted the councilors, administrator, and city attorney all seated around a conference table in the middle of the room.

"Hello, Mayor," Attorney Micah Stanley greeted me.

"Hi, Micah, and everyone. Do you know Sandy Gibbons is camped out in the hallway waiting for an announcement?"

"She was the first one here," Administrator Gary Lunden said.

I took the empty seat and nodded at my cohorts. Gary set a small tape recorder on the table. "Our meeting is confidential, but we need to record it in the event we get a request for it down the road. Or there's a legal question about the way we conducted the meeting." He pressed a button on the recorder. "It's January twenty-second and the Brooks Landing City Council is meeting in closed session to discuss the appointment of an interim police chief following the death of Chief Aaron Newel yesterday. We'll go around the room and identify ourselves. I'm Gary Lunden, city administrator." He turned to Stormin' next to him.

She took a breath. "Rosalie Gorman, city council."

"Wendell Lyon, city council."

"Camryn Brooks, city mayor."

"Gail Spindler, city council."

"Harley Creighton, city council."

"Micah Stanley, city attorney."

"Thank you. Let it be noted all councilors are present," Gary said.

Wendell raised his hand. "I'll start and cut right to the chase. Clinton Lonsbury has my vote. He's bright, level-headed, educated. Lonsbury has proven himself more than capable the last months when he filled in the times Newel was gone."

Gail went next. "I echo what Councilor Lyon said. Assistant Chief Lonsbury has my full support."

Harley nodded a bunch of times. "I agree. Plus he served our country in the Army for four years. Let's not forget that."

"And he's served the people of Brooks Landing for eleven years now. He'll do the city proud," Stormin' said.

Micah Stanley looked at me. "Mayor?"

"I think the councilors expressed their support very well, but given my relationship with Assistant Chief Lonsbury, I need to recuse myself and abstain from making any comments or weighing in on the decision."

Micah zeroed in on Gary. "Administrator Lunden?"

"I think Clinton Lonsbury is a fine choice. As a bonus, there's no need to do a background check, psychological and physical exams, or train him in. It seems Council has decided, and I think it's a win-win all around," he said.

"A reminder this is interim," Micah said. "We're a government agency so you'll need to post the position, open it to interested candidates. Keep in mind, a number of qualified candidates could apply that you'll need to interview."

It was a more complex process than I'd thought. Harley and Rosalie shrugged, and sent me looks I read as, "We'll cross that bridge if we come to it." Wendell raised his eyebrows and Gail jotted something on her legal pad.

Gary pulled at his top shirt button. "Yes, we will, if the need arises. In the meantime, the next step is to ask Clint if he'll accept the interim position along with the added responsibilities it entails," Gary said.

"One way to find out. Call him and invite him over here," Stormin' said.

Gary nodded. "We will recess and continue this closed session to a date and time we can meet with Assistant Chief Clinton Lonsbury." He turned off the recorder and had Clint on the phone a minute later. "Clint, Lunden here. As you know, the council met in closed session, and would like you to join them in chambers. . . . Now, if you're available. . . . Good, we'll look for you then. Oh, and Clint, come in the back way. Sandy Gibbons is waiting outside chambers."

He disconnected. "He'll be here in ten minutes, thereabouts."

Stormin' leaned forward and rested her ample bosom on the table. "How did he sound to you, Gary?"

He shrugged. "Like Clint."

We speculated and chatted until Clint let himself in the back door seven minutes later. He wasn't on duty and looked as good in jeans and a flannel shirt as he did in uniform. Even better, more rugged. His brows creased in a slight frown as an apprehensive look crossed his face. I imagined his mind had run through different scenarios after he got summoned by the administrator.

Gary stood and indicated the empty seat at the table for him. Clint gave a slight nod, sat down, and cast his eyes on mine for a split second. I glanced around and noticed all the councilors had their full attention on Clint with positive-looking expressions, perhaps to ease his mind, show their support. My heart thumped in anticipation. Would Clint accept the appointment?

Micah Stanley pointed at the recorder. "You can go back into your closed session, Administrator Lunden."

Gary turned on the recorder. "We are back from the recess. Everyone previously noted is still in the room, along with Brooks Landing Assistant Police Chief Clinton Lonsbury who has joined us. Clint, I'll get straight to the point. The councilors met and after a brief discussion, agreed they'd like to offer you the position of interim police chief, until we can make it official, or in the event something changes in the meantime. We all hope you'll say yes."

I was surprised when tears formed in Clint's eyes, and it choked me up. He squeezed his eyes together, used his thumbs to slide the tears into his sideburns, then sniffed a couple times before he spoke. "I am honored, Administrator Lunden, Mayor Brooks, council members. The last twenty-four hours have been the most surreal ones of my life, my career. I didn't expect to get so emotional, but your offer drove home the reality that Chief Newel has passed on. I haven't fully processed that fact, by any means."

I heard others snuffle as I brushed tears from my own cheeks. Gary made a choked sound then cleared his throat. "Clint, this is a tough one, all right. For all of us. He was your boss, so you had more contact with him than any of us. But we'll get through this together, and one of the first steps is to appoint a new chief. It will be an interim position, for now, until we can cross all the legal Ts and dot all the legal Is. When you said you were honored, does that mean yes you will accept the appointment?"

Clint's eyes were red-rimmed with more tears ready to spill as he looked from one to the other around the table. "I will. And I thank you for your confidence in my ability to do the job. I promise to do my best."

It was a bittersweet moment. The city council was gathered under tragic circumstances to select Newel's successor and had the best candidate ready to step in as the next police chief.

"Thank you, Clint." Gary looked around the table. "If there are no further comments, we can end the closed session. Ms. Mayor, when would you like to start the public meeting?"

I glanced up at the clock on the wall behind the dais. "It's five fifty, so let's start at six o'clock. Does that work for everyone?"

They all agreed.

"Very good. This meeting has ended at five fifty." Gary pushed the off button and stood. As did everyone else. We formed a circle of sorts around Clint, thanked and congratulated him.

"After you vote to appoint Clint, I'll administer the oath of office," Micah said.

"Thank you," I said.

"I better open the chambers door. I'm sure Sandy is chomping at the bit," Gary said.

When the door opened, Sandy wasn't the only one who came in. Jake, Mark, Pinky, and Erin fell in behind her.

"*Mark,*" Clint and I said together.

His face was ashen and his bright spirit had dimmed. "After Clint broke the news about Chief, I headed straight for home. He was always one of those larger-than-life kind of guys. I don't believe he's dead."

I threw my arms around Mark for a big hug. "We're all having trouble with that."

When I stepped back, Jake put a hand on Mark's shoulder. "Why don't we head to our favorite watering hole later, decompress over a beverage?"

Erin and Pinky moved in alongside Mark. "Good idea, Jake,"

Erin said.

I locked eyes with Pinky and mouthed, "What are you and Erin doing here?"

She motioned her head toward Mark. They were his support team. It was nice our friends were nearby, for Mark and Clint and Jake and me.

"Mayor? It's five fifty-eight," Gary said loud enough for everyone to hear.

I nodded and climbed the two steps to the dais with the other councilors in tow. We took our appointed seats. Gary sat behind his desk to the right of us, and everyone else sat in the visitors' chairs.

At 6:00 sharp I tapped the gavel and called the special meeting to order. "The purpose of this meeting is to appoint an interim police chief for our city. Council met in closed session and selected Clinton Lonsbury for the position. Assistant Chief Lonsbury has accepted, and we're here to make it official. Is there a motion to appoint him?"

"I'll make that motion, Ms. Mayor," Wendell said.

"I'll second the motion," Stormin' said.

"We have a motion and a second. Is there any speaking to the motion?" When no one responded, I added, "I need to recuse myself from the vote." No reason to add why. "All in favor, signify by saying 'aye.'" Four assented. "Motion passes. Congratulations, Chief Lonsbury. If you and Attorney Micah Stanley will come forward for the oath of office."

The two men met and faced each other in front of the dais. Micah held a printed sheet with the oath in his left hand. He lifted his right hand and instructed Clint to do the same, which he did. Micah said, "Repeat after me. I, Clinton Lonsbury, do solemnly swear to support the Constitution of the United States, the Constitution of the State of Minnesota, and will discharge faithfully my duties as Police Chief for the City of Brooks Landing, to the best of my knowledge and ability, so help me God." Micah paused after each phrase so Clint could speak the words. I was moved by the commitment, the solemnity behind the words. I had taken the oath as mayor two weeks earlier. When they finished, Micah shook Clint's hand. "Congratulations, Chief."

Lights from cell phone cameras captured the moment. Everyone in the room stood and applauded their approval. I somehow managed to keep my tears at bay. The councilors congratulated Clint and chatted for a bit before they said their goodbyes and left for prior commitments. They had yet to learn the details of Newel's death.

Sandy Gibbons moseyed her way to Clint. She produced a pen from behind an ear her professionally coiffed hair had secured in place, and pulled a memo pad from her hip pocket. "Chief Lonsbury, what do you think of your appointment?"

Clint studied her. "I'm grateful for the support and confidence the city council has shown me. I've been honored to serve Brooks Landing for the last eleven years, six of them as the assistant police chief. I'll continue my commitment to the city as long as I'm able."

Sandy swooned toward him, whether it was from exhaustion, or from her proximity to the hunkiest guy I knew. Clint caught her under the elbows and steadied her. Pinky and Erin stepped in and guided her to a nearby chair. Sandy waved her hand. "Thank you, but there's no need to fuss over me. The excitement got to me, is all."

My heart went out to Sandy. Her husband had died a few weeks before after a long illness. Expected, but just as sad, nonetheless. I had a strong suspicion she was lonely beneath the brave front she put on. She was likeable, but most people went out of their way to avoid her, whether she was after a story or not. I'd never seen her with friends or family members. Her only daughter flew the coop after high school and had returned only a handful of times the past two decades. I'd ask Sandy about the why behind that when the time was right.

I moved over to Clint, pulled him aside, and quietly said, "I wish I could have voted to appoint you, but you know you have my full support."

He touched my arm. "That's all that counts."

"The guys mentioned grabbing a beverage. It'd be nice to see if anyone else here wants to tag along. Maybe Sandy most of all," I said for his ears only.

His eyebrows shot up. "You're serious?"

"Why not? I wonder how many invitations she gets in a month."

"You make a good point." Clint whistled to get everyone's attention. "We've been to hell and back since last night, and I think the suggestion to get a burger and a brew would do us good. Who's up for some down time at Sherman's Bar and Grill?"

"I'd like to," Gary said, "But I was at that conference last night, and best head for home."

Micah shook his head. "My son's got a wrestling match, so I gotta skedaddle myself."

Sandy got up from her chair, her mouth downturned. Sad. "Have fun," she said.

I nudged Clint and he called out, "Wait, Sandy. You're coming with us, aren't you?"

Her face brightened and the corners of her lips lifted. "Me?"

"Of course. The invitation includes you."

"Really, well I—"

"I won't take no for an answer," Clint said with a grin.

Her smile made her face shine. "Then I'll have to say yes."

I caught the surprised look on Pinky's face. Her eyes were wide, and her mouth was open. I shot her a slight frown in return, a "be good" caution.

Sherman's Bar and Grill was a popular spot for people of all ages. Sherman's placed more emphasis on food and less on alcohol, and if patrons got too rowdy, they were asked to quiet down or leave. That kept the dining and social experience more pleasant for everyone else.

Our group gathered near the front reception desk to check in. The place was already hopping since people tended to go out earlier in the winter. When the sun set in the late afternoon, it seemed later than it was. Sherman's had been a department store in its former life, and the large area had been converted into several smaller dining spaces with a large horseshoe bar in the main room.

It was decorated to resemble a ski chalet with old, dark wood planks that ran at different angles and formed designs on the walls. A stone fireplace in the largest room made a cozy place to eat in winter.

Winter sports equipment hung on the walls, and were propped in corners: antique sleds, ice skates, toboggans, snowshoes, skis, and hockey pucks. They changed the wall hangings with the four seasons, and next would have baskets of flowers, metal spring décor pieces, and watercolor paintings that depicted the season.

We were escorted to our favorite section, the fireplace room, and directed to the large round table to the left of the hearth.

Servers set menus, water glasses, and baskets of honey mustard pretzels and popcorn in front of us. Their service was as fine as their food.

We settled in and passed the snacks around. When a server returned, we ordered beers, some preferred craft ones on tap, others liked bottled. We chatted, and my eyes were drawn to Sandy time and again. She looked like she'd won the lottery. Why hadn't I thought to invite her out before?

When our drinks arrived, Mark held up his glass. "Here's to our boss, Chief Newel. May he rest in peace." We raised our glasses and bottles, clinked them, and uttered words of respect for Newel.

Mark had toasted Chief Newel in death so it seemed a bit inappropriate to toast Clint in congratulations, since he'd been appointed to fill Newel's vacated position. But that didn't stop Sandy. She lifted her pale ale as high as her short arms reached. "Here's to our new chief!" *Interim chief, for the time being.* Our clinks were as quiet and reverent as they had been for Newel, our smiles subdued. Except for Sandy's, of course. We would have another celebration for Clint down the road.

A measure of guilt swirled inside me and dampened my mood when I thought how only four of us—Clint, Mark, Jake, and I— knew the truth about Chief Newel's death. And were sworn to secrecy until Detective Garrison made his announcement the next day. I exchanged a guarded look with Clint. He may have read my mind.

The officers told war stories and talked about work incidents they could share, then Sandy piped up, "I don't want to speak ill of the dead, but I have to say I never could quite figure Chief Newel out. He kept things closer to the vest than anyone I've ever known in my entire life. And that's a *lotta* years."

"He was a private man," Clint said.

"Very," Mark added.

I suspected that character trait would pose extra challenges for investigators on his case and felt compelled to get to the bottom of Newel's secrets, for my own piece of mind. I'd discovered in my private investigations that detectives faced obstacles as a matter of course. From what I'd learned over the years, most people had at least one dark secret they didn't want exposed. Most were not criminal in nature. Some were indiscretions. Many were stupid mistakes they regretted.

Clint put his hand on mine. "We lost you for a minute."

"Sorry. Did I miss anything?"

"No, we're thinking of calling it a night," he said.

"Ah, yes," I said as the others stood. "It was nice to be together."

We exchanged hugs, and Sandy's was extra tight.

Clint walked me to my car. "Is it okay if the interim police chief kisses the mayor?"

"Way more than okay." His kiss was hot enough to warm my entire body in the bone-chilling cold.

11

I drove to Chief Newel's house Thursday morning before Detective Garrison's noon press conference. It was four blocks northwest of city hall, a pleasant 1940s one-and-a-half-story tan house. I parked on the street in front and pondered the mystery man and what his personal life was like. What had he done for fun and relaxation? Had he interacted with his neighbors, was there a special someone among them he'd confided in?

Banks of snow were piled next to Newel's driveway and sidewalk, but the surfaces were clear. It had snowed the day before he died and it dawned on me shoveling snow was likely one of the last homeowner tasks he'd performed. He had attended to personal and professional duties right up till his unexpected end.

At 11:39, I headed to city hall. Garrison had phoned earlier and asked if I'd join him and Clint in front of the dais when he addressed the crowd. "Let's meet in the audio room next to council chambers a few minutes prior," he'd said.

I spotted news vans from three Minneapolis television stations, and one from St. Cloud, parked on the street and in the city hall parking lot. I knew Sandy Gibbons and the local radio station newscaster would be there, but hadn't expected reporters from outside Brooks Landing. Had Chief's manner of death somehow leaked out?

Mark Weston and Jake Dooley had been appointed guard duty. Mark held the front door open with a glum look on his face. We exchanged hand pats and nods. Jake took my arm and escorted me toward council chambers. When we were in the corridor, I asked him, a breath above a whisper, "Have city staff been briefed about what Garrison plans to say?"

Jake turned to me and glanced around to be sure no one was in eavesdropping range. "Yeah, Clint cleared it with Garrison to let our officers and staff know before the public press release, with the understanding they were under a gag order until then."

"Margaret too?"

He nodded. "She took it hard, passed out in her chair for a minute."

"Oh, no. How is she?" Margaret needed a thorough physical exam to uncover what caused her spells. It was the second one I knew of and figured there'd been others.

"She's okay now. She wanted to mind the office, didn't want to be in there." Jake moved his head toward council chambers.

"Poor thing. None of us do."

Rosalie Gorman hustled down the corridor in her storm's-a-brewin' fashion. "I don't think I slept two hours last night. Our chief's gone, now a press conference, and all those vans outside, besides. I have a bad feeling about this."

With good reason because it's about to get worse. Chatter from several conversations spilled out from council chambers. "We should get inside," I said.

Jake looked at his watch. "It's a full house with about fourteen minutes to the top of the hour. I'll check with Mark, but I don't think we need crowd control at this point. Seems like all the necessary parties are here. And then some."

Stormin' and I stepped inside. People talked with raised voices at different decibels that hurt my ears. Administrator Gary Lunden stood near his desk, next to the dais. Forty or fifty chairs sat in the visitor section, and after Stormin' took a seat, it'd be standing room only. Reporter and camera crews along with local radio station news director Kip Jones were set up in the back of the room ready to roll. Sandy Gibbons sat front and center in the first row. She touched my arm as I walked by, and I gave her a small smile.

I exchanged nods with Gary as I passed him and stepped into the audio room. The detective's and interim police chief's sober faces set my heart to hammering. As if the gravity of the situation wasn't enough in my already hyped-up state.

Garrison lifted a hand to greet me. "Mayor, glad you made it. I wasn't sure given the way you hesitated when I asked you."

"Sorry, you caught me off-guard. I'm still adjusting to my role, and what I should and shouldn't do. After I thought about it, I realized you were right. It's appropriate for the mayor to be with you and the police chief for this meeting."

We were silent a while. Garrison opened his folder and studied the paper inside. Clint kept checking his watch, and after the umpteenth time, sucked in a breath. "Eleven-fifty-nine."

Garrison straightened his shoulders. "Mayor, Chief, you can stand on either side of the podium. Your pick."

I caught Clint's attention and shrugged slightly. He lifted his eyebrows in return then opened the door. The podium was in front of the dais and equipped with a microphone. I followed Garrison and took my place on his right side. Clint filed in and stood on his left. Which of us dreaded the painful situation most?

Garrison laid his folder on the podium and flipped it open. The microphone was set at the right height. He stood for a few seconds and surveyed the crowd. "I'm Detective Garrison with the Buffalo County Sheriff's Office. With me are Mayor Camryn Brooks and Interim Police Chief Clinton Lonsbury."

I nodded and in my peripheral vison saw Clint remained still.

"Thank you all for being here. I hadn't expected such a large turnout, but should have, given the circumstances. It's rare to have a police chief die in office, thankfully. Chief Aaron Newel was with Brooks Landing Police for ten years and respected in the city, the county, and in the law enforcement community across greater Minnesota," Garrison said.

I scanned the faces in the packed room; many were unfamiliar.

Garrison continued, "On Tuesday at seventeen hundred hours, or five o'clock p.m., Chief Newel was pronounced dead in his office after an EMS team's valiant efforts were unable to revive him. Newel was taken to the Central Minnesota Medical Examiner's Office. The exam and tests revealed he died from a toxic chemical overdose. I'm not able to release specific details at this juncture, but suffice it to say, we are investigating Chief Newel's death as a homicide."

The room exploded with gasps and "whats?" and it seemed every hand in the room shot up. I did my best to maintain composure in front of the people and their stunned expressions.

Detective Garrison pointed at Sandy. "Ms. Gibbons."

"Detective, I'm flabbergasted. You're saying you have evidence that leads you to believe someone killed Chief Newel?

On purpose?"

"Yes." Garrison nodded at a TV reporter in the back.

"You caught something on camera?" the young brunette woman asked.

Garrison dodged the question. "Sorry I can't answer that." He pointed at Kip Jones.

"This question is for the mayor." Kip paused. "Mayor Brooks, I understand you're the one who called nine-one-one when you found Chief Newel. Did you see the chemical evidence that caused his death?"

Garrison cut in and saved me. "The mayor can't answer that." Then he indicated the St. Cloud television reporter.

"Thank you. Another question for the mayor. They introduced Clinton Lonsbury as the interim police chief. Does that mean you'll be posting the position, looking for another candidate?" the middle-aged man in gray asked.

"Go ahead and answer that, Mayor," Garrison said.

I didn't know if my voice would work with the tight band around my throat. I pushed out a breath to loosen it. "Our city council met last night and selected Assistant Chief Clinton Lonsbury to step in as the interim chief until we can go through a formal hiring process. He accepted. The council voted in favor, and Lonsbury was sworn in last night. But to maintain transparency and fairness, the position will be posted, yes."

Garrison waved at another news reporter. "Chief Lonsbury, do you have any comments?" a tall man with jet black hair asked.

"Nothing on the investigation, but I will tell you our department and city will grieve for Chief Newel a long time. I am humbled and honored to serve as the interim chief."

Garrison pointed at a thirtyish redhaired woman.

"Had Chief Newel received any threats on his life?" she asked. *Had he?*

"I can't answer that. In fact, we're not able to take any further questions at this time. When our investigation leads to the arrest of the person—or persons—responsible we'll release that information to all of you. Thank you." Garrison turned and headed to the audio room. I wasn't sure whether I should stay or go so I went, and Clint followed.

We formed a three-point circle. Garrison shook his head. "I hate press conferences when you can't tell the full story. But at least they know Newel's death was not natural and down the road they can't accuse us of concealing the truth."

"But there will be lots of speculation about his death and who killed him," Clint said.

"Of course," Garrison said.

"The killer would know they'd run a tox screen on the chief's blood," Clint said.

"You'd think. But the killer planned it so he wasn't there when Newel died. The perfect alibi, right?" I said.

"Carefully planned, no question," Garrison said.

"And what about cameras in the PD? There's one facing the chief's office, isn't there?" I asked.

Garrison raised his eyebrows. "Yes, and our investigation will be thorough. I'll leave it at that." He turned and tilted his head toward the back door. "I'll make my escape out that way."

"Don't blame you. And thanks, Detective. You did a fine job with the press," Clint said.

I was tempted to either follow Garrison or stay in the sanctuary of the audio room until everyone had cleared from council chambers. But I owed it to the councilors to join them. A

112

knock on the door solved my dilemma. Clint opened it and the four councilors and Sandy Gibbons piled in.

"I am beyond shocked," Stormin' said.

Harley stared from me to Clint and kept shaking his head. It unnerved me even more.

The twinkle was gone from Wendell's eyes. "Frosty killed just last month and now Chief Newel? I don't know what to think."

"I know. *Which one of us is next*?" Stormin' screaked.

Gail with her tranquil presence and soothing voice said, "What happened to Chief Newel was terrible. But there's no reason to believe any of us are in danger. Right, Chief Lonsbury?"

Clint nodded. "That is correct. No reason. The sheriff's office will conduct a topnotch investigation, and if they uncover anything that concerns them, we'll be notified immediately."

Harley found his voice. "Has anyone threatened you, Rosalie?"

"Well, no. I mean, people get mad at us for different reasons and the decisions we make they don't like," she said.

"Nobody gets *that* mad at the city council," Sandy said, reminding us she was in the room.

I lifted my hands. "Gail and Clint are right. This is really difficult, but it's in our best interests to stay as calm and clearheaded as possible. Maybe talk to someone, a professional. I know some I can recommend. And ministers are trained to counsel people."

"There are great psychologists right here in town," Gail said.

"Think about it, and we can talk later. For now, we should get back to chambers so people don't think we're in a secret, unauthorized meeting," I said.

"As a witness here, I can vouch that you weren't," Sandy said.

"Sandy, that being said, what we talked about here needs to stay *here*," Wendell cautioned. "We don't know what will turn up in the investigation, and some of our comments might lead to conjectures."

Sandy raised her right hand. "I understand and will not repeat a word of it." I imagined she twitched all over thinking she would've had a juicy scoop under different circumstances.

When my phone buzzed, I glanced at its face. "I need to take this. I'll join you in a minute." They all trooped out except Clint. When I mouthed, "It's my mother," he nodded and left.

"Hi, Mom." She and Dad were minding the store again.

"Cami, I'm glad you answered." She spoke faster than usual. "We weren't sure when to call. Oh, my! We have the local radio station on and it's all over the news, the press conference and everything. Chief Newel was *killed*? How is that possible? You were with him. Did someone poison him then sneak out the back door?"

I pinched the back of my neck to loosen the muscles. Oh, boy. "Mom, even if I knew anything, I wouldn't be able to tell you until the investigators figure it all out."

"I suppose. Gracious, such an *awful* thing. We'll pray no one else is at risk, that someone doesn't have a beef with the Brooks Landing Police Department."

That gave Stormin's comment a specific bent. "A good thing to pray for. Mom, sorry but I gotta go and need to be here a little while yet."

"Take all the time you need. A couple people checking out the January sale is about all that's going on here."

"Okay, see you soon."

Cold fingers walked up my spine as I hoped against hope

114

Clint's and other officers' lives were not in danger. I stepped into council chambers and saw Sandy in conversation with Kip Jones, the radio guy. The news people had packed up their equipment. I circulated among the people and thanked them for coming.

Pinky burst into the chambers and made a beeline for me. "Jiminy Christmas, Cami. What in the world? You were with Chief Newel when he died! How could someone poison him with you standing right there?"

Pinky, did you not see all the news folks here? I tried to pull her aside, but the media surrounded her like they were magnets, and she was the north pole. Camera crews moved in behind them.

"Mayor, is that true? Were you with Chief Newel when he died?" A Minneapolis reporter asked.

When Pinky realized her blunder, her eyes opened wide and her brows shot up close to her hairline. If I tried to respond to the reporter, I suspected it would come out like Jackie Gleason's response in the classic Honeymooners show when he was asked questions he couldn't answer: "Hmm a hmm a hmm a."

Administrator Lunden tuned in to the uproar and came to the rescue. "Is everything okay here? Mayor, you look a little pale."

Pinky picked up on the cue. "Sorry, Gary, it was my fault. I said something I shouldn't have, based on something I heard. I must've misunderstood. Or something. Sorry, Cami. Mayor, I mean."

I couldn't tell an out and out lie, and "No comment" seemed like a cop out. "It's all right, Alice. I can confirm I happened to be in the building when Chief Newel died. I didn't see anyone else there. And that's all I can say at this point. It's an open investigation and Detective Garrison with the sheriff's office will let us know of any developments."

Gary slipped his hand under my elbow. "Mayor, sorry, but there's something that needs your attention."

I glanced at the expectant reporters' faces. "Excuse me, everyone." Gary led me away before anyone tried to pump more out of me. When we reached my office, I said, "Pinky blurted out I was with Chief when he died. Loud enough for the reporters to hear. I can't believe she did that!"

Gary shook his head. "Ah, that's what got everyone so stirred up. It added fuel to the simmering fire."

"At least Pinky realized her major slip and back peddled as best she could. It caught me between a rock and a hard place. The truth would've come out eventually and what I said was the truth, just not the whole truth."

"It's okay. You didn't lie, you're good," he said.

"Thanks, Gary. I'll hang around here a while, give people a chance to clear out."

"It shouldn't be long. The reporters will need to get back to work. This is a major news story, but not much more for them to report on yet. They might look for people in town to get comments about Chief Newel or his murder. Get something quotable for their stories."

"I hope Pinky went back to her shop and no one tracks her down there. If she gets questioned, I'm afraid she'll give 'em answers. She can't help herself." That brought up a point. "Gary, can you go back to chambers, make sure the reporters haven't gotten hold of her?"

"Sure, I'll take care of it."

He hustled away as my office phone rang. I wasn't prepared to talk to a reporter or inquiring member of the public, so I let it go to voicemail. In case. My friends, family, colleagues, even Sandy

116

Gibbons, had my cell phone number if they needed to reach me. I turned and stared at the watercolor.

Pinky slinked into my office, bent over, threw her arms around my waist, and tucked her head in my side. "Open mouth, insert foot. I'm *so* sorry. I saw you and didn't really notice anyone else."

I pulled at her arms, reached for her hands, and took a step back so we faced each other. "It's okay, Pink. We covered it fine, got through it."

She gave me a hug then bopped her forehead with the heel of her hand. "Will I ever learn to stop, look, and listen before I forge ahead?"

I chuckled. "You keep life interesting, and I love you the way you are. We can expect the unexpected and that usually leads to fun or mischief of some kind. I've told you before I'm a little jealous of how spontaneous you are."

"And I'm a little jealous how you think before you act. Wanna trade?"

We both laughed and the rest of my exasperation dissipated like smoke.

12

After Pinky left, my thoughts turned to poor Margaret. If Chief Newel's death wasn't bad enough, the extra jolt he'd been killed had made her pass out. Ever since I'd scared her half to death, she'd pulled at my heartstrings. I needed to check on her, see how she was. Margaret should've been among the first people Detective Garrison talked to. Since he'd revealed Newel died from a lethal overdose, it seemed he'd need to get into specifics when he interviewed key people. And Margaret was key.

Had Garrison asked her about the mysterious envelope? When I figured the media people had left the building, I headed out city hall's front door. Detective Garrison was leaving the police station, and we met in the common atrium entry area. He'd left via the back door after the press conference and must've gone around to the front entrance. The person with answers.

"Hi, Detective. You did a nice job with the press. Thank you. But I need to tell you what happened in council chambers after."

"What's that?" he said.

I shared the Pinky incident and how we'd handled it. "Bottom line is, the press already knew I'd found Chief's body. Although I didn't admit to being with him when he died, I did admit I was in the building and hadn't seen anyone else there. Just so you know, Pinky feels awful."

Garrison rolled his eyes. "It sounds like no harm, no foul. Thanks for filling me in."

"Detective, I have a question. Since you announced that someone poisoned Chief Newel, did you plan to tell anyone how he got it?"

"That's a fair question. I spoke to both management and staff on all three shifts at Fresh Start last night and this morning. I informed them there was poison on an envelope from their facility but didn't disclose what the chemical was. I made each one promise to keep their interview under wraps until I've interviewed everyone who works there."

"I take it no one admitted knowing anything." When he didn't respond, I braved another question. "Did you ask the CEO if he wrote the personal note to Chief Newel?"

One eyebrow lifted. "I need you to keep this confidential."

"I promise."

"The answer is yes. I showed it to Matthew Anderle, and it turns out he had written the note, but it was a few months back. He didn't think to add the date at the time. In fact, he said Chief Newel sent a donation in the return envelope back then.

"Mister Anderle has no idea who would've sent the recent request for a donation, or how they'd gotten a hold of the old note he wrote. Unless Newel had it in his desk drawer since then and pulled it out for some reason. Maybe he was going to toss it. Again, an unknown someone sent the envelope with Fresh Start's address on it," he said.

"Hmm. But most likely, someone had gotten a hold of the

119

note and re-sent it with the deadly drug on the envelope. But who?"

"The answer we need to chase down," he said.

"Detective, did you find out Chief Newel's connection to Fresh Start?"

He evaded the question. "It's early days yet."

"And none of my business." I glanced at the police station door. "I'm on my way to see Margaret. Can you tell me if she knows about the drug on the envelope? So I don't say anything I shouldn't."

"I asked her and the other two secretaries if they remembered seeing a letter addressed to Chief Newel from Fresh Start. Without getting into specifics, I told them there was a chemical on it that caused his death."

Before I had a chance to ask Garrison how they answered, a woman entered the atrium and ended our conversation. Garrison took the front exit, and I went into the police station. Red blotches dotted Margaret's face. She pushed the button and released the door latch so I could get into the office area. Two secretaries were in their cubicles in the center of the room. "Margaret, do you have a few minutes to talk to me in the break room?"

She nodded and asked the secretaries to watch for visitors until she returned. When I offered the women my sympathies, they thanked me with quiet voices. Once in the small room, Margaret collapsed on to a chair.

I laid my hand on her shoulder. "Detective Garrison talked to you, told you about the drug Chief Newel got from the envelope."

She buried her face in her hands. "It just keeps getting worse. Bad enough that he died, but that someone killed him is just plain unreal."

I took a seat next to her. "Do you know how that envelope got

120

into his office?"

She lowered her hands, and her eyes met mine. "No. I think I would have noticed when I sorted the mail. But I can't swear to it. We get mail from different charities and groups delivered here, seems like about every day."

"Yeah, I do too, at my house and the shop. The secretaries didn't remember that particular envelope either?"

"No." She dabbed her cheeks with a tissue.

"Did the chief ever say anything to you about Fresh Start Rehab, their program?"

She shook her head. "Not to me. Not to the other girls, either, from what they said."

"Well, Detective Garrison will figure it out. Sorry if I'm being too nosy. My curiosity gets the best of me," I said.

"I don't blame you. We want to find out what happened."

I brushed a crumb off the table and leaned in closer. "The other thing . . . Margaret, I'd feel much better if you'd see a doctor, get a physical."

She looked at her hands, eyebrows drawn together. "You heard I fainted?"

"Yes."

"I know why. It's happened maybe six times in my life. The first time was when I was ten and my father died of a sudden heart attack at the dinner table. Our family was eating together, and then he was gone. I passed out from the shock."

I put my hands on hers. "Margaret, that's awful. I'm so sorry."

"Thanks. The doctor back then said that trauma caused it. I had a few more after that for different reasons. It was years since the last one, and then when you rushed in with your hand all full of Mayor Frost's blood, it triggered it again. And then today . . .

you'd think at my age I'd have built up a tolerance for unexpected things like that, especially given where I work. But I guess not." I was curious about the other times she'd fainted, but had no reason to ask.

We stood and hugged. "It shows you care. And thanks for sharing your history with me. It makes me worry a little less about you," I said.

She squeezed me tighter. "I know we got off on the wrong foot somehow, and I'm glad that's changed. You've been a good friend the last weeks."

"Thanks, so have you."

I met Sandy Gibbons on my way out the door. She puffed out a breath. "Cami, how are you doing with the whole Newel ordeal? When Detective Garrison dropped that surprise bomb, my heart pounded to beat the band for the *longest* time."

I nodded. "It was a big shocker, but we'll work our way through it."

"Yeah. Oh, and to change the subject, going to Sherman's with you and your friends was the best time I've had in years. I mean it. Despite what happened to Chief Newel, and all."

The memory of how happy Sandy looked at Sherman's brought on a smile. "I'm glad you came. We'll have to do it again sometime soon."

Her face beamed. I suspected Sandy was even lonelier than Margaret, and it struck me they might make good companions. To go places and do things together. Margaret was quiet and introverted but would not have to worry about initiating a conversation or deal with moments of uncomfortable silence. Sandy was never at a loss for words, always had questions about something. No dead air when she was around.

After our goodbyes, I headed south to the shop, and Sandy headed north to her car. The wind was minimal and the cold air refreshed me, felt good on my face, cleared my thoughts after the tense hour plus at city hall. I was half a block from the shop when I spotted a television news van parked out front. I picked up my pace and dashed into Brew Ha-Ha ready to run interference for Pinky, but found my mother behind her service counter instead. I saw a reporter and cameraman at a table with muffins and beverages.

The brunette female reporter waved at me. "Hi, Mayor. Here for a cup of java?"

I was at a loss for words the second time that afternoon and smiled instead. Mom with her great instincts picked up on the cue. "I'll get you your usual," she said.

Whatever that was. A surprise usual. "Thanks."

Seconds later she set a hot chocolate with peppermint on the counter. "On the house," she said.

"Thank you. Sorry I have to rush off. Bye." I waved at the news people and exited the way I'd entered. Did they know my connection to the shops? Not likely. I walked the few steps to the Curio Finds front door, went in, and made a shushing motion before my dad called out my name.

We met, and I whispered, "Tell me when the news people leave Pinky's. Did she go home?"

Dad took my arm, led me to the back office, and opened the door. Pinky sat hunched in a chair. Her eyes opened wide when she saw me. "I'm hiding," she said in a stage whisper.

Was she kidding, or had she experienced a blast from the past moment? "What?" I said.

My dad closed the door behind me.

"When I saw the news van pull up to my shop, I asked your mom to take over, and scooted back here."

My face was close to hers when I said, "You were afraid they'd wheedle some information and facts out of you, huh?"

Her head bobbed up and down. "And I don't even know that much. At least not the kind of info they'd be looking for."

"But you knew you'd have to say something, maybe something best left unsaid."

"Exactly. It's happened before." *About a million times.* "And the last thing I need is a visit from Detective Garrison because of it. So I'm hiding."

I snickered quietly. "So am I. Hiding, I mean."

She scrunched up her face. "What?"

I filled her in, and she joined me in a hushed laughing spell. When she stopped, the sides of her mouth turned down. "Cami, tell me the truth. Do you think you or Clint or Jake or Mark or the other council people are in any kind of danger?"

"I don't think so, but I'll feel better when they find Newel's killer and he confesses to why he did it."

"For sure. Chief Newel was the biggest mystery man I knew. Not that I knew him much at all. Because he was a mystery man."

"Has he gotten coffee or treats at your shop?" I asked.

"Yes, but not for a long time now."

"Not since I've been back in town. Did he come in alone, or with someone?"

She glanced down at her hands. "He and Rosalie Gorman used to come in together, here and there, a couple years back."

"Stormin' was here with Newel, like more than a couple times?"

"Yes. It crossed my mind that maybe they were having an affair, but I kinda doubted it."

"Stormin'?" I said again.

"Yes."

"Huh. Maybe that's why she didn't want to have *the talk* with Newel. Because of their past together."

"Could be." She picked up the drink I'd set on the desk. "You gonna drink this?"

"Go ahead, I've got to eat real food first. That's like dessert," I said.

"You've heard that Barbra Streisand saying, 'Life's too short. Start with dessert.'"

"I've heard it but didn't know who said it."

She took a sip. "The perfect winter afternoon treat."

My stomach growled. "You hear that? It's asking for some comfort food to settle its nerves."

"Like pot roast or spaghetti?" she asked.

"Maybe. I just had a burger at Sherman's last night, but a thick juicy cheeseburger would hit the spot about now."

Pinky picked up the office phone and punched in some numbers. "Hello? Yes, I'd like to order four cheeseburgers and two orders of fries to go. . . . Alice Nelson. . . . Thank you, I'll be there to pick it up." She hung up. "Sherman's has the best third pound burgers in town and none of us have had lunch yet. I'll slip out the back way to the parking lot."

"Where's your coat?"

She snapped her fingers. "Shoot, in my back room."

"I'll have Dad see if the coast is clear." I peeked around the office door and spotted him alone at the checkout counter. I crept closer to him and cleared my throat. He turned when he heard me, and I waved him over.

"Are they still in the coffee shop, the news people?" I said in a quiet tone.

"I believe so. I'll wander over." He strolled to the archway between the shops and when he came back, we joined Pinky in the office.

Dad shook his head. "They're still there, all right. Girls, I'm not used to all this espionage stuff. Or the two of you playing hide and seek like when you were kids."

Pinky and I looked at each other and shrugged.

"All right then, if you fly, I'll buy," Pinky said.

"No, I got it. I'll fly *and* buy."

I headed down the back steps and out the door.

Another news van was parked in Sherman's lot. It must've been a slow news day for two, maybe three, metro television stations to hang around town more than an hour after the press conference ended. Maybe they'd hoped to shake some insightful stories from our small-town residents. Besides the murder of Chief Newel, that is. The quaint community of Brooks Landing seemed far less so that day.

I pulled up my fur-edged hood so it covered the sides of my face, and slipped on the pair of sunglasses I kept in the center console. I realized I should have warmed them first when the cold frames bit my cheeks and nose bridge. As I pulled open Sherman's door, I prayed no one would recognize me. The immediate problem was it was darker and warmer inside so my sunglasses fogged up and I saw next to nothing.

The reception station was directly ahead, but in my near-blind state I was disoriented, unsure where that was. I was about to slip off the glasses and risk being recognized when I bumped into someone. "I'm so sorry," I said, lowered the glasses, and faced the redhaired female reporter. The one who'd asked the question that made me wonder the same thing. *Had Chief Newel received any threats?*

"Mayor Brooks. I thought that was you when you came in. Can you join us at our table?" So much for my attempt at incognito. Had she seen me leave city hall earlier and recognized me from my coat? But half the town wore midcalf-length quilted coats.

"Um, I appreciate that, but I'm picking up meals I need to deliver."

She pulled a business card from somewhere. "I understand. Please give me a call if you get any updates you're able to share."

I accepted it and stuck it in my pocket. "Will do. Oh, and thanks for staying to have lunch in our town, supporting a local business."

"Sure, of course. The food is amazing here," she said.

"I agree. Well, I better pick up my order."

"Hope to chat again," she said. *Chat?* That was one way to describe volleying tough questions and answers back and forth. Back in my hometown for the past year, I'd lost a lot of the edge I'd had in Washington, D.C.

I sort of smiled, paid for my order, and escaped before another TV station crew showed up. I'd grown used to dodging Sandy Gibbons in Brooks Landing, but not reporters from the Twin Cities and St. Cloud areas.

I was the most popular person in the room when I returned with the bag of food. The reporters had left, so Mom, Dad, and Pinky followed me to a table in Brew Ha-Ha. I set the wrapped burgers and fries on the table as we sat down. The burgers were a handful, and Pinky had a knife on the table to cut them in two. We divided the two generous orders of fries, enough for six people.

Mom swallowed her first bite of burger. "How could Chief Newel get poisoned before your very eyes? And to think someone actually killed him. He's been a police officer for a long time, and they go through a lot of training."

"That's what I wanna know," Pinky chimed in.

I couldn't escape tough questions even from my family and friends and did an extra swallow so the food didn't get stuck in my throat. "All I can say is Detective Garrison is working on that."

Pinky squinted her eyes at me. "You know more than you're admitting to."

I rested my elbows on the table and lifted my hands, palms up. "No comment."

Pinky shook a French fry at me. "I knew it. You know but you can't tell us what it is."

I couldn't lie and raised my eyebrows instead.

My dad laid a hand on Pinky's arm. "Cami will fill us in as soon as she can. Right, sweetie?"

"Right." I bit into the burger and tried to clear my brain of everything except how tasty it was.

13

Friday morning, I was in the middle of nightmare and awoke in a panic, my heart thumping against my ribs. I was with Chief Newel in his office. We both seemed to spot an envelope on his desk at the same time. When he reached for it, my instincts told me he shouldn't touch it. I shouted, "*No,*" and tried to grab it from him. He held it out of my reach and sneered as he said, "I should have expected this, but it's too late now, the damage has been done. You need to find—"

What? No clue what Newel was about to say, and even though it was my dream, I was curious what in the world it might've been. A chill ran through me as my mind's eye focused on Newel's sneer. That and the eerie words he spoke. I threw back the covers, reached for the robe on the end of the bed, and slid my arms into its warmth.

His words played again on my way to the kitchen. "I should have expected this . . . it's too late now." *Cami, it's your dream for heaven's sake*. But it made me wonder if Chief was involved in something, knew someone who had a motive to kill him. I shook my head in hopes the dream and its possible meaning would disappear.

I dropped a teabag in a cup and filled it with water. As it heated and steeped in the microwave, I pulled a pen and notepad out of the drawer and set them on the table. Questions popped into my mind and I needed to record them before they faded away. When the tea was ready, I sat down and wrote:

Persons of interest to talk to:

Rosalie Gorman. Pinky said she and Newel spent time together at Brew Ha-Ha, and she must know more about his personal life than she'd shared. I had no reason to suspect she'd harm Newel. She, along with the other councilors, had wanted me to talk to him. And she'd seemed genuinely distressed when he died. Unless she was clever enough to pull off a plot like that, and a good enough actress to appear upset.

Gina. She knew more than she was willing to share, but what? She'd given me little gems like Newel was handling things and she "kind of" respected him for that. He had confided in her but she couldn't say what it was because of the people involved. And she felt sorry for him. What in the world did it all mean? Maybe Garrison would wheedle it out of her. But I wouldn't be privy to what she told him.

Chief Newel's brother. From what I'd gathered from others, and the fact that he lived in South Dakota and felt badly he'd lost contact with Newel, it was safe to cross him off the list.

Clint. I needed to ask him who'd had access to Newel's office. That information would either narrow or expand my list of potential suspects. Margaret and the other secretaries had not recalled an envelope from Fresh Start, but couldn't swear to it with all the mail they handled.

Margaret. I had already asked Margaret a lot of questions, but more might come up along the way. She'd given me an important tidbit, namely about Newel and his ex-wife, Elissa Warne.

Elissa. I would forgo Pinky's muffins for a week, maybe a month, if Elissa would reveal the reason their marriage had crumbled after a few months. From what Margaret indicated, it'd been more serious than finding out they weren't compatible, couldn't live together after all. Newel must have done something egregious, but what? A problem with gambling or a drug habit he managed to keep secret, even from his astute police officers and other staff? Or was it the same thing that'd cost him his last position, an affair with the wrong woman? That was the path my instincts directed me toward.

Fresh Start Rehab. Their stationery was central in the investigation. The drug-laced envelope was used as the murder weapon by somebody who had access to their stationery, whether it was an employee or a client. And that somebody hated Aaron Newel enough to kill him in a painful way. I planned to check on the center myself, without interfering in Detective Garrison's case. He had talked to management and staff.

I knew the law enforcement community worked with treatment centers on a regular basis. A large percentage of rehab clients were court ordered to treatment. The reason Chief Newel had contributed to Fresh Start might be as simple as he liked their program and how they helped people recover.

Perhaps his generosity was known among other contributors and the staff at Fresh Start. Maybe word got out to the wrong person who had a deep-seated grudge against Newel and who plotted a way to end his life. Garrison had told me Matthew Anderle, the CFO and CEO, had written the note to Chief. But it was months before. Had Anderle dated it, it wouldn't have been used again.

Another question remained. Why had Newel missed so much work? His strange absences and bizarre death posed mysteries, and I had to believe they were connected.

Brooks Landing had a human resources team who attended to employee issues for all the departments: police, fire, parks, public works, and administration. They handled employee benefits and tracked sick and vacation time.

Human Resources. I needed to sit down with HR director, Jill Patel. I liked the rhythm of her name. She'd have the records on Aaron Newel. The times he'd been absent could show a pattern.

I looked over my list, more names might be added later. I debated whether to talk to Jill in human resources or someone at Fresh Start Rehabilitation first, and settled on Jill. She was in the office by 8:00 a.m.

"Brooks Landing Human Resources. Jill speaking," she answered with an upbeat voice. I could take lessons from her.

"Hi, Jill, it's Camryn Brooks."

"Hi, Mayor. Hope you're doing okay."

"Yes, thanks. I'm wondering if I could come to your office, have a look at Newel's sick and vacation time records."

It took her a few seconds to respond . "That should be fine. When do you want to come by?"

"Twenty minutes okay with you?" I asked.

"That works, see you then."

As I drove to city hall, it dawned on me that in addition to Chief Newel's appalling death, the seven mostly cloudy days in a row, coupled with subzero temperatures, had worn me down. I pulled into the back parking lot, saw Clint's police car in his designated spot, and pulled into mine. A nice perk for us both. I didn't have keyed access to the police station and called to see if he'd let me in the back door. He opened it a moment later.

"Good morning, Chief," I greeted him.

He gave a slight nod. "Mayor."

"Got a few minutes? I'm on my way next door but have a question for you."

"Sure, let's go into my office." We walked past Newel's closed door to Clint's. "I'll stay in here for the time being, as the interim chief. Plus, Detective Garrison and his team will be back later today to take a deeper dive into Newel's papers, whatever, for any leads."

"Wow, a big job, I'm sure."

"You have a question?"

"I do, but I wanna tell you about my dream first."

A quizzical look crossed his face. "Your dream?"

"About Chief Newel. It scared me, and I'm embarrassed to admit this, but it made me wonder if it was prophetic."

"Prophetic? You got me curious."

Clint trained his eyes on me as I shared every detail. "I can see why it'd scare you. It'd scare me, too. As far as prophetic, you do have that thing with the pennies you find. Who knows?" he said.

"Who knows? And there is one other thing."

His eyes narrowed. "Do I dare ask?"

"I'd tried to forget it, but then we found out Chief had been poisoned, and it freaked me out."

Clint touched my hand. "What did?"

I sucked in a breath. "Okay. After Chief died, I was in the shower later that night and the word 'poison' came to me out of nowhere."

"You don't say."

"The crazy question I had—don't shoot the messenger here—had Newel reached the end of the line and took poison right before I got there? We later found out it was on the envelope, so no it wasn't after all."

"Maybe someone from above whispered the word 'poison' to you."

I shrugged. "In that case, it would've been good if they'd sent the guilty one's name."

"No doubt." We were silent a moment, then Clint said, "Back to your question."

"Oh, right. I wondered who had access to Newel's office."

"Tell me it's not because you're doing a little detective work of your own?"

Little? "Looking for answers is not necessarily the same as investigating, Clint."

"Garrison will have both our heads if you compromise the investigation," he said.

"I won't do that. Even if I did a *little* investigating, that kind of thing happens more than you think. The police go through their process, and families hire private detectives to have another look at it."

His eyes were mere slits. "Where'd you hear that?"

My nerves tingled. "Around. And you know they sometimes work together. PIs sometimes take unconventional routes law enforcement can't."

"Give me an example." I think he played dumb to see what I'd say.

"I know of a detective from a large metro police department who hired a private detective to scope out places and people and then gave him anonymous tips so the police detective could get warrants."

One eyebrow lifted. "You don't say."

"Maybe Buffalo County doesn't, but you never know."

"You've helped in a few cases with those unconventional methods of yours, I'll give you that. But you are not a licensed private investigator." He tapped my hand.

"I don't pretend to be. Anyone can ask questions."

"That depends. The last thing I want is that you get hurt . . . or worse."

"Me too." I gave him a sweet smile. "Clint, you didn't answer my question."

He tipped his head to the side and scratched his cheek. "And that was?"

"Who has keys to the chief's office?"

"Me, as assistant chief, Margaret our office manager, and Gina our cleaner, since she's here after hours."

Gina. "Did Gina get special clearance for that?" I asked.

"Of course. Everyone who works here goes through a background investigation. Not that the chief left any confidential documents laying around after hours, or when he was gone. They'd be locked in his files or his desk."

I made a mental note. "And how about access to your office?"

"The chief, Margaret, and Gina."

"Hmm. Clint, that brings up another question. You've no doubt thought about who you'd want as assistant police chief, right? I guess it'd be interim for now?"

He lowered his voice. "What do you think about Mark?"

I smiled and nodded a few times. "Very good choice. I've known him almost my whole life. And he's served our city well for a lot of years."

"Yep, fifteen of 'em. Mark's got a level head on his shoulders, does well with people. He's more of a people person than I am, so I think we'd make a good team."

"Agreed. You'd be a great team. Well, I best get next door. Thanks and see you later."

"Bye."

I slipped through the common area, past Margaret's unoccupied desk to the administration offices, and stepped inside Jill's office. She was at her desk reading a form. A diffuser on a nearby shelf filled the air with a eucalyptus scent. Jill noticed me and stood. "Come in, Mayor."

"Thanks. Smells good in here, and it's opening my sinuses at the same time."

She chuckled. "It does help, especially since winter air is so dry."

I indicated her piles of papers. "Looks like you've got lots to take care of."

She patted the top of a stack. "Always something in HR."

"True. Jill, as I said over the phone, I'd like to have a look at the dates Aaron Newel took time off. I've been told there were a lot the last six months."

"Yes. The report lists the dates, and if they were taken as sick or vacation. Employees aren't required to give reasons, of course. It's their business unless someone volunteers the information."

"Sure."

"I gave the report to Councilor Gorman last week. You know since the council planned to talk to him about his absences. She wanted documented proof." That must be why Jill hesitated when I asked for the information. She'd already given the report to Gorman.

It took me aback. "Really? It's funny she didn't share that with me and the other councilors—that I know of, anyway—when we discussed Newel's absences. They said he had missed at least ten days a month the past six months."

"That's true, and I thought Councilor Gorman got the records for all of you to review. I'm not sure why she didn't," she said.

Another thing to talk to Stormin' about. "I'll ask her about it some time. I should've thought to get the documents before I met with Chief Newel. It took me by surprise when the councilors appointed me for the job, and I didn't think of it. I'm still trying to navigate my way around."

"There's a lot to learn, Mayor. And there'll be things you won't know you need to know until they come up."

I nodded. "I'm finding that out. And I question why the councilors decided I should be the one to talk to Chief Newel. Me, the one who knew the least about him, had never even met him."

Jill's shoulders lifted. "They must've had their reasons."

"Yep. Meanwhile, is that the report?" I pointed at a file folder.

She nodded, picked up the folder, and handed it over. "I thought you'd like the record for the whole ten years he was here. FYI, Councilor Gorman only got the last year's."

"Good to know and I appreciate this, Jill."

Thank you, Jill, I thought as I unlocked the Curio Finds back door. She'd told me more than I'd asked for. And what was up with Stormin'? If she'd wanted to protect Newel by covering up his extensive absences or making excuses for him, she could've voted against the council's inquiry, or volunteered to talk to him herself. I climbed the stairs to the main level of the shop and called out, "Hello, Pinky!"

She appeared in the archway between the shops and pointed at the file. "Hey, what are you holding on to for dear life?"

I pulled the folder tighter against my chest. "Just a little research project."

"Do tell."

I mouthed, "Is there anyone in Brew Ha-Ha?"

She shook her head a little too vigorously.

"I collected some information on Chief Newel's work history to check how much time he'd really taken off."

"And?"

"I don't know yet and can't share the specifics, of course. But it's no secret he missed a lot of work. It seems like the whole town knew that."

"There had been chatter all right. But does it make a difference now that the poor guy is dead?" she said.

"Not sure. Most personnel records are private and none of my business, but I'm curious about these."

"Yeah, I get that, and it makes me no never mind."

I turned the open sign and shop lights on and carried the file to my office as Pinky trailed behind.

"Where is everyone?" I laid the file on my desk.

"A lot of merchants already got their goodies and went off to their stores. The early birds are commuting to their jobs, or are there by now." She glanced at her watch. "Soccer moms should be here any minute."

I hung my coat and purse on a hook. "I'm going to do some research until I get a customer, or you need help."

Brew Ha-Ha's doorbell dinged, and Pinky turned around.

"Holler if you need me," I called to her back.

She lifted her arm and wiggled her fingers.

14

I decided to work on the report at the checkout counter so I could watch for customers and be close at hand if Pinky needed help. It was easy enough to slip it under the counter if people were around. I pulled a notebook and pen from the drawer to take notes.

Chief Newel had accumulated more sick and vacation time than he'd taken his first nine years with Brooks Landing. All that changed last July. I had discarded last year's calendar when the new year arrived, so I turned on the computer and signed on to the internet in search of one. When I located the calendar, I printed the July-December months.

I circled all the missed workdays on the months and marked an S or a V on the days to indicate if he'd taken them as sick or vacation, and to look for a pattern. The marked days raised some questions. I phoned Jill.

"Brooks Landing Human Resources, Jill speaking."

"Hi, Jill, it's Camryn with a question, or two."

"Sure, what is it?" she said.

"When the chief took vacation, did he put in for it ahead of time?"

"Not when it was for a day or two, like in the last six-plus months. Typically, the city likes some lead time when it's more than one day, but it was a little different with Chief Newel. He had an assistant to step in for him, so he was covered per se. With other employees, we like at least two weeks' notice so we can adjust schedules as needed. And most people plan vacation times well ahead of that."

I tapped my pencil on a calendar page. "True. I see Newel took off the last week in December through the first week in January. Two weeks. Was that planned in advance?"

"Yes, he put in for that in November."

"How about the one week that started on November twenty-eighth?"

"I believe he requested that about two weeks ahead of time," she said.

"Okay. Is it fair to say Chief took some last-minute vacation days as well? There are a bunch scattered throughout the months."

"Yes. It actually happened a lot with those single days off."

"And what about sick days? Sometimes they were right before or right after vacation days. Especially the recurring weekends," I said.

"Yes. Forgive me if I'm speaking out of turn, but I'd say he played the system. Chief Newel had accumulated lots of sick and vacation days over the years, as you can see. And then he started burning through them."

"I noticed that, and it looks like he planned his days off that way. And took them before and after his regular days off."

"Yes, that was my point. It seems obvious when you look at the whole picture in black and white. It bothered me the way he shifted more and more of his duties to Assistant Chief Clint. You

140

know the city's policy, when employees are out sick three days in a row, they need a doctor's note. Certainly, if someone gets injured, or has a scheduled surgery, we don't hold to that same requirement. But Newel never took three days in a row of sick time. Maybe I told you more than I should've," she said.

"You're fine. I'll keep your opinion between the two of us."

"Thank you."

"Sure. Thanks again."

I smiled with appreciation after we'd disconnected. If everyone was as candid as Jill had been when I posed questions, it surely would save time tracking down answers. The shop's doorbell alerted me a customer had arrived. I flipped the calendar sheets over and shoved the report into the drawer.

I worked on the calendar pages between customers, grateful it was a quiet day, overall. My mind focused on Newel. What had caused him to "play the system?" No one seemed to know. I laid the pages side by side on the counter. Newel had taken the first full week of July off. Then starting the second week, he'd taken every other Thursday, Friday, and the following Monday off through the middle of November. A definite pattern.

What had triggered those long weekends off that started in July and ended in November? Had Newel taken another job every other weekend? No. As the police chief, he had a scheduled Monday through Friday work week, but there were events weekends and evenings he was expected to attend. And he would've been on call if something major happened. He'd been charged with the overall responsibility as the chief law enforcement officer for the city. In his absence, those things fell on Clint's and the other officers' shoulders.

There were other scattered days off each month with no notable pattern. A Tuesday or Wednesday here and there. Then he'd taken off the last week in November that ran into December, along with the last week in December and the first week in January. It was rumored he was in Mexico those last two weeks. Either he'd mentioned it to someone, or it was the assumption when he'd returned with a tan.

When Garrison gained access to Newel's credit card records, any flights he'd taken would show up.

A lot of people, me included, found it strange that Newel had left on vacation shortly after Mayor Frost's death. According to Jill, he had announced in November he planned to take those weeks as vacation time, and hadn't changed his plans, even though one of his bosses had died. Whatever had been going on in Chief Newel's life, it was apparent his career had taken a back seat to it.

I counted the days Newel had been gone from work. There were twenty-seven sick and thirty-five vacation. That totaled sixty-two days, out of one hundred and thirty-three work days. Nearly half. I picked up my calculator and punched in numbers. Sixty-two times eight equaled four hundred and ninety-six. The number of hours he'd taken off without explanation.

I respected a person's right to privacy, and no one needed to disclose personal medical problems, but most people gave the reason when they called in. Employers had the right to ask why if they didn't. Newel's absence every other long weekend for four months was strange, to say the least. If he hadn't had a part-time job, what was it?

Clint mentioned he'd looked haggard and more distracted during those months, but he'd assured Clint he was fine. My question when I looked at the proof in "black and white," as Jill

142

had phrased it, why hadn't Newel been brought to task months before? Administrator Gary Lunden and the councilors had concerns. Mayor Lewis Frost had been a kind man who liked to smooth things out, settle conflicts. As long as the police department was well run, he in all likelihood hadn't wanted to make waves. For all we knew, Frosty'd had a talk with Newel and they'd come to some sort of agreement.

The long weekends off ended after the first week in December. The last two weeks Newel had taken a vacation was the straw that broke the camel's back. The reason I'd been appointed to talk to him.

His death had turned the issue into a moot point. Still, I wondered again if the reason behind his extensive absences had factored into his murder. Gina said Newel wouldn't do anything illegal. His staff had considered him a good boss. They had mutual trust. So why would Newel have kept his possible medical condition or activities—whatever they were—private?

My phone rang and broke my concentration. I took a breath before I answered, "Hi, Clint. How are things?"

"Peachy Or not. To let you know, I got a call from Detective Garrison. He said Aaron Newel's brother Adam is coming to town tomorrow to make the funeral arrangements. Garrison asked if I'd meet him at Chief's house. As next of kin and only known relative, Adam can go through his brother's personal things without a search warrant. Garrison cleared it with Adam. Of course he wants to do what he can to help track down his brother's killer. I hope and pray we come across something there that helps solve Chief's murder," he said.

"Garrison told Adam about the poison?"

"Yeah, he did."

"Clint, if it's not too much to ask, I'd like to be there. I promise not to touch anything or say anything you don't want me to. I was with the chief when he died, so Adam shouldn't object. In fact, it might help if he talks to me, maybe give him a measure of closure."

It seemed a full minute passed before Clint answered. "That should be fine. I can't think of a reason Garrison would object."

"Good. When will Adam get here?" I asked.

"By noon tomorrow, estimated time. He hasn't been to Brooks Landing in almost ten years. Chief was new to the job and didn't bring his brother around to introduce him to us back then. Anyway, he'll come to the PD first. We'll talk over whatever, then head to Chief's house."

"Okay. Should I meet you at the PD, or his house, or where?"

"His house. You have the address?"

"I do." I didn't add I'd sat outside his house a while before the press conference.

"Good. I can text you after we get there. Adam might need some time to process things before he starts digging in," he said.

"Sure. Clint, on a personal note, will I see you tonight?"

"Oh. I scheduled a meeting with my officers at seven. We'll have our own debrief and discuss next steps. On that note, I ran the interim assistant position by Mark and he's in," he said.

"I'm glad to hear that."

"The meeting could go pretty late."

"No worries. Take care of what you need to do," I said.

"Thanks."

When I considered what helpful information we might uncover at Chief Newel's house, waves of apprehension and anticipation rolled through me. Not to violate his privacy, but in hopes something emerged and shed light on who'd killed him. If Newel hadn't utilized the calendar in his phone, he would've had a personal planner or calendar to note his days off work, what he did, where he went.

It felt good to close up shop for the day. I waited in my car for the engine to warm and thought of Newel's ex-wife Elissa Warne again. Clint was tied up for the evening so it might be a good night to pay her a visit. I hoped she'd be willing to talk to me, that she'd tell me what happened between the two. It might feel good to get that load off her chest.

It was nearing 5:40 when I pulled to a stop in front of her house. We likely shared the same contractor when that side of town had been developed in the 1950s. What they called either starter or retirement homes. My next-door neighbor had a reverse floor plan from mine, with the living and dining rooms swapped, but otherwise was the same. Homeowners had remodeled over the years. Some had built additions, so the original designs had changed somewhat.

Lights from the front room were visible over the tops of her closed curtains. I decided to take a chance she would invite me in after I identified myself. As I approached the house, it triggered a bright motion detection light above the door and almost blinded me when it flashed in my eyes. I blinked a few times as I climbed the front steps. They had been shoveled, but I took care in case they were slippery from a thin ice coating.

I rang the doorbell and perked my ears for any sound inside. I heard something, but it could be a cat jumping from the couch. I knocked on the door and listened again. The sound of the back door shutting carried through the small house to where I stood, yet the front room lights stayed on.

Either Elissa chose to not answer the door, or she was about to leave and didn't have the time. I got down the steps and sidewalk to my car as fast as I could safely navigate. Her garage was in back, next to the alley, like mine. She could head either north or south. Her house was closest to the south street, so I started my car and headed that direction.

As I was about to take a left, a small white SUV pulled up to the end of the alley. Perfect timing. Except she took a right toward me. We met, and I looked in the rearview mirror to see which direction she went. North. I did a quick U-turn and took a right to follow her, in hopes she was none the wiser. She took a left at the next intersection then a right onto Central Avenue that ran on the east side of Green Lake into downtown Brooks Landing. I held back as she approached a red at the only stop light in town. Her left turn signal blinked and when the light turned green, she turned west onto County Road 53 and into Chatsworth Township.

Where was she off to? Two of the larger draws in Chatsworth were a large apple orchard and a riding stable, but both were closed for the season. It was supper time, so maybe she was off to meet someone at the biker bar and grill. Or the ski lodge if she was one of the brave souls that flew down slopes despite sub-zero temperatures. She passed both establishments and after another mile signaled a left turn. I was some distance back, but I could read the spotlight-illuminated sign: Fresh Start Rehabilitation Center.

My heart rate doubled in seconds. Elissa was on her way to *Fresh Start*? Why? Was she about to start treatment, or had she been there before and relapsed? She could have left a light on in her home so it would appear occupied while she was away.

I knew a registered nurse who had her license suspended after she was convicted of driving while intoxicated. The review board approved her reinstatement after she successfully completed treatment. Drug use and related offenses, like procurement for themselves or others, meant serious criminal charges and punishment.

If either scenario were true, Elissa would most likely have a revoked license. She could be on her way to visit a friend or relative who was in treatment at Fresh Start. Someone Aaron Newel knew? Maybe a friend they had in common. Once again, it struck me as an odd coincidence Newel had sent large contributions to the facility and died because someone had poisoned one of their return envelopes. As a visitor, would Elissa have access to their envelopes?

I gave her a head start then turned and followed the long drive to their sprawling facility. I'd been back in Brooks Landing for almost a year and never had reason to check out Fresh Start before Chief Newel's death. I planned to visit them at a later time. I pulled in the parking lot and shut my car off to kill the headlamps. Through the picture windows I saw a large gathering space with a few men around a table playing cards, another in a chair reading, still another with his eyes closed in a recliner.

A few minutes later, the woman I recognized as Elissa from her social media pictures walked into the room in medical scrubs with a stethoscope draped around her neck. She went to a table of card players, smiled, and started talking. She wasn't a client or a visitor, she *worked* there? Last I knew she was employed by a hospital in the Minneapolis metro area.

I drove home wondering who she really was. Was there anything sinister beneath her outward caring persona? She moved up on my persons of interest list.

15

Pinky had been in a tizzy all Friday morning. "I feel bad about Chief Newel, I do. But what happened makes me more afraid for Jake and Mark and Clint." She paused. "And the other officers, too." She'd repeated her concerns many times.

I wanted to tell her it appeared Newel had been the single target, anything to ease her angst, but couldn't. It was natural for her to make up all kinds of scenarios and reasons and think others in the force might be in harm's way. And in fact, we didn't know with complete certainty they weren't. That thought blasted a shiver through my body.

"Pink, they're police officers and that makes them cautious and suspicious and on the lookout for any sign of danger," I said to assure us both.

She leaned in closer and narrowed her eyes at me. "Why did your eyes blink like that when you said that?"

"Like what?"

"They fluttered like you were either nervous or lying."

Now that she mentioned it, I guess I was. "Not lying, but I am concerned, like you are. It's only natural. We don't know why

Chief Newel was killed, but we do know he kept secrets about why he was gone so much. And I think it's possible, even probable, those absences had something to do with his murder."

She threw her arms up. "Murder. That means it was planned, doesn't it? Like the detective said, it's being investigated as a homicide."

I tried to steer her thoughts in another direction. "You're thinking premeditated, but not all murders are planned. Like our friend Archie Newberry. He didn't plan to kill Jerrell Powers last fall."

"Yeah, poor Archie. What an awful deal. He didn't know what he was doing. At least now he's getting the mental health help he needs, even if it is in jail."

"That's for sure, and the times we've visited him he seemed to be doing well," I said.

"I agree. Well, I better grind some coffee beans before I get more customers."

"Not much going on in either shop, so I'll keep an eye on Brew Ha-Ha while you're in the back room."

"Thanks." She headed that direction. I grabbed a cup of coffee and carried it to a back table. My thoughts returned to Elissa Warne. *How long had she worked at Fresh Start, and was it full time, or did she moonlight there?* She'd left the lights on in in her house, likely to discourage burglars. Not that Brooks Landing was fraught with crime. Aside from the rash of homicides, accidental and intentional, over the past months.

If Detective Garrison had gotten a list of employees who worked for Fresh Start, he would have Elissa on his radar. It didn't seem like a coincidence to me, but would she be dumb enough to kill her ex-husband by putting a dangerous substance on a return envelope that had her employer's name on it? On the other hand, that might be her alibi: it was too obvious. She could claim someone knew she worked there and was trying to frame her for his murder.

I finished my coffee, set the cup in the sink full of sanitizing solution, and glanced up at Betty Boop. Her hands pointed at ten and eleven. 10:50. A little over an hour until noon and no word that Adam Newel had arrived in Brooks Landing. My parents were set to fill in for me all afternoon. They liked helping, especially since I'd taken on new responsibilities as the mayor. I think they considered it their way to pay it forward.

Mom was healthy again, but Dad still watched her like a hawk to ensure she didn't overexert. On the one hand, Mom thought it was sweet of Dad. On the other hand, she didn't think it was necessary. She listened to her body and knew when it was time to kick back and rest. But she kept her protests quiet until she could no longer contain them.

My parents arrived promptly at noon. "Thanks for all the extra help lately," I said and slipped into winter gear.

Mom patted Dad's arm. "Glad to do it. It gets us out of the house and gives your father something to think about besides me and my health."

Dad's eyebrows lifted. "I've got plenty to think about. But you're at the top of my list, Beth. Along with our children and grandchildren."

I gave them both hugs. "I don't know how long my duties will take."

"Not to worry. We'll lock up at closing time if you're not back by then," Mom said.

Pinky poked her head into the shop. "Beth and Eddie! I thought I heard friendly familiar voices. All I can say is it sure has been nice having you here more often lately. It's almost like the old days."

I waved at them. "As much as I hate leaving this mutual admiration society party, I best take off."

They called out "byes" on my way out the back door. I drove to city hall and noticed Clint's car wasn't in the parking lot. He phoned as I stepped into my office. "Hi, Chief."

"Camryn. At your shop?"

"No, city hall."

"You free to meet Adam and me at Aaron's house?" he said. *Aaron's?* "Sure."

"Adam got in earlier than he thought so we've been here a while. Whenever you can make it is fine." Clint's voice was softer, more casual, called Chief "Aaron," maybe to lighten Adam's heavy load.

My insides started to flutter. Clint cared and that warmed my heart, but I was also apprehensive how things would shake down when Adam Newel went through his brother's things.

"See you shortly," I said.

Clint's police car sat in Newel's driveway in front of the attached garage. I pulled in and parked behind it. A white SUV with South Dakota plates was next to it. I made my way up the walk and rang the bell.

Clint opened the door with a small smile. "Come in."

"Thanks." I stepped inside and scanned the living room décor. It was nice, almost artsy; the furniture and rug were in tasteful shades of gray and mauve. Perhaps the abstract painting on the wall

152

behind the couch had determined the color and style of the room. Elissa's touch? If Newel had done the interior decorating, he had an unexpected talent.

I shrugged off my outerwear. Clint hung my coat in the front closet, and I set my shoes on a mat by two other pair. "Adam's back there." Clint waved his hand at an open door off the living room and led me into the office/guest bedroom. Adam Newel stood in front of a two-drawer file cabinet that sat on a small tabletop and turned when he heard us. I would not have guessed he was Chief's brother. He was inches shorter with a leaner build. Adam was perhaps six feet tall and weighed around one seventy, ninety to a hundred pounds lighter than Chief. And had a more agreeable presence.

He closed the gap between us, reached for my hands, and held on tight. His dark brown eyes seemed to peer into my very soul. His voice, a breath above a whisper, uttered, "Thank you."

Thank you? I didn't know what he meant or how to respond. The expression on my face must've revealed my confusion because he said, "You were with Aaron when he passed. Seeing you now, it makes me feel better knowing in his last moments on earth your sweet face gave him a glimpse of what heaven must be like. You have a glow about you." *I did?*

Clint cleared his throat. I swallowed and finally answered with, "Oh, um, thank you, what a nice thing to say. Adam, I hope this gives you some comfort, some reassurance—if your brother felt any distress or pain, it was only for a few seconds until his heart stopped."

He blinked and slowly released my hands. It was one of the most unusual interactions I'd experienced with someone I had just met.

Clint waited a moment and cleared his throat again. "Camryn, to bring you up to speed, Adam thought his brother's files were a good place to start. We've all wondered about the generous check he was about to send to Fresh Start Rehabilitation."

Adam nodded. "Yes. Aaron kept a file on Fresh Start. He sent them a very large contribution six years ago and then a smaller amount once a year after that."

"Can you say how large?" I asked.

"Five thousand dollars."

My throat closed for a second. "Wow. A good chunk of his annual income. Any explanation why?"

"Not that I found. Aaron was a generous guy. He might've been helping someone in need. He gave me money a few times back when and wouldn't let me pay him back. I sent him checks he never cashed."

"The question is, if he was paying someone's bill, you gotta wonder who that was. Who was he that close to?" Clint said.

Adam rubbed the back of his neck. "Aaron's death is more difficult for me to accept because we'd drifted apart. I knew next to nothing of what was going on in his life these last years."

"How did that start, the two of you losing contact, if I may ask?" I said.

Adam gave his neck a squeeze then dropped his hand. "I got dragged into his personal life against my will, is one way to put it." He paused and shook his head. "I went up for a visit when he lived in Ironwood, a little over ten years ago. I'd taken a run to the store and guess I got back quicker than he'd thought I would.

"He was cuddled up with a woman on the couch. He introduced us and we talked for a bit. I didn't think much of it. A while later there was a loud pounding at his front door and a guy yelled, 'Newel, is my wife in there with you? Send her out!' The woman jumped up and ran out the back door.

"When Aaron opened the door, a guy rushed in and shouted, 'Where is she?' Aaron told him she wasn't there. He could look around. The guy turned to me and asked if Aaron was telling the truth. I said he was and felt guilty for not saying she had just left. He let out a disgusted sounding grunt, threw his arms down at his sides, and left.

"I asked Aaron what it was all about, and he admitted he was having an affair with the city administrator's wife. I asked him why in the world he would do that. He said they had fallen in lust. I'd been proud of my big brother, and his career as a police officer, then as police chief, but lost all respect for him that day. I felt like I didn't know him. In my world, there are certain lines you don't cross. And an affair with a married woman you don't even love, that's one of the biggest ones. He was so flippant about it."

After Adam delivered his eyewitness account, Clint said, "You know he lost his job in Ironwood over that affair?"

"I suspected as much when he told me he had taken the chief's position with Brooks Landing not long after that incident. I paid him a visit when he first moved here, but that was it. He knew I didn't approve of his affair, his personal lifestyle. I'd told him as much. We called each other on our birthdays, and a handful of other times. I got married eight years ago, and we're blessed with a daughter and son. Aaron never came to see us, and I didn't invite him either.

"You could say we had a mutual parting of ways. In all honesty, I didn't trust him around my wife, didn't want my kids to get to know him. I hate to say this out loud, but it wouldn't surprise me if it turns out a jealous husband killed him. So there you have all the sordid details." His shoulders lifted in a shrug.

"Sorry to hear the way things went down, Adam," Clint said.

All I did was nod. I was stuck on the jealous husband comment. I hadn't heard Newel had been involved with anyone of late, married or not, but there were guesses and suppositions, given his unexplained absences. I wanted to hear what Elissa had to say, why she'd left him after a few months. Did Aaron Newel have a girlfriend on the side? Gina admitted Elissa had a good reason to leave him.

Adam went back to work on the file drawers. He withdrew file after file and paged through them. It seemed his brother had kept things well organized. Clint and I gave Adam plenty of space, didn't peer over his shoulder. He noted each file's subject as he pulled them out. Auto insurance and repair records, utility bills. He held up a file. "He owned his house free and clear. Paid off his mortgage last year."

When Adam removed a file of bank statements, he sat down at the desk for a better look. After a few minutes scanning a short stack of papers he said, "Very strange. Aaron withdrew ten thousand dollars from his savings account every month, from July to December. Plus an additional five thousand the last week in December. And there are other large amounts here and there. The January statement isn't here yet."

"Last July? That's when he started taking a lot of time off work. And he was gone the last week in December too," I said.

Adam's eyebrows drew together. "What do you mean?"

Clint nodded at me so I took Adam through his brother's absences, some for days in a row and other single days here and there. I ended with why I'd been with him when he died. "So, I

156

never got to ask him about the reason, or reasons, he was gone so much. We may never find out."

Adam looked from me to Clint. "We need to keep digging until we do."

A little zing of hope zipped through me. "Do you think your brother had a drug or alcohol problem? You mentioned he gave five thousand dollars to Fresh Start six years ago. And then withdrew ten thousand every month starting last July. You think he was paying for treatment? I know it's very expensive."

Adam shook his head. "No. He never drank, and I doubt he *ever* took drugs. His weakness and big downfall was women."

"Maybe he was close to someone with an addiction problem," Clint offered.

"It's possible. I have no idea who that'd be, having so little contact with him all these years."

Clint nodded. "Right. I worked with him and knew next to nothing about his personal life. I didn't even know he was getting married until the week of the wedding."

Adam's upper body jerked back. "Aaron was *married*? When was that?"

"I figured you knew. It was about six years ago, and only lasted a few months," Clint said.

"And he never told his little brother. Maybe he knew it wouldn't last," Adam said.

"From what I heard, something unexpected happened, and it was big enough for his wife to leave him," I chimed in.

Adam focused on me. "Is she still around here?"

"Yes. I haven't met her, but I just found out she lives two blocks from me."

"I want to meet her, talk to her." He shook his head. "But maybe she won't feel the same way."

"She might," Clint said.

"But would she attend Aaron's funeral?" He sucked in a breath, and went back to his task. "What in the world?" He pulled out a file, laid it on the desk, and flipped it open. Inside were photos of a young girl. A dark-haired, dark-eyed beauty with dimples. He picked up one photo after the other, studied them, and looked at the backs.

Clint and I watched and waited. After a minute Adam said, "Sylvie, newborn. Sylvie, three months, Sylvie, six months. Who is this?" He passed each photo to Clint who passed them to me.

"No idea who she is," Clint said.

"So you don't recognize her, either of you?" Adam said.

"I sure don't," Clint said.

"Not at all," I agreed.

Adam handed over the last photo in the file. "Four photos from newborn to twelve months, then one for each year after, until age six. No one else with her. No dates listed. No explanation of who she is. Just her name and ages. And it's not in Aaron's handwriting."

The first photo looked like it was taken in the hospital nursery. The kind they capture of baby's faces. She had a little pink bow on the side of her head. In the second Sylvie was on a blanket, the third in a bouncy walker, the fourth she stood with her hand on a chair, a proud grin on her face. For the rest of them, she sat in the same overstuffed chair. The age six photo revealed she had a missing front tooth.

"She's darling, that's for sure. Looks like she could be of Latino descent. Maybe your brother sponsored her through an organization like Compassion International. There are other organizations like that out there," I said.

Adam raised his eyebrows. "I guess that's possible. But there would be something in his files or bank records to show that."

He made a good point. My parents supported two children from other countries and the money was automatically withdrawn from their bank account each month. Who was Sylvie, and why had Aaron Newel kept a small stack of her photos in a file, and not on display? Unless there were framed ones somewhere in the house.

16

Adam discovered another file with a handful of photos of him and his brother and their parents, along with some school photos of childhood friends. He spread them out on the desk. None of them included Chief's ex-wife Elissa or other women who may have been in his life.

Adam started on a journey through the house in search of framed photos of Sylvie, family, or friends. He found none on display or in drawers. He pulled a small plastic tub from Chief's bedroom closet shelf, set it on the bed, and popped off the cover. "Athletic awards and yearbooks from high school. He kept a piece of his past anyway. But what about the years since?"

"One thing I knew about your brother is that he loved sports, and followed the Twins, Gophers, and Vikings. Never mentioned going to a game, and I figured he watched them on TV, like most of us do," Clint said.

He left the storage tub on the bed, and continued his search. Like before, Clint and I hovered in the background to give him space, yet close enough if he needed us. Over the course of an hour, Adam had shaken his head about a hundred times. "Who was

Aaron Newel? Besides being a public figure who buried secrets so deep that even a look through his personal files doesn't give many answers."

"No question your brother was a private man. It makes me think after that fiasco in Ironwood those years back, he didn't want negative things from his past, or his present, to trip him up again," Clint said.

Adam pulled on his ear. "So he either shaped up or got rid of evidence to cover things, you're saying?"

Clint lifted his hands. "Just throwing that out."

Adam appeared lost in thought on the way back to Chief's home office. He picked up the most recent photo of the little girl and stared for a moment. "I must be losing it because the more I look at her face the more I think I should know her."

Clint put a hand on his shoulder. "Maybe she seems familiar because you've looked at her photos so many times."

"You're probably right."

I studied the family photos Adam had spread out on the desk. One was his mother holding baby Adam with Aaron standing by her side. "Adam, it might be because Sylvie has a smile kinda like your mother's. They both have those cute dimples."

"You're right, Camryn. I loved when my mother smiled. She lit up the room, and it looks like Sylvie would too. Again, the question, who is she and how can we find that out?"

"We can ask people at work, council members, his ex-wife to look at her photos, see if they know anything about her," I said.

"Good idea. Detective Garrison took your brother's phone to go through his calls and messages. I wonder what photos he might have on it. I didn't see cell phone records in his files, so I wonder if he just had a work cell, the one issued by the city?" Adam asked.

"As far as I know. It's the only number I had for him, never saw him with a personal one besides," Clint said.

"Clint, why don't you look through his files, see if anything jumps out at you, something I might've overlooked, " Adam said.

"You were doggone thorough, but I guess it doesn't hurt." Clint took care to page through each file, and then slid his hand under the files to check for papers that might have slipped underneath. "Aaron might've had a safety deposit box."

"Sure. I didn't think of that. It makes sense 'cause we didn't find a safe anywhere in the house."

"We haven't looked in his garage yet. How about we take a look out there?" Clint said.

Adam nodded. "Good idea."

We trooped out to the attached garage. Newel's personal SUV was parked in the closest stall. An electric heater mounted on a corner wall kept the garage above freezing. Adam peeked in the SUV then opened the passenger side door. "Keys aren't in it, of course."

He climbed inside, opened the glove box, pulled out a few papers, looked at them, put them back, and closed it. Adam opened the sliding back door and surveyed the vehicle's interior with his eyes. "Clean as a whistle," he said and closed the door.

The three of us searched, but aside from a lawnmower, snowblower, garbage cans, and neatly hung tools, we didn't spot much else. No hidden safe.

Clint got paged over his police radio when we were back in the home office. "I need to leave, and will catch up with you later."

Adam and I stood and stared at each other. "Do you want to do any more here today?" I finally asked.

"No, to tell you the truth, it's more exhausting than I thought it'd be. I have the names of companies I need to contact in the next day or two: insurances and utilities. My wife and I can take a deep dive into Aaron's things at some point. No real rush. We'll set the thermostat just high enough so the pipes don't freeze."

"I know Clint and others will be happy to keep an eye on the house. I surely can, if you'd like."

He glanced around the room. "I'd appreciate that. One less thing to worry about."

"Adam, how about we get a beverage and muffin at my friend's coffee shop? It's connected to my parents' Curio Finds shop."

"That sounds good. We could both use a pick-me-up." He gathered a stack together and slid the files into the briefcase that rested on a chair. "I'm glad I thought to bring this with me. I was sort of a mess when I found out about Aaron."

"You had good reason. Why don't we ride together in my car? I can drop you off here later."

"Sure."

Adam followed me into Curio Finds. My parents were nowhere in sight. A glance into Brew Ha-Ha told me why. Pinky had a large crowd for mid-afternoon treats, and they were assisting. Mom and Pinky were behind the counter; Dad was at a table pouring coffee for a couple.

"Looks like a popular spot," Adam said as we crossed the threshold between the shops.

"Yes. It was quieter during the cold snap, so it's nice to see a full house again."

Mom and Pinky spotted us at the same time, and both raised their eyebrows at the good-looking man with me. Dad finished at the table and joined us. "Hi, Cami. And you must be Chief Newel's brother."

"Yes, sir, I'm Adam."

"Adam, this is my dad Eddie, and my mom Beth is with my friend Pinky behind the counter."

Dad and Adam exchanged greetings then Dad said, "Sorry for your loss, son."

Adam nodded. "Thanks."

"We're here for some goodies." I pointed at the day's menu on the wall. "What would you like, Adam?"

He read for a minute. "The pumpkin cream cheese muffin, and for coffee? Pinky's blend sounds good to me."

"Coming right up," I said.

Pinky and Mom were taking orders. I squeezed behind them, put a few muffins on a plate, filled two coffee cups, and set them on a tray. I passed the tray across the counter to Dad who carried it to a table with Adam in tow.

"Need me to help out?" I asked Pinky.

She winked at me. "Thanks, but we're good. Take a load off; join your new friend."

With just two people left in line, I headed to the back table where Dad and Adam sat. My dad was skilled at making people feel comfortable, and the two looked like long-time buddies. Dad stood as I joined them. "Mom just signaled we have someone in our shop, so I'll catch you later."

Adam swallowed a sip of coffee. "Your dad's a nice guy."

164

"He sure is. He can act like a grizzly bear when he's riled up but turns into a teddy bear the next minute. He says it's in his Vanelli blood."

"Vanelli? Is Brooks your married name?" he asked.

"I'm not married. It's my given name." I told him my maternal aunt and uncle had adopted me after my biological parents died when I was five. "My parents kept it as my last name because my ancestor founded the town, and I was last in the Brooks family line."

"Lots of history there. Sorry for what you went through as a young child."

"Sometimes, when I think of my birth parents, I still feel like a sad, lost little girl."

He gently squeezed my hand. "I think of my own daughter, and it breaks my heart to imagine what that was like for you."

"Thanks. I have the best parents, sisters and brothers, nephews and nieces, who all love me." I chuckled. "Sometimes a little too much, is all."

"Good to hear." Adam took a bite of his muffin. "Wow. Really good. I'm glad you put more than one of these on the plate."

"Everything Pinky makes is really good." I pointed at the plate. "Try the blueberry cherry walnut one next."

If someone had told me three days after Chief Newel died—a man who'd intimidated the best of them, the councilors and me included—that I would be in Pinky's shop having coffee and muffins with his congenial brother, I wouldn't have believed them.

He swallowed a bite of a second muffin. "I think it's important to meet my ex-sister-in-law. She wasn't married to my brother long, but I know she can shed some light on what ended their marriage."

165

Mom stopped by our table. "Adam, this is my mom, Beth," I said.

Adam stood and smiled. "Nice to meet you. Your daughter has been a big help to me this afternoon."

Mom smiled back. "Well, good. Very nice to meet you. We've got more customers next door, but I wanted to say hi, and give you my sympathies."

"I appreciate that," Adam said.

As Mom left, Pinky swooped in, and dried her hands with her apron.

"Adam Newel, this is Alice Nelson," I said.

She sat down. "Gosh, I guess we have the same initials. But everybody calls me Pinky. How is everything going with . . . everything?"

Adam half shrugged. "Pretty good, all things considered." He held up a muffin. "Pinky, I need to tell you, these are the best muffins I've ever had. But don't tell my wife I said that."

Pinky's face colored the same shade as her name. "I promise. Is she here in Brooks Landing?"

"No, she's home in South Dakota with our kids."

"Ah. Well, my not-so-secret ingredient is butter. I'm in the 'it's better with butter' camp," she said.

"I have to agree with you," he said.

"I guess you know this, but you don't really look or act anything like your brother, um, did."

I gave her leg a gentle kick under the table.

"I didn't mean that in a bad way. Just speaking my observation out loud."

"You're right. Aaron and I talked about how we were a study in opposites," Adam said.

166

"Oh, I like that, 'a study in opposites.' Are you a teacher or something?" Before he answered her Pinky's shop doorbell dinged, and she jumped up. "Duty calls."

Adam's smile appeared for a second then faded. "I need to meet my ex-sister-in-law, get her take on things."

I shrugged. "And she might know who the little girl in the pictures is."

"I hope so. You have her address; can we just show up?"

I considered a minute. "I know someone we can ask." No one was in earshot so I pulled out my phone and called the PD.

Margaret picked up right away. "Brooks Landing Police. Camryn?"

"Hi Margaret. I'm with Adam Newel, and we plan to visit Elissa Warne—"

She cut me off. "Why?"

"Adam hasn't met her yet."

"I suppose," she said.

"I called to get your opinion. Do you think we should call Elissa first or just stop by? Expected versus surprised?" I asked.

"Hmm. Would she be more likely to answer the phone or the door? I didn't know her that well. But seeing how things ended badly with Chief Newel and Elissa, I think you should call first. You can leave a message if she doesn't answer," she said.

"You're right. Do you have her number?"

"I do, and I guess it's okay to tell you, seeing how you're the mayor." Margaret rattled off the number before I was ready.

"Can you repeat that so I can add her to my contacts?" I punched in the numbers as she repeated them and typed in Elissa's name. "Thanks, Margaret."

"That's fine, and good luck to you."

167

I held up my phone when we disconnected. "Margaret says call first. Elissa might be at work, but I'll give it a try." After a few rings, I was about to leave a message when Elissa said, "Hello?"

"Oh, Ms. Warne. This is Camryn Brooks, the mayor here."

"Yes, Mayor. Is this about Aaron Newel?"

Perceptive of her. "It is. I'm with his brother, and he'd like to meet you."

"Adam? Why?" She knew about him, anyway.

I mouthed, "Will you talk to her?" Adam nodded. "Here he is." I handed the phone over.

"Elissa, hi, um, Adam. Elissa, it would mean a lot to me if we could meet and talk for a bit. It's been a tough few days." The way he phrased it how could she say no? He was silent while she spoke then said, "Thank you. The mayor and I will be over in a bit."

Adam's eyes glistened with tears he blinked away. "Sorry, I didn't expect to get emotional over a minute-long phone call." He handed me the phone.

"It *is* emotional, Adam. Like you told her, it's been a tough few days. And meeting the sister-in-law you didn't know you had is a whole other deal." I picked up my coat from the back of the chair and slipped it on. "Should we go?"

"Let's do it."

I stuck my head in Curio Finds, and told my parents we had an errand and hoped to be back before closing.

"Take your time," Dad said.

As we climbed into my Subaru, I got a text from Clint. *Be tied up for a while yet.*

No worries. On our way to visit Elissa, I wrote.

Good luck!

"Clint is still tied up, and wishes us good luck."

Adam bent his head a moment like he was praying. When he lifted it again he said, "I'm ready for whatever comes."

17

We were at Elissa's door minutes later. Adam rang the bell. I hung back so they could greet each other first. When Elissa opened the door, they stared at each other a few seconds until she took a step back. "Come in."

Inside, Adam set his briefcase by the door, and Elissa took our coats. Elissa and Adam were silent as they studied each other a second time. Two was company, and I made it a crowd. Adam took Elissa's hands in his and said, "I don't know what my brother did to you, but whatever it was, I hope you were able to forgive him. There were things about him I struggled with and had trouble forgiving myself."

The floodgates opened. They embraced and cried together. I dabbed at my own tears. It was a time for them to shed whatever bad feelings—and maybe come up with some good ones too— they'd felt for Aaron Newel. Since I lacked the magical ability to disappear, I moved further into the living room, and sat down on a side chair.

Their immediate connection surprised me to say the least. I knew Adam was genuine, and Elissa's touching reaction seemed sincere. Nurses were caregivers by nature, so she was bound to have some empathy for Adam no matter how she felt about Chief. Or was there more to it? Sadness over her failed marriage, or guilt because she'd had a part in his death?

They pulled apart after a drawn-out minute. Elissa left the room and returned with a box of tissues she offered to Adam. He acted nonchalant as he pulled out a couple, dried his eyes, and wiped his nose. Like it was a regular thing for him. Elissa did the same. Adam turned around when he remembered me. "Sorry, Camryn."

I shook my head. "No need to apologize. It's good to get things out."

Elissa waved at the furniture. "Let's sit down, get more comfortable."

Adam retrieved his briefcase, carried it to the couch, and took a seat. Elissa sat down in the comfy chair.

"Would you be more comfortable if I left?" I asked.

"No reason to as far as I'm concerned," Elissa said.

"Same here," Adam agreed.

Good because curiosity has gotten the best of me. And I needed to find out how long she'd worked at Fresh Start.

Adam reached into his briefcase and pulled out files. "Elissa, I have a few pointed questions, but you don't have to answer them if you don't want to."

Elissa lowered her head. "All right."

"How did you meet my brother?"

She raised her head and met his eyes. "At a fundraising event for a treatment facility here: Fresh Start Rehabilitation. I support their mission, and so did Aaron."

That piqued my interest.

"When was that?" he asked.

"Just over six years ago. Aaron could be charming, and literally swept me off my feet. We got married a short time later."

"But something happened," Adam said.

Elissa looked at her hands and nodded. "A big something. Aaron found out he had fathered a child with someone else."

I sucked in an involuntary breath at the revelation. *Sylvie.*

Adam's face colored. He stood and shifted his weight from one leg to the next a few times. "No."

Elissa blushed in kind. "The blood test proved it. When he told me about it, that he needed to support his daughter, I couldn't deal with it. I didn't know the scope of it, what it all meant. I just knew I couldn't share Aaron with the baby's mother." She paused a moment. "He should've told you that you have a niece out there somewhere."

Adam sunk onto the couch again and leaned forward. "Did he say who the mother was or anything about his daughter?"

"No, aside from the fact that he'd just found out and he was in love with me, not her. To tell you the truth, I didn't want to know because I didn't want to care." Elissa shrugged.

"You think the little girl is about six. Do you know where her mother's from, where they are now?" Adam inquired as if he hadn't figured it out.

She shook her head. "I have no idea where they're from. It might be here in Brooks Landing. The news ruined our marriage when we were still in the honeymoon stage."

"That would have been a big blow. I understand why you felt the way you did. Betrayed," Adam said.

"Betrayed is right. I left, filed for divorce. And that was that."

"Did you talk to Aaron after you left?"

"Not much during the divorce process, or since. But I did send him a text on his work cell maybe a year ago that said, 'Sorry it didn't work out.' He didn't answer me."

Adam's eyebrows drew together. "What did you think about that?"

"I just shrugged because I'd honestly convinced myself I'd lost all feelings for him. I just wanted to wave a white flag in case there was anything he wanted to say to me, to tell me," she said.

Adam nodded. "We went through a lot of Aaron's papers today, and found he sent very generous donations to Fresh Start Rehabilitation."

"That doesn't surprise me. I do too. Like I said, we met at a fundraiser there."

That meant she'd receive donation request letters, and may even get a personal thank you note from Anderle, like Chief did.

Elissa continued, "I'm a nurse and do some fill-in shifts for the center when someone calls in sick. If I'm available." That answered one question.

"Oh, you do?" Adam said. The news must have struck a chord with him, as it had with me. I hadn't told him—or anyone—I'd seen her at Fresh Start on my spying expedition.

"Yes. In addition to being full time at a hospital in Minneapolis." And that answered my other question. She still worked there.

"Wow. How long have you been at Fresh Start?" I couldn't resist asking.

"Three months." Not long. But long enough to have access to stationery if she so desired.

"With your busy schedule, we're lucky we caught you at home." Adam opened a file, withdrew photos, and handed them to Elissa. "Have you ever seen this little girl?"

She studied one after another. "Cute little thing. Striking dark eyes." She glanced up at Adam. "Aaron's daughter?"

"I just found out he had a daughter, but my best guess is it must be. Her first name and ages are written on the backs of the photos. There was nothing else about her in the files, not that I found, at least."

Elissa turned the photo over. "I agree she must be Aaron's daughter. Sylvie. She's six in the latest photo, so the timeline fits. He would've found out a couple weeks after she was born, as I recall."

Adam stood again and circled the room a few times. "He didn't tell me he was married. He didn't tell me he had a daughter, but it wasn't with his wife. There was nothing more in his files, no birth certificate, no documents about her at all, including who her mother is."

"Aaron did that on purpose, I'm sure. He kept very few personal records. Plus he paid cash for groceries, gas, hygiene products, and just about everything else. No paper trail on what he bought. He also used cashier's checks for some expenses he didn't want to show up in his bank account. But he sent checks for utility bills and donations he made, for the tax deductions."

"Why all the secrecy?" Adam asked.

"I don't know, but after I found out he had a daughter, it made me wonder if someone was blackmailing him."

That put me on the edge of my seat.

Adam's eyebrows lifted. "Why do you say that?"

"His paycheck was deposited automatically every other Friday, and he'd withdraw the bulk of it, some in cash, some he transferred to savings." Elissa shook her head. "I found out by snooping, not because he told me any of it. And I was his wife. Yes, for a very short time. But like you said, why all the secrecy?"

"Last July, Aaron started missing a lot of work. At that same time, he withdrew ten thousand dollars from his savings every month." Adam said.

I was glad he told her.

Her jaw dropped. "Ten thousand *dollars?* Every *month*? For how many months?"

"Six. July through December. Then he took an additional five thousand out the last week in December. Besides other amounts those months."

"That is very odd. Maybe someone *was* blackmailing him, after all," Elissa said.

"The detectives should be able to find that out. Maybe through the contacts in his phone. I understand he just had the one phone."

"The main work cell phone. But he used those disposable ones too. He called me from different cell numbers when we were together."

I butted in. "Really? I wonder if the detectives found any other phones."

Elissa's eyebrows lifted. "I'd be curious. I asked Aaron why he used disposables, and he told me he liked them for personal calls, separate from his work cell. He had every phone number he needed memorized. Amazing."

"That makes some sense, about the disposables. In case his phone ever got confiscated, like for a data request by a member of the public for a specific reason, or from an agency working on a case," I said.

"Oh. Why would that be?" she asked.

"If they'd need to interrogate his phone after an incident in question. I learned that working for a U.S. Senator. We'd get data requests from time to time. Emails, mostly, regarding certain issues."

"I guess I never knew about that," she said.

My shoulder lifted. "Maybe it was something like that with Chief. In case his phone was taken for a while. But that could've been solved by having a personal cell, and a work cell."

"Aaron took it a step further using disposables, I guess," Elissa said.

"I wish I'd kept better track of my brother. It sounds like he was kind of paranoid. Disposable phones, cash transactions, what else?" Adam said.

Elissa tapped her chin with her pointer finger. "That reminds me. We flew to the Gulf Coast of Texas for our honeymoon. Aaron asked me to put the flights and hotel room on my credit card because he had cut his up. Then he reimbursed me the full amount, in cash."

"We didn't find any credit card receipts in his files, either. So I doubt he ever got another one," Adam said.

I thought of one last question. "Elissa, before we go, I was wondering if you told Gina, the cleaning lady at city hall and the police offices, about Aaron's baby."

Her eyebrows drew together in a slight frown. "I never met Gina. Aaron never mentioned her, and I didn't know who did the cleaning service there."

I drove Adam back to his brother's house, and pulled in the driveway. "You have no idea how much I want my brother back. I want to talk to him, find out why he changed so much, ask him a growing list of questions," Adam said.

"I didn't know him, but what I know of him, he was a complex man. I also know he was a good boss. Staff told me that."

"Thanks, I need something positive to hang on to," he said.

We sat in silence for a moment, then I said, "What are your plans for the evening?"

"Head to the hotel, have a long conversation with my wife, talk to my kids to remind me how blessed I am. If I'm hungry, I'll order a pizza. Spend some time trying to process everything."

"Okay. You reach out to Clint or me if you have a question or think of something else, all right?"

"I will, and thanks a million for your help. Having good people with me today made it way better than if I was trying to navigate this alone." Adam reached across the seat and grasped my hand. "All I can say is thanks again."

"Glad to help. Adam, may I have a copy of Sylvie's photo? I could ask a few people if they know her."

"Sure. In fact, I'll give you one now, and you can get it back to me at some point." He reached in his briefcase, withdrew the one of Sylvie at age five, and handed it over.

I slipped it in my purse. "I'll see what I can find out. Take care, Adam."

"You too. Night."

18

After Adam was in his SUV, and I saw exhaust trailing from the tail pipe, I drove back to Curio Finds, opened the door, and called out, "It's just me," when I noticed the deserted shop.

"We're in here," Pinky yelled from Brew Ha-Ha. It was almost quitting time. Pinky and Erin were at a table with steaming mugs in front of them.

I plopped down on a chair between them. "Mom and Dad go home?"

"Yeah, it was dead, so I told them I'd keep an eye on things till you got back, or lock up if you weren't back by closing time. Which is about six minutes from now," she said.

"Good. I smell minty chocolate."

"You want one?" Pinky asked.

I propped my elbows on the table, and dropped my head into my hands. "If it's spiked with some kind of alcohol."

"Minted chocolate with a shot of beer, mmm," Pinky said.

Erin leaned in close and pulled at my hands. "Hard day with the chief's brother, huh? Pinky said you were gone all afternoon. Back for a little while, and then gone again."

When she released my hands, I used them to scrub my face. "Emotional is the best way to describe the afternoon. It seemed way longer than five and a half hours. Not that I can say a lot about it, but Adam went through his brother's files for a few hours, bank records, some pictures. Then we met Chief Newel's ex-wife at her house."

Pinky swallowed with a gulp. "Get out of town! You actually met her? Fill us in on every single detail."

What should I say? "Well, Elissa is an RN at a metro hospital, and also fills in at Fresh Start Rehabilitation outside of town." They didn't know the murder weapon was on a Fresh Start envelope. "She and Adam actually hit it off well. Maybe because the chief had kept secrets from both of them."

"Like what kind of secrets?" Pinky asked.

"Like Chief hadn't told his brother he'd gotten married."

"What, *why*?" Erin said.

"I don't know. Maybe he wanted to see if it would last. And it didn't. I think it was secrets he kept from Elissa I can't talk about until the investigation is over." I wanted to show them Sylvie's photo, tell them about her, but needed to check with Clint first.

"Because you think Elissa had something to do with his murder?" Erin said.

Maybe, but that's not the reason. "I just don't know what I can and can't say without getting into trouble with Detective Garrison. Not until they get everything wrapped up." *Besides, I have things to check out myself.*

Pinky waved a napkin at me. "Cami, you're no fun."

Erin shook her head. "Pinky, as the most ardent rule follower at this table, I can appreciate Cami not saying something she shouldn't, and letting the detectives do their job. She got into enough trouble the last few cases she stuck her nose into. No offense, Cami."

I tried to slough off the guilt her words brought on. "No offense taken. I guess I have gotten a little too close to some bad guys in the past."

Pinky raised her eyebrows. "That's one way to put it."

I got home a little before 6:00, and found a package of chicken breasts in the refrigerator. I'd make a quick and tasty dish I liked. While the oven heated, I put the chicken in a glass baking dish, poured lemon juice over the tops, added garlic salt, pepper, oregano, thyme, basil, and paprika. I washed four potatoes, pricked them with a fork, and put them, along with the chicken dish, in the oven.

I hadn't heard from Clint for a couple hours, so it was a nice surprise when he phoned and said he was in my driveway.

"I'll open the back door." He'd implored me to keep my doors locked whether I was home or away, and I was mostly good about it. Growing up in Brooks Landing, nobody locked their doors, except when they went to bed at night. So when I returned to my hometown, I'd fallen back into the old habit. Until I met Clint, that is. We had a low crime rate in our small town, but bad things still happened, like everywhere.

A cloud of cold air surrounded Clint when he stepped into the kitchen. "Something smells good."

"Lemon herbed chicken and baked potatoes, so far."

I helped him out of his coat. Clint hung it over a kitchen chair then took off his boots. He rubbed his hands to warm them, put his arms around me, and held me a moment. He leaned his torso back, searched my eyes, then he put his cheek on mine, lightly brushed my lips with his, back and forth until I couldn't stand it. I threw my arms around his neck, and locked my lips on his.

A beeping sound interrupted us. It took me a few seconds to break the moment. "Um, it's the timer."

"What?" Clint's voice was huskier than normal.

I reluctantly slipped away, silenced the timer, and turned off the oven. "I hope you're hungry. I made enough for four."

"Are you psychic? You knew I'd turn up at your door? Let me rephrase that, given what you told me about your poison thought in your nightmare."

I shrugged. "I often make extra, and if no one's here to share it, I have a meal for another day."

"Sounds like an invitation I can't refuse. Be back after I get washed up."

As he made his way to the bathroom, I dug through the refrigerator freezer for another side dish. I found a blend of broccoli, cauliflower, and carrots, cut open the bag, poured it in a glass bowl, added a little water, covered it, and put it in the microwave for five minutes. I set plates, napkins, eating utensils, butter, and sour cream on the counter next to the stove.

The vegetables had steamed to perfection by the time Clint returned. I removed the chicken and potatoes and set them stovetop alongside the vegetables. "A simple meal served buffet style."

Clint put his hands on my shoulders and squeezed. "Looks like a feast to me."

We dished up and carried our plates to the dining table. When we were situated, we gave thanks for the food, and dug in. Clint was a fast eater, a habit he'd picked up in boot camp, and finished his plateful while mine was still two thirds full. "Help yourself to some more."

"Thanks." He left and returned with seconds. "Tell me how the rest of the day went with Adam. And Elissa."

I summed up our last minutes at Chief's house, the time at Pinky's, and jumped right into the embrace Adam and Elissa shared when they met. "I was the odd one out for what seemed like forever. Adam asked questions, and then Elissa delivered a news bomb."

Clint lowered his chicken-filled fork. "Oh?"

"The reason she left Chief was because he had a *daughter with another woman*—it must be Sylvie, the one in the pictures—born around the time they got married."

"He *what*?"

"I know, it's a shocker all right. The two hadn't been married long when they found out he'd fathered a baby girl. Besides what Chief did, Adam was upset he never told him he had a niece."

"That weasel. He had a daughter, didn't tell his brother, didn't tell any of us. What did Elissa say about the mother, who she is, where they live?"

"She didn't know anything about her. She said she didn't want to know so she wouldn't care."

"Humph. Nothing in the files about the mother, the daughter?"

"Not that we found. Adam took some files, bank records. Maybe Chief had a safety deposit box or a home safe we didn't see."

"Could be."

I went to the kitchen, brought my purse back with me, found Sylvie's photo, and held it up. "Adam said I could make a copy, show it to whomever, see if anyone recognizes her."

"We have a high-quality copier at the PD, so I can make copies."

"Thanks. I can get one from you tomorrow."

"Who are you going to show it to?" Clint asked.

"Not sure yet. The councilors, maybe Pinky and Erin. Margaret, Gina."

Clint's eyes narrowed. "*Gina*, why?"

"Just a hunch. She seems to know more about Aaron Newel than anyone else."

"How so?"

"The comment she made about Elissa having a good reason to leave Clint. Elissa didn't even know Gina—I asked her earlier—so Chief Newel must've told her. She knew at least one of his secrets no one else did."

"You gotta wonder why." He thought a moment. "I'll talk to Adam tomorrow, see if he's come up with a game plan of sorts."

"That might take more time, Clint. He was pretty shot by the time we parted ways. Sounds like he wanted to talk to his family and chill out. Adam needs to take care of things, notify companies, pay bills. I said we could keep watch on the house."

"Of course. That's easy enough with our officers on patrol twenty-four-seven," he said.

"Did you know Elissa met Chief at a fundraiser for Fresh Start Rehab?"

"I didn't, no."

"She said she wasn't surprised he gave large donations to them. She does too, in fact. And get this, she even works part time at Fresh Start," I said.

Clint's eyebrows lifted. "You don't say. That adds a new wrinkle now, doesn't it?"

"The detective didn't say anything to you about that?"

"No. You know we're not working together on this, per se. The sheriff's office can be more objective than the PD, and that includes me."

"I guess that's true. I just thought they might brief you on any updates, like who they've interviewed."

"No."

"Or if they've ruled out any suspects."

"At this point it's difficult to say they would've ruled out anyone," he said.

"I can see why they wouldn't have ruled out Elissa."

"Because she had a fall out with Chief? That was years ago."

"Things fester with people all the time until something finally snaps," I said.

I woke up Saturday morning with Stormin' Gorman on my mind. Maybe it was the gusting north winds in the night that reminded me I had yet to talk to her. Her explanations would determine what I'd ask the other councilors.

After a cup of strong coffee to fortify myself, I phoned Stormin'. "How are you doing, Rosalie?"

"Oh, Camryn, I'm a mess. A good thing it's a slow time of year for real estate. Or maybe it's a bad thing. If I was busy it might distract me. I can't stop thinking about Aaron, and wondering if anyone else is in danger." She sounded distressed.

"I know. It's like a nightmare we can't wake up from."

"That's a good way to put it."

"As far as others being in danger, the Buffalo County Sheriff's Office would tell us if they thought so," I said.

"I guess."

"Rosalie, I'd like to meet with you, run over some things."

"Like what?"

"We can talk about it in person. Are you free this morning, before my shop opens at nine? Or we could talk over coffee sometime today at Brew Ha-Ha."

"I need to get ready to face the world, so does nine thirty at Pinky's work? That will give me the push I need," she said.

"Sure, see you then."

I phoned Clint next. "Morning," he answered.

"Morning," I said, leaving out the 'good' as he had. "Checking in. Did you have a chance to make copies of Sylvie's photo?"

"I did. They're here on my desk. Want me to drop one off?"

"I can pick it up before work. I'm meeting with Stormin' at nine thirty."

"About anything in particular?" he asked.

"Just a couple questions is all."

"Tell me you aren't treading into verboten territory."

"You speak German? And the answer is no." At least I didn't think it would be.

Clint let me in the police station's back door. I followed him to his office where he picked Sylvie's envelope-enclosed photo from his desk, and handed it over.

I removed it and studied her face. "Clint, would it be okay to show her photo to a few people, besides the employees here? Like Pinky who sees a lot of people in her shop. Or Erin. Maybe she's seen her at school."

"I don't see the harm in that. We can't go public with her photo. We need to protect her privacy, her mother's privacy," he said.

"Of course." I smiled at Sylvie's smile. "I love her dimples. I wonder if she got them from her mother or from Newel's mother. If she is his daughter, that is."

"I never like to assume anything, but it seems safe to presume she is."

"What a mess. They might live in another state, another country. Mexico maybe. Word is that's where he was over Christmas. Might explain why Sylvie's mother hasn't come forward with a paternity suit. She hasn't heard Chief is dead." I said.

"One possibility. Wherever she is, they must've led separate lives."

"She did send Sylvie's pictures to Chief. Annually, from the time she was one," I argued.

"That might've been all Sylvie's mother let him have. I'll ask Detective Garrison if there are photos in Chief's phone. That could give us—them—a lead," he said.

"But would it lead them to the killer?"

"Never say never."

19

Rosalie Gorman was not her usual stormin' self. As she slinked into Curio Finds, I didn't recognize her at first. She wore a stocking cap pulled down to her eyebrows, sweatpants, and a jacket that looked decades old. Her green eyes gave her away. "Rosalie, is that you?"

She kept her cap on. "It's me. I'm having a down day so I'm glad you called to get me out of the house."

It was the first I'd heard of her "down" days. Her appearance and demeanor concerned me. I picked the file folder off the counter. "I'm glad you're here. Let's chat over a cup of coffee."

Pinky's eyes widened when we walked up to her service counter. "Rosalie, are you undercover today, or what?"

"More like under the weather." Her voice was quiet.

"Oh, I'm sorry to hear that. So you could use a little pick-me-up. How about a Blue Jamaican?"

Pinky, really, did you have to say "blue?" I frowned at her.

She tried to smooth things over. "From the Blue Mountains there. People think it's the finest coffee in the world. Very smooth, almost creamy with a hint of chocolate, and no bitterness. Rare and expensive . . . and my treat today."

Did she have to say "expensive" when the price was listed on her menu? I gave Stormin's arm a gentle nudge. "Hey, that will be a treat. What do you say, Rosalie?"

"Um, okay." Far less robust than usual.

"What kind of muffin or scone would you like? Rhubarb looks good to me," I said.

"I'm not very hungry, but any kind of muffin might be nice."

"Two rhubarb muffins?" Pinky asked, and we both nodded. "Coming right up. Take your choice of tables before the coffee break crowd shows up. I'll bring your order in a minute."

I followed Rosalie to the back table. She slipped off her jacket, but left her cap in place, and shrugged. "Bad hair day."

"Can you tell me what's going on?"

She looked down at her hands and remained silent.

"Is it Chief Newel's death?"

"Mostly. That made my SAD disorder all the worse." Seasonal Affective Disorder, depression not uncommon among people in winter when days were shorter, with less sunlight. There were different degrees, and Stormin's looked pretty bad from where I sat.

"I'm so sorry. Do you take anything for it?"

She shook her head. "Like meds? No. I have a sun lamp that helps a lot. So does getting out of the house, and thanks for that."

I hoped she felt the same when we'd finished talking. Pinky brought our tray of goodies. "Here you go, ladies. Enjoy!"

When Stormin' and I took sips of our coffees, she almost smiled. "I don't know why I never tried Blue Jamaican before. It's my new favorite," she said with a little more energy.

188

"It is about the best there is." I swallowed a bite of muffin. "You mentioned you can't stop thinking about Chief. Forgive me, but did you have a personal relationship with him at some point?"

She choked on her coffee, and it took her a bit to recover. "Yes, but not in *that* way, if that's what you're thinking."

Did I have a guilty look on my face? "It's just that you've been protective of him, so it made me curious."

"When my husband left me a few years ago, Aaron saw how hard it was on me, and we met a couple times—in public places I might add—to talk. He helped me through a rough patch, and I admit I've had a soft spot for him ever since. Personally speaking. Professionally, I admit he was intimidating."

"Sorry about your marriage."

She nodded.

"Did he talk about his wife leaving him?"

"No, and I was on the council when it happened. He didn't tell a soul why she left, as far as I know," she said.

I pulled Sylvie's photo from the file, and slid it in front of Stormin'. "Do you recognize this little girl?"

She picked up the photo for a closer look. "I don't, but she is a cutie. Who is she?"

"Chief Newel's brother found it in his files. Since you've known him for some years, I thought maybe you knew something about her."

"I don't. No info about her in the files?"

"Just photos from the time she was born to age six. This is her at age five. This isn't public yet, but she may be Chief's daughter."

"*No.* Very strange if he kept his own child a secret." She laid the photo on the table, teared up, found a tissue in her purse, and

189

dabbed at her eyes. "He left behind so many unanswered questions. They say you never know, and they're right. You *never* know."

A common sentiment when the unexpected, especially an untimely death, occurred. "Rosalie, something else I wondered about."

"What's that?"

I opened the file, and handed her Chief Newel's sick and vacation leave data sheet. "I understand you got this information from HR a while ago."

Stormin' glanced at it. "Yes."

"Did you share it with the other councilors?"

She nodded. "I did."

"Yet you didn't tell me. I'm the one you all chose to talk to him, and I realized after the fact I should have gotten the info before our meeting. You decided to send me in blind. Why? I'd be angry if Chief was still alive." I tried to keep my voice level, but it rose with each sentence.

Tears rolled down Stormin's cheeks. "It wasn't fair, I see that now. You were right when you said I was protecting Aaron. I didn't want you to know how bad it really was, all his absences I mean, and I asked the other councilors to keep the report quiet until after you'd talked to him. I pleaded with Aaron over a month ago to spill the beans, but he didn't.

"Then he went on another vacation, and Frosty died, and we didn't know what to do next. After you got appointed mayor, with all your experience dealing with folks in D.C., I thought you'd be the perfect one to wheedle out whatever Aaron's deal was. And the others agreed." She took a well-deserved breath after all that poured from her mouth in about ten seconds.

190

I covered her hand with mine. "Rosalie, it's the past, and we have more important things here in the present. The detectives are working to find Chief's killer, and if we have any information that helps, we need to tell them."

"Of course. Detective Garrison talked to me, but I didn't have much to say. In fact I felt ashamed I knew next to nothing about Aaron's private life. He had secrets, big ones I figured, but what were they?" She leaned closer to me. "I even hired a private detective agency a couple days last summer. You know, for some of the days he took a scheduled vacation."

That surprised me. "Really?"

"Yes. In August." She pointed to days listed on the report. You see he was gone the eleventh through the fifteenth? I only knew of the eleventh and twelfth ahead of time to give to the detectives. You'll never guess this, but Aaron didn't leave home, at least not for the sixteen hours each day the guys kept watch."

"Really?"

"Same thing on the twenty-fifth and twenty-sixth," she said.

"That is odd."

"Tell me about it. Lights came on in the house early mornings. The blinds were drawn, but they could see lights inside. And they went out late in the evenings, around ten."

"The fact that he took every other weekend off for all those months baffles me. If he was home that means he wasn't moonlighting at another job somewhere else," I said.

She shook her head. "I never thought of that, but I'm with you. I wondered about PTSD, and thought maybe he was doing in-home counseling sessions, like over the phone or something."

"His home phone records should show that." I couldn't tell Stormin' about the large cash withdrawals. Maybe it was for counseling services. Someone knew about Chief's secrets, besides Elissa. At least one other did.

"Well, I feel better coming clean with you. It wasn't fair not telling you what I knew about Aaron. I hope I can rebuild your trust."

I smiled. "Sure thing."

"Thanks, that lightens my burden." She grinned at me. "The coffee helped, too."

I noticed Stormin's spine was straighter as she left Brew Ha-Ha. Pinky swooped in as I stood, and gathered our dishes. "What was that all about? I didn't even know it was Stormin' at first when the two of you came up to my counter."

"It took me a minute to recognize her myself."

"Honestly, Cami, you were talking so quietly back there, it made me even more curious than normal. I had a heck of a time trying not to eavesdrop."

I chuckled. "Well, I had a couple questions for Stormin', and didn't want any *eavesdroppers* to hear what we were talking about, or she might not have answered me." I carried the dishes to the sink then turned to Pinky. "All right, so I found out the city council was given a report of all the days Chief missed work a while ago. I needed to ask Rosalie why they didn't show me the list, didn't tell me."

"Wait. So they had the list, didn't tell you about it, sent you in to talk to Chief Newel blind?"

I nodded. "That's what happened all right. Turns out they didn't want me to know the full extent. They thought I'd be less biased, more open to what Chief had to say, and maybe he'd come clean about his reason. Or reasons."

"I kinda get that logic, but that's not the way I would've handled it."

"No, and it's one of the things I admire most about you. You're forthright."

Pinky's eyebrows lifted. "Forthright, huh? I like that. It's sad though, now that the chief's dead, you might never get those answers."

"Garrison and his team are investigating, and should get to the bottom of it. They just need to find the right people to talk to."

"Yeah, someone knows something."

"Pinky, I have a photo to show you." She followed me back to the table. I withdrew Sylvie's photo from the folder, and handed it to her.

"What a little doll. Who is she?"

"We don't know for sure, but think she might be Chief Newel's daughter," I said.

"Get out of here, *what*?"

"Adam found her photos in Chief's files. It turns out he'd fathered a child with a woman—whose identity is unknown at this point—and found out after he'd married Elissa."

"Get out of here, *what*?" she repeated.

I lifted my hands. "That's the reason Elissa left him."

"Hmm. Can't say I blame her." She shook her head. "Did you happen to find out anything about Stormin' and the chief?"

"Actually, yes. She told me Chief Newel was a friend to talk to through her divorce," I said.

"Well, I guess we can give him credit for that, at least."

The doorbell in my shop dinged, and I left to greet the customers.

193

Adam Newel stopped by Curio Finds after lunch. His brow was creased, like he was perplexed. "Good morning, Adam." I waved him to the back office, a quiet place to talk.

"Hey, Camryn. I just came from a meeting with Detective Garrison. I gave him Sylvie's photo."

"What'd he say?"

"He was intrigued, but told me that finding out who she is, and where she lives is more what a private investigator does. Unless she's involved in the criminal case," he said.

"But what if she is involved somehow? What do you think?"

"That's the issue; I have no idea how she would be. It's out of my league, all this undercover stuff. My biggest ask is that they catch and punish Aaron's killer is. My second ask is that we find my niece. We only have photos to go on so far, but you'd think Aaron had more information about her somewhere."

"Like in a safe or safety deposit box," I said.

"Right. I can't check with his bank until they open again on Monday." Adam drew in a loud breath. "I had a dream last night that other children, and young adults, showed up claiming Aaron was their father. I woke up in a cold sweat."

I wasn't the only one with nightmares. "Adam, you only found the one file with Sylvie's photos, so let's count on the fact she's his only child."

"That's true, and I hope you're right." He looked down and shook his head.

"So what've you got planned for the rest of the day?"

"I'll head back to Aaron's. After yesterday, I didn't think I could, but when I woke up, I knew that's what I had to do."

20

Clint stopped by in street clothes a little after 3:00. His face was drawn, bags under his eyes. I put my warm hand on his cold cheek. "No offense, but you look like you need about twenty hours of sleep."

"More like forty, but I'll settle for eight." He sat down on the stool behind the checkout counter. "Detective Garrison called me; said he'd met with Adam Newel."

"Yeah, Adam was here earlier, told me he'd shown Sylvie's photo to Garrison, and Garrison said it was more of a private detective's job to look for her."

"True, unless she's involved with, or connected to, a criminal case. According to Garrison, a little girl named Sylvie, or the fact that Chief had a daughter, hasn't come up in their interviews."

"So they haven't talked to Elissa yet?"

"No. I asked him about her, and he's going to meet with her later today. It's the first time that worked with their schedules," he said.

"Wow. Adam and I were lucky we caught her at home yesterday."

"You were, yes."

"Did he say who all they've talked to?" I asked.

"You know they went to Fresh Start right away, interviewed the CEO and staff, me of course, the other officers in the PD, our office staff, both in Admin and the PD. They're the ones I know of. They might've gotten tips to follow I'm not privy to."

I touched his chin. "Does it make you feel bad, not being in the thick of things?"

"A little, sure. But when another agency takes the lead, it's best to stay out of their way. I can still poke around, and if I learn something, I'll let them know. I suggested they check with the Ironwood administrator to cover that base."

"Good. I see the administrator is still with his wife. Would he have a motive after all this time?" I asked.

Clint's eyebrows lifted. "How'd you find that out?"

"The easy way, social media."

He grinned. "I went that same route. They do present themselves as a happily married couple, at least in the eyes of the public."

"Married couples hit rough patches along the way. Chief might've been there at the right, or the wrong, time when the two got together."

"Still wrong, by my standards," he said.

"Clint, Adam's number one priority is finding his brother's killer. Then he can concentrate his attention and efforts finding Sylvie. He had a dream that his brother had more children, some were even adults."

"You don't say. Lord help us." Clint shook his head. "I hope for his family's sake it was only a dream."

"You think Sylvie's mother will come forward, and ask for her daughter's share of Newel's inheritance?"

"You gotta wonder. Like we talked about before, could be she doesn't know he's dead. Could be Chief was never in their lives to speak of, so she didn't expect anything from him, dead or alive."

"What a mess. And those large chunks of money Chief Newel withdrew is another big mind boggler. Adam's going to check with Newel's bank to see if his brother had a safety deposit box there."

"Yeah, he mentioned that. I know we didn't do as thorough of a search of Chief's house as we could've. Adam got overwhelmed, and I didn't want to push him. Could be Chief has a well-hidden safe there after all."

"If you find one, and it turns out it's filled with answers to the secrets Chief kept, that'd also be the answer to prayers. Adam's at his brother's house now, and I think he'd appreciate some company, if you're up to it," I said.

"Sure, happy to help, do what I can. If we uncover something significant, all the better."

Since we were alone, I took the opportunity to give him a big smooch.

"Now that hit a sweet spot," he said, and rested his forehead against mine a moment.

"Mmm, ah ha," I agreed.

The sun was low on the horizon as I approached the front door to lock up. A man of average height and build had his head bent down as he looked at the snow globe window display. If he was in the market for a gift, I'd keep the shop open until he found one. I lifted my hand, and waved to get his attention. He glanced up for a second then ducked his head away from me, turned, and hurried off.

I'd gotten a quick glimpse of his face, enough to guesstimate he was in his late thirties or early forties with a ruddy complexion, either from a skin condition or the freezing cold. His stocking cap covered his head and hair.

As I locked the door I muttered, "That's odd. He acted like he didn't want me to see him eyeing the merchandise." The lights in the shop flickered, turned off, then came back on again. "Molly, really? What are you up to now? It kind of freaks me out when you do that, especially when I'm alone here." The lights went off, and came on again.

I half-smiled and shook my head at her response. If that's what it was. Not that we could prove Molly's spirit did, in fact, hang out at our shops. But we had no way to disprove it either. The electrician had found nothing wrong with the wiring, so that's what we had to go on.

Several things flittered through my mind. I wanted to talk with Elissa again, see if she'd reveal anything enlightening, woman to woman, something she hadn't wanted to say in front of Adam. With her ex-husband gone, there may be other secrets she needed to get off her chest. Positive or negative.

Gina was the other person I needed to chat with again. She knew one of Chief Newel's secrets, maybe more. There should be no reason to keep them now that he was gone. And it could help the investigation.

I also planned to visit Fresh Start Rehabilitation, see what kinds of vibes were floating around the facility. Was there a viable suspect who either worked, or was a client, there? I didn't know

Matthew Anderle, but Clint did and he would've mentioned anything questionable about him.

Anderle hadn't dated the note he'd written a few months back. And said he hadn't sent out the deadly one. In his position, he would be too smart to do something that dumb. Unless that was his angle. "Why would I send a personal note if I intended to kill Chief Newel?"

Something to find out: was Anderle in cahoots with Elissa?

My head started to spin as I thought of different scenarios, possible suspects, and how Chief Newel's killer would get flushed out.

I glanced at the time on my phone. 5:34. I hadn't heard from Clint since he'd left my shop and sent him a text, *Still at Newel's house?*

Yes, wrapping up. Catch you later.

Okay. I didn't know what "later" meant. Hours, minutes? What to do in the mean time? Matthew Anderle likely wasn't at work on a Saturday evening. I phoned Gina to see if she was available for a chat. My call went to voicemail after seven rings. I didn't leave a message. She'd see my number on the missed calls list, and could call back.

The frigid air bit my bare face as I walked to my car in the back parking lot. It was dark, and I was tired, so it seemed all the worse. *Brrr! No wonder so many people escaped Minnesota cold over the winter months.*

I decided to swing by Elissa's, check if she was home. She'd had a day to process the visit from Adam, and if her stirred emotions brought up something confidential she was willing to share, I'd be grateful for any clue to follow up on.

199

I drove down the alley to the back side of her house and parked by her garage. A light was on in her kitchen, but the rest of the house looked dark. On my way to her door, I resisted the urge to look in the garage window for her car. I knocked on the door and listened for sounds inside. I waited, heard none, then knocked again, in case. Nothing.

On the walk back to my car, I brushed aside the thought someone might see me, and peeked in Elissa's garage window. No vehicle. I drove home longing for Clint. His strong arms wrapped around me would help settle my unease about the murder. After spending time with Adam Newel, I empathized with him. His brother's death seemed more personal to me. Estranged brothers who led vastly different lives, but still family after all.

The chill I felt as I entered my house was caused by more than the low setting on the thermostat. It felt lonelier than usual. I needed friends, family, Clint.

Pinky phoned a short time later. "Cami, it's been a really hard week for all of us. How about we get the gang together for a spur of the moment meal tonight, something simple? My house. I started making a kettle of chicken and bacon wild rice soup, and it got to be enough for ten. I have two loaves of crusty bread I baked and put in the freezer to have on hand. If anyone wants to bring something else, that's great. If not, no biggie. If no one wants to eat we can just hang out later. But I'll have a *lot* of leftover soup."

"I would love that. A meal together, I mean. And nobody makes better soups than you," I said.

"Except you."

I chuckled. "Whatever. I'm waiting to hear from Clint, and as far as I know, he doesn't have plans. I'll come alone if he does."

"Super. I already talked to Jake since we were trying to decide what to do. I'll check with Erin and Mark."

"Still hoping those two will rekindle their love, huh?" I said.

"We both know they never lost their love. It just got sidetracked because he's a cop, and she's a worrywart over him. More than she needs to be, I always thought. But then Chief Newel got killed."

"Pinky, the investigators haven't come across anything to make them think other officers in the Brooks Landing PD are in danger. That's what I'm holding on to."

"Yep. Let's say my house at seven for whoever can make it."

"Sounds good. I'll send Clint a message."

Before I could, a knock sounded on my back kitchen door, and Clint stepped inside. "I was just about to—"

He interrupted me. "Camryn, you need to keep your doors locked." Clint was safety-minded to a fault and persistent with his reminders.

"I know, I was a little distracted—"

"The very reason it's critical that it's a built-in habit, something you do automatically so you don't think about it. You just do it."

It put me off when he got after me, but he made a good point. "Yes, sir." I looked down at my feet.

He stomped the snow off his boots then reached over, and lifted my chin with his fingers. "I didn't mean to sound gruff, sorry I barked at you."

His brown eyes softened as I searched them, and it made my pique melt away. "I can't argue with you, Clint. I always kept my doors locked in D.C., but after I moved back to Brooks Landing, it was like I reverted to my childhood when we locked the doors at night before we went to bed. Maybe. And that was about it."

He snaked his arms around me. "It seemed safer then, but being a cop has changed my attitude, even about that. Every so often a person you least expect gets caught doing something nefarious."

"You're right." I rose on tip toes, and gave him a peck on the lips. He returned the kiss with enough fervor to take my breath away. When we came up for air, I asked how Adam was, if they'd found anything special at his brother's.

"Nothing enlightening. He decided to drive home, come back Monday when the banks open, see where that leads. His wife called, said she and the kids missed him, so off he went."

"Good. He's got a lot to process, that's for sure." I paused a second. "Pinky called, and wants the gang to get together tonight. She's cooking, if you need any coaxing."

"I sure as heck don't. I could eat a horse about now."

"Can you hold out until seven?"

"No problem, it'll give me time to shower. What should I bring?"

"Beer, maybe? I'll pick up a pre-made relish tray at Greta's Groceries. I love their fresh dill dip. They grow the plants year-round."

"You don't say." He looked at his watch. "How about I pick you up in forty minutes, and we'll stop for our humble offerings on the way."

Erin, Mark, and Jake had arrived ahead of us, and were in the kitchen with Pinky. Her kitchen was filled with the mixed aromas of soup and warm bread. Yummy. And something else. "What have you got in the oven?" I asked.

"Brownies."

Be still my heart. I set the relish dish on the counter, and gave her a half hug. "You are a baking queen."

She held up a wooden spoon, hummed a few bars of Abba's *Dancing Queen,* twirled around, and sang out, slightly off key, "I am a baking queen, young and sweet, only seventeen. Ha! Baking queen."

Erin took over in her sweet alto when Pinky stopped, "You can bake, you can jive, having the time of your life. Ooh, see that girl, watch that scene digging the baking queen."

The rest of us joined in with some classic disco moves. Arms, hips, feet, rocking to their a cappella song. It lightened our moods, made us laugh.

"Hey, after we eat we should find some music from that era and dance the night away: the Bee Gees, Kool and the Gang, Donna Summer, Marvin Gaye, the Jacksons," Mark said.

"KC and the Sunshine Band," Jake added.

"You guys are good. I know a lot of songs from the seventies and eighties, but not most of the artists who sang them," I said.

"No. I gotta admit, I've never done any disco dancing," Clint said.

Pinky giggled. "There are tutorials, I'm sure. And you sorta did okay trying out those moves a minute ago."

Even Clint laughed at that. "Pinky, I should find you a disco ball on Ebay to hang in your kitchen. That way we can get the full effect when you break into an impromptu song and dance number."

"Good one, boss," Jake said.

Pinky snorted, and the rest of us laughed again. Things were getting sillier by the minute. The timer on Pinky's oven dinged, so we switched our focus. She put on mitts, removed the pan of brownies, and set it on the ceramic countertop next to the stove.

"Soup's on. How about you grab a beverage and dish up?" she said.

We all got a beer from Clint's twelve pack, and popped off the tops. Clint held up his bottle. "Sorry if this is a mood changer, but I have to say it. This has been the worst week of my life as a cop. Mark and Jake said the same thing." They both nodded, and Clint continued, "Let's salute Chief Aaron Newel again. He ran a top-notch office, a tight ship. He shouldn't have gone out the way he did, and that will always be about impossible to accept." He took a breath. "Skol, my friends."

Good health. Cheers. We saluted with him.

After a moment of silence, Pinky ladled soup into bowls, and set them on the counter next to the relish tray and small plates. "Don't be shy." Mark nudged Erin to start then fell in behind her. The dining table was set with silverware and napkins, along with baskets of bread, crackers, and butter in a dish. Pinky insisted on being last in line, and the rest of us waited to dig in until after she'd joined us.

As I savored my first spoonful of soup, I knew I needed the recipe.

After our earlier moments of levity, we ate and talked in a more contemplative mood. Clint had saluted Chief Newel and wished the rest of us good health. I was touched by both. One by one, we reflected on Newel's life and career. And each other's safety.

Clint said, "I want to reiterate there is no reason to believe other officers on our force are in danger. The sheriff's office has found no evidence to support that speculation."

Pinky lifted her spoon to get his attention. "But who killed Chief Newel, and why? That's what everyone wants to know so we can sleep better at night." She stopped, and glanced around the table. "You are three of the city's finest, not to mention our best peeps. We can't help but worry about you."

Erin tipped her head down, her eyes on her lap, a sign Pinky's words had upset her. "Let it go, Alice. Please."

Alice. Confirmation they had. Pinky's eyebrows lifted, and her lips turned down. She reached her long arm across Mark's chest, and touched Erin's shoulder. "I got carried away. Sorry, Erin."

Erin turned toward her. "It's okay. I know you're one who processes your thoughts through verbalization."

Pinky's cheek muscles moved back and forth while she thought that over for a minute. "I guess."

I cleared my throat. "My hips won't let me hide how much I love good food, and your soup and bread are *really* good, Pinky."

Everyone agreed with nods and kind words.

Pinky beamed. "Wait till you taste my decadent double chocolate brownies."

Be still my heart, I thought again.

21

It snowed most of Sunday morning, a gentle fall with huge flakes. The kind you'd see on Hallmark movies. Picturesque. Perfect. I did something I hadn't done in years. I found a sheet of black construction paper, stepped outside, held the paper in front of me, and watched snowflakes land. The fact that each was a little different was nothing short of a miracle in my mind. The weather was mild, almost balmy after the polar vortex temps the week before.

The weather forecasters predicted an upcoming few days of "January thaw" when temperatures rose above freezing. I remembered one year when it stayed in the fifties for a week. It felt so warm, people went for runs in shorts and tee-shirts, like they did in spring when temps hit the high forties.

I stayed out for a while, looking at the snowflake designs. Snow caught on my eyelashes, and I blinked them away every so often. I went back inside, and set the paper on the kitchen counter. Within seconds the flakes were small wet dots on the paper. I brushed snow off my clothes and hair, picked up the coffee I'd left on the kitchen table, and carried it into the living room.

CHRISTINE HUSOM

Sunday was traditionally a day spent with family or friends or relaxing before the next work week. Adam would be back in Brooks Landing the next day. Elissa didn't have a nine-to-five job, and I hoped to connect with her soon.

Gina could wait. She hadn't returned my call. She was either avoiding me—or to give her the benefit of the doubt—was otherwise occupied. I'd track her down tomorrow evening at the city offices. I nursed my coffee and thought about my strategies.

Clint phoned midway through my plans. "It was nice Pinky threw that dinner party, a good night for all of us."

"For sure. Plus the leftovers she sent home are great. I had a brownie for breakfast, and will eat the soup at some point today."

"It sounds like Pinky—and Erin especially—are worried about our officers' safety."

"I think you helped relieve some of their worries, but it's an intrinsic thing for Erin, why she didn't want to marry Mark. She's been fearful forever, long before Chief Newel was killed. She thinks it's separation anxiety from her babyhood. Since she was adopted from an orphanage in Vietnam, she doesn't know what happened to her biological family, why she was taken there."

"Hmm, maybe that's it." He took a moment. "Mark is putting his fish house out on Green Lake today, wants Jake and me to join him for an afternoon of fishing."

"It'd be good for you guys to decompress a while," I said.

"Mark lured me by guaranteeing we'd catch a meal or two of walleye."

"Lured you? Bad pun."

"Accidental bad pun."

"Whatever."

We laughed, and disconnected.

My mom checked in a short time later. "Your sisters and brothers all send their love. They're hoping we can get together soon. Your father and I—well, mostly I—know how it can overwhelm you when we're all in the same house and the volume goes through the roof, what with three or four conversations going on at the same time."

"Thanks, Mom."

"It's wonderful when everyone's home, and a relief when they all leave again," she said with a chuckle.

We'd had a similar conversation off and on since I was a small child. "Thanks, Mom. As soon as they solve Chief Newel's murder, things will settle down again. I hope."

"Does being the mayor add too much to your plate?" she asked.

"It adds to it, but I don't think it's too much. When we get on the other side of this, things will be more routine again."

"That's what we're praying for."

"Thanks, Mom."

I tried to get back into the mystery novel I'd started reading the previous week but couldn't concentrate on the fictional murder case. Not when we had a real one on our hands. I'd try Elissa instead. Should I ring her doorbell, or call first? A phone call would save a step if she wasn't home.

One, two, three rings and she answered. "This is Elissa."

"Elissa, it's Camryn Brooks. Checking to see how you are."

It took her a moment. "Um, okay. A little numb, to be honest."

"I'd like to talk to you some more, if you're available."

"About what?" she said.

"Aaron Newel."

208

"What about him?" Her voice was flat.

"Nothing special. But you might remember something that would help the sheriff's office find his killer."

"I can't imagine what that'd be, but you're welcome to come over."

"Would now be okay?" I said.

"Give me fifteen minutes, I'm still in my pajamas."

"Thanks."

Elissa appeared tired and tense when she opened the door. Her eyes were half-closed, and the crease between her eyebrows was deeper, like she had a headache. "Come in. Want a cup of coffee?"

"Sure, thanks."

She poured coffee in two mugs, and set them on the kitchen table. "Cream, sugar?"

"Thanks, no. I drink it straight," I said with a smile.

"Yeah, I'm hoping another shot of caffeine will chase away my headache."

I was right. "No fun. Is it from the barometric pressure change in the weather today? I know it affects a lot of people."

"No, it's from a different kind of pressure. Tension, all the memories brought on by Aaron's death. Meeting his brother—a really good guy, by the way—reliving our divorce when we had barely said 'I do,' the affair that caused the break up."

"Lots for you to deal with," I said.

"I thought I was over Aaron years ago, but don't think I will ever be. Even with his privacy quirk, he was the love of my life. It devastated me to think I *wasn't* the love of his. It took me years to find him, and then it was over, just like that."

I nodded. "I can't comment except to say, he didn't marry before you or after you, not even the mother of his child. So maybe you were the love of his life."

Tears formed in her eyes. "Maybe I was at that. Camryn, I thought of something before you got here, something I'd put out of my mind, all but forgotten after Aaron gave me that news. It was the same day he told me about the baby. Minutes before, actually."

She stopped, and time passed with no words between us. Finally I said, "What was it?"

Elissa brushed the tears with her thumbs. "I heard Aaron on the phone in the other room. I was curious because he was talking in a hushed tone, like he didn't want me to hear. As it turns out it was something he knew he had to tell me. And later did."

"Did you know who he was talking to, hear what Aaron said?"

"I don't know who was on the other end, but it sounded like it was the husband of the woman who'd had Aaron's baby."

"Wait a minute. That woman was married?" I said.

"That's what I surmised from the conversation, but didn't ask because I didn't want to know for sure. It made it seem that much worse."

"What made you think that's who it was?" I asked.

"I heard Aaron say, 'I'm not in love with your wife, and two wrongs don't make a right. I'll help, so you won't have the extra financial burden.'"

How could Elissa have not asked Chief to explain, to clarify. "You think he was talking about the baby?"

"It had to be. Aaron said he wasn't in love with the guy's wife, and that he'd help them out financially. I have no idea what happened to the man or his wife after that. If they split up, or what.

Aaron probably paid child support. He'd want to do that much, at least." Chief had gone through a lot of cash, maybe he'd been bribed, paid money to keep a big scandal from surfacing.

"It sounds like it," I said.

"If I'd forgiven him at the time, we would've made it work, could've had a child together. My anger and jealousy put a wall between us I couldn't climb over."

"It was a big shock. When you've been betrayed, it's not always easy to forgive, move on."

"No. But you know what? I did eventually forgive him, and sent that text I told you about, the one he didn't answer. I couldn't really move on in my personal life. I haven't wanted to. Aaron Newel, with all his faults, set the bar high. Never met a man quite like him," Elissa said.

I went home, and puttered around, did laundry, cleaned, and thought. Elissa was front and center in my mind. She hadn't hated Aaron Newel after all. He was the love of her life. "Never met a man quite like him." Her sentiment was unexpected and made me curious. Even married women fell for him. Like Jeni Fischer. Like Sylvie's mother.

Elissa had overheard the call between Newel and Sylvie's mother's husband, and pushed it to the back of her mind. Oh, my. Who was Sylvie's mother? I wondered for the umpteenth time. And was she still married to the man who had called Newel back when? Chief had said he'd give them support money. Unless he'd stopped payments, what would be the motive for either the mother or her husband to kill Chief Newel? He'd spent big money on something the last months that no doubt included child support.

Chief Newel had kept a file of Sylvie's photos, so he must have cared about her.

Adam, Newel's files, Elissa. The large amounts of money Newel had withdrawn from his bank account, all the time he'd taken off work. The more I thought the harder I cleaned.

When I started to feel weak and lightheaded, I realized I hadn't eaten since the brownie for breakfast, and it was nearly supper time. I opened the fridge and smiled at the bowl of Pinky's specialty soup. Clint phoned as the dish warmed in the microwave. "Hungry for some fresh fish?" he said.

"You caught some, huh?"

"Oh, yeah. Nice walleye, crappies. They're all fileted in a big bowl of water in the refrigerator."

"Sounds good, but I'm about to enjoy Pinky's leftover soup. Maybe tomorrow. So the three of you had time to relax a bit?" I asked.

"Yeah, and toasted Chief some more. Lots of memories over the years, all the cases and the crazies we'd dealt with. We laughed and—I'll admit it—we cried too."

"I'm glad. It's healthy to laugh, and to cry. Does the soul good," I said.

"What will really do the soul good is when they find his killer."

"True. Clint, I had an enlightening chat with his ex-wife Elissa this afternoon."

"You don't say." His voice had an edge to it.

"She remembered a phone conversation she'd overheard between her husband and an unknown person. It was right before their break up."

"Unknown person?"

212

"According to Elissa, it was the husband of the woman who'd had Newel's baby, who we believe is Sylvie."

"Hah. I'm a little slow on the uptake here. The woman who had Chief's baby was married to someone else at the time?" Clint said.

"That's the way it sounded to Elissa." I filled him in on the details.

"Did Chief not learn his lesson from the Ironwood fiasco?" he said.

"Doesn't sound like it."

"So Chief was supporting his child, yet not part of the family. The mother of his child *and* her husband knew the truth, so why did he keep it secret from all of us?"

"Elissa knew."

"Right, but none of his colleagues did."

"Maybe it was to protect his daughter and her parents, if they were still together. Maybe he was paying the family hush money, in addition to child support," I said.

"Hush money? Why would he do that?"

"His affair in Ironwood had cost him his job there. Maybe he didn't want to risk losing his Brooks Landing one, too."

"It wouldn't look good, that's for sure. It'd turn into a scandal among the good folks in Brooks Landing," he said.

"Two other things I thought of. Maybe he wanted to protect Elissa from the public humiliation it could've caused her. And maybe his daughter doesn't know Aaron Newel was her father."

"You've come up with some possible scenarios, Camryn, I'll give you that. If they're true, it's a very tangled web," he said.

213

"And a nightmare to untangle that web and get truthful answers to questions left by a man who went to great lengths to keep just about everything in his life a great big secret."

"Yeah. In all our years together, you'd think he would've confided in one of us at the PD. We commiserated about that again today. Between Mark, Jake, and me, we concluded one of his secrets got him killed. Trouble is, we don't know what on earth it could be."

"Between the detectives' investigation and Adam doing some digging on his end, they're bound to find out, right?"

"Yeah." He was quiet a moment. "How is Newel's ex dealing with his death and dredging up unhappy memories from the past?"

"Believe it or not, Elissa said she wished she'd forgiven Chief earlier than she did. She's still in love with him and told me she hasn't been able to move past that. It caught me a little off guard. I'd gotten the impression she didn't care about him."

"That surprises me. I'm glad she forgave him, for her own peace of mind. And maybe she'll be able to move on, now that . . ." The rest went unsaid.

"Hope so."

22

It surprised me when Elissa phoned Monday morning.

"Hello, Camryn. Is this a bad time?"

I glanced at the clock. "Not at all. I've got plenty of time before work."

"I want to apologize for dumping all my old baggage on you yesterday. About Aaron, I mean."

"No worries. I'm glad you told me what you've been through. What you're still going through."

"What kind of a fool am I to still have feelings for Aaron Newel?" she said with a little hiccup.

"I've learned when it comes to love, our brain is not the organ that's the boss. It's our heart. I blame it for making a fool of me a few times in my life. I've told myself I was smarter than that, but it didn't make any difference to my heart. It wouldn't listen to my brain's logic."

Elissa laughed. "I can picture that image, like something a cartoonist would draw. And I realized after you left I'll continue to grieve for Aaron, but in a different way. No longer what the two of us lost as a couple. Our relationship. Now it will be that I'll never see Aaron again, hold him in my arms. That old expression, 'It's better to have loved and lost than never to have loved at all,' keeps running through my mind. I need to concentrate on savoring those precious months we had. And they were *good*."

Her reflections pulled at my heart strings, and I cleared my throat. "Hold on tight to the good memories."

On my way to the shop, thoughts of Adam and Elissa took turns in my mind. I liked and trusted them both. They had a lot to come to grips with, loose ends to tie up, and a great deal of healing. It would take time and engagement on their part.

I unlocked the shop door and headed to Brew Ha-Ha for a muffin. Pinky looked at me with a flushed face. She looked like she'd run a marathon. "Are you okay, Pink?"

She wiped her forehead with the back of her hand.

"You won't believe it, Cami. I had the busiest early morning rush in weeks. I guess it was the warmer weather that got droves of people out of their hibernation."

"You should've called me in," I said.

"Actually, Emmy was one of the customers and offered to help me through the rush and would only take a muffin and coffee as payment." Emmy had worked part time in our shops for the Christmas season.

"She is a gem."

Adam Newel stopped by a short time later. "Hi, Camryn. I was at Aaron's bank when they opened. I found out he didn't have a safety deposit box there after all."

"What a disappointment."

216

"Tell me about it. They suggested I check with the other two banks in town, which I did. No boxes at either one of them," he said.

"Have you been in contact with Detective Garrison?"

"Every day. I shared the whole ball of wax with him, how I couldn't find much in the way of records in Aaron's files. You know we talked about Sylvie. He said they didn't find any personal information, like photos or documents, anywhere in his office. Or on his phone. I can't imagine why my brother acted like he was in the witness protection program, or a spy from another country, or a secret agent."

"It is more than your run-of-the-mill curiosity, that's for sure," I said.

Adam shook his head. "I'm going to go back to Aaron's house, do some more digging. Move furniture, look under rugs, see if there are any hidden drawers."

My eyebrows lifted. "Secret passages?"

He laughed. "I might just find one."

"Mind if I tag along later? I'll see if my fill-in worker can come in today. She was in Brew Ha-Ha earlier, so I know she's been out and about," I offered.

"It'd be great if you'd come over. I can tell you that going through Aaron's things seems less daunting when someone's with me. And less lonely too."

Emmy walked in with a sweet smile half an hour later and unzipped her coat. "How are you, dear? What with the police chief dying, and all?"

I gave her a warm hug. "Hanging in there. Thanks for bailing me out today. I have something to work on, and it could take a few hours."

"I'm glad you called me, Camryn. When I stopped by Pinky's this morning, it reminded me how much I enjoyed working here. Not to mention that it's good to get out of the house for a while. Days can get long when you're cooped up. Take as long as you need," she said.

"Thanks, Emmy. I'll be back before closing, for sure."

I knocked on Chief Newel's door and stepped in the house when Adam yelled, "Come in!"

I took off my coat. "Looks like you're hard at it."

He was on the couch with a stack of papers on his lap. "Yeah. I've gone through his file cabinets and decided to box up most everything in case something is questioned down the road. Like an unpaid bill claim, or the like."

"You haven't come across any hidden drawers, or whatever yet?"

He set the pile on the couch and stood. "Not yet. Clint and I did that quick walk through of the two bedrooms upstairs on Saturday before you got here, before we concentrated on the main level. They appeared empty, but I wanted to take a closer look. Nothing. Like they've never been used," Adam said.

"No extra stuff, huh?"

"There's an attic access panel in the hall, so I checked that out, and it's filled with insulation, that's it. No secret rooms upstairs. No rugs to look under."

"Less to go through, right?"

218

Adam clapped his hands. "Come join me on a treasure hunt. We'll start in Aaron's bedroom where I found the box of his high school stuff." He picked up a three-step stool and carried it down the hallway to the bedroom. He opened the bi-fold closet doors and set the stool in the space. Some ball caps sat on the shelf above the clothes pole.

Adam leaned his head inside and looked up at the ceiling and walls. "No access doors." He got off the stool and moved clothes to peer behind them. "Nothing special in here." We looked under the bed, behind the dresser, two bedstands, and checked for any cuts in the carpet. A thorough sweep of the room.

Same thing in the office, kitchen, living room, even the bathroom. But didn't come across a safe or hidden packets of papers. Adam opened the basement door and flicked on the lights. "Ready to tackle the lower level?"

"I'm game." I didn't sound as enthusiastic as I could've.

He went ahead of me and proved the steps were solid. I held on to the railing on the way down. It was a large, open, unfinished area. A furnace stood in the middle, with a washer, dryer, water heater, and water softener against one wall. Otherwise, it was bare.

"Not too much to dig through down here. Not even a basket of dirty clothes. He must've finished his laundry before he went to work the day he died," Adam said.

We searched behind the appliances and around the furnace. I glanced up and a glint from a shiny black object propped in the ceiling rafters caught my eye. I pointed. "Adam, look."

He found the spot. "What is it?"

"I don't know, looks like some sort of package."

"I'll get the stool." He went up the stairs and came back down in short order.

"Can you reach it?" I asked as he stood on the stool's top step.

"Think so." Adam lifted his arms, put one hand on the bottom of the object and one on the top. "Feels like a cardboard box wrapped in a garbage bag."

"Careful," I cautioned when he gave it a gentle tug.

"It's not heavy." He pulled and released it from its resting place.

"I'll take it," I said.

He leaned over the stool's top bar and handed it to me. It was the size of a boot box, and the plastic bag around it made it a little slippery.

Adam peered at the rest of the rafters. "It's either where you least expect it or always the last place you look."

"That's what my mom used to say, 'it's always the last place you look.' When I got older it hit me, of course it is."

He stepped off the stool and took the box.

"Pay dirt, you think?" I asked.

He tipped his head. "Let's take it to the kitchen and find out."

As we trekked up the stairs, I wondered about the treasures that awaited us. Adam set the box on the table like it was a delicate piece of glass. It was encased in a thick plastic bag, sealed on the open end with a large black clip. We stared at each other a moment, then Adam removed the clip and set it aside. He slid his fingers inside and got a hold of the cover.

"I'll hold the corners so you can pull the box out," I said.

Between the two of us we freed the package from its wrap. It was a work boots box. Adam removed the cover and handed it to me as he stared inside. I set the top on the counter and peeked in the box myself.

He lifted out wads of cash held together with rubber bands and set them on the table. "My Lord, it looks like a small fortune here." He picked up a stack and flipped through it. "All hundred-dollar bills. We'll count them later." He withdrew a stack of papers, several inches thick. "Medical bills, with the facility names and patient name blacked out with a sharpie." After he looked at each one, he handed them to me.

I scanned the pages. "Looks like they're from three different medical facilities. The account number, amount due, amount paid, and dates aren't blacked out. All last year. Maybe your brother was undergoing medical treatments. Chemo? These statements indicate he paid serious money the months he was absent from work. Coincidental, or not."

Adam shook his head back and forth a few times. "The nightmare continues. Do you recognize where any of these statements would've come from?"

"No, but I haven't been to a doctor since I moved back from D.C., almost a year ago."

"D.C., as in Washington? I thought—"

I cut him off, "Yes. I grew up here, attended college in Chicago, and worked in D.C. for over a decade. Long story that I'll tell you some time. Right now we have a box full of mysterious documents and lots of money."

He blew out an exhale. "Right."

"Adam, my mother went through cancer treatments and I wonder if she'd recognize the statements from one or more of the facilities. She went to the Mayo Clinic, but that's just one. There are a *lot* of hospitals in the metro area, and we have two right here in Buffalo County. Authorities can find out."

He pulled his phone from a pants pocket. "I'll see if Clint can come over. He should see this anyway."

"And Detective Garrison."

He nodded and found Clint's number in his contacts. Their conversation was short. "Clint will get in touch with Garrison, and be over here shortly himself."

"Was your brother big into hide and seek, or hiding things when you were kids?"

"Can't say he was. We played cops and robbers a lot. Aaron always wanted to be the cop, so guess who had to be the robber?" Adam smiled at the memory, then the corners of his mouth turned down as he waved at the stack of papers. "In a million years, I wouldn't have thought my brother would do anything this bizarre. Redacted medical statements and thousands of dollars in cash, hidden in his basement rafters."

"Strange, all right. Maybe he kept the statements in case payments were ever questioned. Or for tax purposes," I said.

"Speaking of which, we never found his tax records."

"Hmm." I pointed at a statement. "Say he was the patient, why black out his own name? And why hide the box—sort of in plain sight—but still. He wouldn't disclose the reasons for his time off from work. If I needed treatments, depending on what for, I might not want everyone in town to know, but my family and friends would need to. And I'd feel obligated to tell my employer."

"Same here." He rubbed his forehead. "I hope to run across a document where Aaron explains the reason he treated important records like classified information."

I bumped his arm with my elbow. "Just had a thought. If your brother had a will, an attorney would have a copy."

"But wouldn't the attorney have contacted me by now?"

"Good point."

We heard a knock at the front door and Clint's voice sounded a second later. "It's me."

"In the kitchen," Adam called back. When Clint joined us Adam said, "Welcome to the mystifying Aaron Newel's home."

Clint went to the table, visually scanned the money and papers. "You found all this in a box in the basement?"

Adam nodded. "Yep. Like I said on the phone, a box filled with money and redacted medical statements."

"How many sheets did you touch?" Clint asked.

"I don't know, ten or so."

"All right." Clint withdrew a pair of disposable gloves from his pocket and pulled them on. He picked up a page and held it to the light. "The sheriff's office will want to check for latent prints, see if anyone's besides Aaron's are on these. Maybe someone gave them to him for safe keeping."

I hadn't considered that possibility. "What about the person's prints who sent the statement?"

"They're generated electronically," Clint said.

"Oh." I should have known that.

"And the money?" Adam asked.

"Must be Aaron's. We've come to find out he paid cash for just about everything. For all we know he has another stash hidden somewhere else."

Adam shook his head. "Clint, do you know if my brother had an attorney?"

"He never mentioned it, why?"

"Wondered in case he'd have answers to Aaron's secrets. Or has some of his records in his office."

Clint picked up another statement. "It's been downright confusing, especially for you, Adam. If your brother had an attorney, they would've been in touch by now."

"Yeah, that's what I told Camryn. Like his daughter's mother should've been."

Clint waved at the papers. "I need to grab an evidence bag for these statements. Adam, find a safe place for the money until you decide what to do with it. Aaron had a life insurance policy through the city, like we all do. I don't know if he paid for extra coverage on his plan or not. HR has that info. But even the basic plan will cover the funeral and help with other expenses."

Adam nodded. "I wondered about a city policy. I talked to a Mister Johnson at the funeral chapel this morning, let him know I'd contact the priest at Aaron's church. We'll meet in the next day or so to plan the service. Aaron belonged to the Catholic church here, but I don't know how faithful he was."

"His job took up a lot of his time, but I think he went as often as he could. A random person would tell me when they saw him at worship," Clint said.

"Good to hear. Even if Aaron didn't mention it, others did, huh?"

"One way I found out about his activities," Clint said.

"We have lunch at our church after funeral services," Adam said.

"So do the churches here," I said.

"Maybe you two can give me an idea of how many people to expect, what to plan for."

"As Brooks Landing Police Chief, you can expect hundreds of people at the visitation, but not everyone will stay for the service and lunch. That's what I've observed at others," Clint said.

224

"Probably two hundred people stayed for the lunch at Mayor Frost's funeral. The priest and funeral director are good at estimating numbers too," I said.

"Thanks."

Clint lifted his hand. "Be right back." He left and returned with a plastic bag. He slid the statements inside, sealed the bag, and wrote the information on the front. "We'll see if the sheriff's office finds latent prints that don't belong to Aaron. If so, and they're in the system, we could catch a break. At the very least, that person can give us answers about the medical bills and what they were for."

When I crossed my fingers, Adam did too.

23

I returned to the shop and chatted with Emmy a while.

"Are the authorities close to finding out who killed Chief Newel?" she asked.

The million-dollar question. "I'm not sure, but I know they're working hard on the case."

"I'm sure they are. It was such a shock, especially after what happened to Mayor Frost." She patted my hand. "And we surely don't want anything to happen to you."

I smiled to give her some assurance. "Me, either."

We closed up shop and I helped Emmy to her car to ensure her safety, then went back inside, sat in the quiet office, and pondered the reason Chief Newel had hidden a box of money and medical statements. For himself or someone else? And why had he picked the basement ceiling rafters as the spot? Why not? It was as good a place as any. In the event something happened to him, it would eventually be discovered. Someone would spot it. Maybe that's what Chief had counted on.

Adam's call interrupted my thoughts. "Hi, Camryn, I'm going to head for home in the morning, after I make Aaron's funeral arrangements. I'll be back with my family this weekend."

"Sounds good. I look forward to meeting them," I said.

"They're my life here on earth. Along with my students. Speaking of which, I should get back to my class the last three days this week, so my kids don't start liking their substitute more than me."

I chuckled. "I don't think you have anything to worry about. If we don't talk before then, safe travels."

"Thanks."

Gina had not returned my call, and the best place to track her down was at Brooks Landing City Hall. She started work at 5:00 p.m., and it was almost 6:00. "Wish me luck, Molly," I called out and flipped off the light switch. The lights came right back on. "If that means 'yes,' thank you and good night." The lights went off again. I stepped outside and locked the door.

I opened the police station's front door and hollered, "Hello!" The day lights were on, and I guessed Gina had started on the police side of the city building. No response, so I yelled louder, "Gina, it's Camryn Brooks!"

I heard a toilet flush from the restroom area in the otherwise quiet office. Gina came into view. Her mouth and eyes opened wide when she saw me. "*Oh*, I didn't hear you come in. You *scared* me!" she said.

"Sorry. I have access to the front door and let myself in. You haven't returned my calls and I need to talk to you." I pulled off my cap.

"I didn't have anything more to say."

"I have something to tell you, something I found out."

She approached the front counter. "What?"

I pulled Sylvie's photo from my purse and held it up. When Gina saw it, her breath caught and her eyebrows lifted. She shrugged. "Who is she?"

"Your reaction just now tells me you know," I said.

"What difference does it make? Someone confided in me, and I've kept the secret."

"Gina, you told me Chief Newel's wife had a good reason to leave him, and it was the baby, right? Elissa told me that's what ended their marriage."

Her eyes narrowed. "She told you about it?"

"She did, but she doesn't know who the little girl and her mother are."

Gina shrugged and shook her head. "Humph."

"Chief confided in you but didn't tell you who the mother of his child was?"

"He didn't, no. And I never asked him."

I didn't think Gina was lying but doubted she was telling the whole truth. There was more to the story than she was willing to share, that I was sure of.

I changed the subject. "Gina, you work here after hours. Did you ever see anyone with Chief Newel who seemed suspicious to you? Someone he had an argument with, or maybe refused to let in?"

"No, no one like that, not that I heard or saw."

228

I pulled my cap on. "Okay, well thanks for giving me some answers. We all want Chief's killer caught, and if you think of anything, please tell Detective Garrison, or your new chief, Clint, if it's more comfortable for you."

When she nodded, I was tempted to say, "Promise me," but wasn't convinced it'd make any difference to her.

I fell asleep that night thinking about Chief Newel's stash of cash, the large amounts he'd withdrawn from his bank account for six months, and his generous contributions to Fresh Start. Elissa said they'd both supported the program. Adam told me his brother didn't have an alcohol or drug problem. Clint said he'd never seen any signs of it on him either. Maybe someone else in Newel's life did, someone Fresh Start Rehabilitation had helped.

When I was fully conscious early Tuesday morning, I felt far from rested. Weird dreams had awakened me at least seven times in the night. In one I found boxes of money in unlikely places, like my kitchen cupboard, my garage, in the front counter drawer at Curio Finds.

In another dream I was in conversation with Sylvie, like we knew each other well. She had a sweet, young voice, with a slight lisp. We were at a party of sorts filled with people I didn't know. I'd tried to ask about her mother, but got interrupted time and again by random men and women before I could.

The other dreams had been pushed to the back recesses of my mind by morning. I sat up and rubbed my face with vigor in hopes I'd feel more alert, ready to face the day. After a shower and two strong cups of coffee, I bundled up and set out for Fresh Start

Rehabilitation to meet CEO and CFO Matthew Anderle. That was my hope since I didn't have an appointment. A handful of SUVs and trucks sat in the parking lot. All four-wheel drive vehicles for better traction on snowy roads. My Subaru was the smallest among them.

I saw people through the windows in the day area on my way to the front entrance. A "Please Press For Assistance" sign was above an intercom speaker. I pushed the button and a chirpy female voice said, "Good morning. How can I help you?"

"Good morning. Camryn Brooks here to see Matthew Anderle if he's in."

"Do you have an appointment?"

"No, I'm the Brooks Landing mayor and I wanted to meet him," I said.

"Oh, Mayor, hang on while I check."

I wiggled my toes in my boots and fingers in my mittens to warm them until a slim young blonde with spiky hair, a nose ring, neck tattoo, and multiple ear piercings pushed open the door. "Come in. I'll take you to his office."

I left my boots on the entry mat and pulled off my mittens. Before we reached his office, a middle-aged man with a trimmed gray beard and ponytail came around the corner. He extended his arm and shook my hand. "Matthew Anderle. Sorry, I had to finish a phone call. Come in. Please." We settled in comfortable wingback chairs in a corner. "I've wanted to call you, but didn't know if that'd be appropriate."

That caught me off guard. "Oh?"

"Detective Garrison was here asking me questions and said you witnessed Aaron Newel's death, that you were with him."

I nodded. "Yes, I was."

He leaned in closer. "I want you to know how sorry I am. I tried to put myself in your place but couldn't even imagine it. Not that I socialized with Aaron to speak of, but I considered him a trusted friend. He had a good heart, and I had a great deal of respect for him."

The side of Aaron Newel not everyone knew. "Thank you, um, for what you said. I won't deny his death was awful. The worst. But I've been trying to focus more on his life outside of work. One thing, I know he was a generous donor to Fresh Start," I said.

"He was, yes."

"Did he have a special reason, that you can share?"

"Aaron took a particular interest in our mission some years back. Five, six, seven. I'd have to look at the records to be sure. He attended a fundraiser and had been a faithful contributor ever since," he said.

"That's where he met his wife, right?"

"His wife?" A puzzled look crossed his face then he nodded. "Oh, you mean his ex-wife. Elissa. I heard they'd married and divorced soon after. I don't like to gossip, but according to the rumor mill it was a whirlwind romance until reality set in a few months later."

Reality was one way to put it. "I just met Elissa, and Aaron's brother Adam."

He looked down and scratched his beard. "Oh. I don't remember Aaron mentioning he had a brother."

"He lives in South Dakota." As if that explained it.

His eyebrows lifted. "I see. Well, Elissa works here part time now. She might've told you that."

"She did." After I'd figured it out myself.

Anderle lowered his voice. "This isn't public information, but you were there, witnessed Aaron's death. Detective Garrison said Aaron had a note with a return contribution envelope for Fresh Start. I wrote that note a few months ago. The detective said there was some kind of poison on it. That's what killed him. It really disturbed me. I've wondered a hundred times who got a hold of that note. Did it give them the idea, a way to kill Aaron? But why?"

I was surprised Anderle had shared that with me. "Everything about his death is mysterious," I said.

"Seems like it. Detective Garrison talked to the staff here, couldn't tell me what they said, of course. But word among the troops is no one suspects their co-workers of any wrong doing."

"It's important to trust people you work with. And you do background checks, I'm sure."

He nodded. "Very thorough ones."

"Did Chief Newel visit any of your clients here over the years?"

Anderle lifted a shoulder. "No one in particular that I know of, but he did check in with some guys here and there to see how they were. Our clients aren't allowed to have family or friends visit the first two weeks, so Aaron often filled that gap."

"But no one special?" I asked.

"Not that I'm aware of. He'd sit in the day area and talk to different people. Some liked to talk, others kept to themselves."

I pressed on. "Anyone ever act like they were angry at him or had a grudge against him?"

"Not that I witnessed or ever heard about from staff." His eyebrows drew together. "You think one of our clients was responsible?"

232

I turned my hands palms up. "I don't know. You keep visitor records, right?

"Of course."

"So you'd know when Chief Newel visited and what clients were in house then?"

"We'd have those records, yes."

I smiled to lighten the tone. "I know you can't give me that information, and I'm not asking for names, of course. Just posing questions. Detective Garrison must've asked you the same ones."

He lifted his shoulders as an answer.

I stood and put on my coat. "I appreciate your time, Mister Anderle."

"Matthew."

"Matthew. If you remember something you witnessed or heard about that struck you as off, please tell Detective Garrison, all right? It could help with the investigation."

He shook my hand again. "I'll do that."

On the drive to work, I thought about Matthew Anderle's candor. I'd hoped when I challenged him to think of anyone with a grudge against Aaron Newel, he'd come up with a name.

Elissa must've known her ex-husband volunteered at Fresh Start, but hadn't mentioned it. Had Newel checked her work schedule to be certain their paths never crossed?

I walked into Brew Ha-Ha and found Pinky wiping off her counter.

"Cami, morning."

"Morning. How goes it?"

"Good." She indicated the people at the back tables. "Down to a dull roar. Before I forget, a man stopped by about a half hour ago, asked when your shop opened."

"A man, as in you don't know who he is? Got a description?" I asked.

"Don't think I've ever seen him before. Around our age, I guess. Could be mid-thirties to early forties, darker skin, dark brown eyes. He looked Latino, or maybe American Indian. He had a stocking cap on, so I didn't see his hair."

I shrugged as I thought of darker skinned men I knew. "What'd you tell him?"

"Nine. The hours are posted for heaven's sake."

"Not everyone notices signs. Since you're open he probably figured I would be too seeing we're on either side of an open archway."

"You're right, lots of people do," she said.

"Did he say he'd stop back, or what he wanted?"

"No. Something I noticed about him is he acted kinda jumpy, like he was nervous about something."

"You've got me curious, anyway. City residents reach out to the council and mayor with issues, or when they need help."

"Then why would he come here, instead of city hall?"

"You raise a good point," I said.

"I hope he's not some sort of stalker dude."

"Pinky!"

"Just saying."

I was behind the checkout counter when a man who fit Pinky's description, and likely the same one I'd spotted looking in the front window on Saturday, came in the shop. "Welcome. How can I help you?"

He stared at me as he pulled off his gloves. Pinky had put a scare in me, and my heart speeded up as I tried to assess the situation, size him up. At least Pinky was only one loud scream away.

"Mayor Brooks?" he finally said.

"Yes."

"I have some information for you."

When he didn't continue, I said, "Maybe you can tell me who you are first."

"I'm Gina Lopez's husband, Juan."

My heart beat even faster. "Oh, um, nice to meet you. What information is that?"

He looked around the shop and spoke in a quiet tone. "I know you talked to my wife. A couple times."

So Gina wasn't keeping my questions about Chief Newel secret from him. "Yes, there were some things about the chief I thought she might have answers to, since she worked at city hall and the PD."

"She knows something she can't tell you."

I knew it. "Why not?"

"She has a reason. But I have the same information and can tell you," he said.

Tell me already. "What is it?"

He looked at me, his brown eyes intense. "*No* one else can overhear me, or know I'm the one who told you this thing."

Confidential information about Aaron Newel? "Okay."

"We need to meet somewhere where no one will see us together."

I didn't want to lose him, so I played along. "Like where?"

"I have a fish house on Green Lake. Not far out. You could either walk or drive to it. And park next to a nearby house. The guy who owns the nearest one to mine is only there on weekends."

He wanted to meet in his fish house? "Why out there?"

"It's public, but private at the same time. I don't know all the guys who have houses by mine because we're not always there at the same times. We can talk without fear of being overheard or seen together."

Juan had it all figured out. "Tell me where your house is and what time you want to meet."

He pulled a paper from his pocket, unfolded it, and smoothed it out on the counter. It was a sketch of the southeast side of Green Lake, the public landing, and where his fish house was. He pointed to the house and said, "It's the only green one around. You can park by the tan one here. Would five fifteen work for you?"

"I'll close at five, and should make it by then."

He slid the paper toward me. "Good."

"One question, does your wife know about this, that you're here?"

He shook his head. "It's best she doesn't until after the two of us talk." Juan turned and walked out the door.

Pinky popped into Curio Finds. "Oh, that was the guy I told you about." She bent over and picked a coin off the floor. "Somebody dropped a penny." She laid it on the counter. My penny from heaven. "Cami, you have a funny look on your face. Did that guy say something to upset you?"

I waved my hand and put on a small smile. "Not at all. A citizen with a concern, is all."

She waved the dishtowel she held. "Did you have any idea of all the things you'd get dragged into as mayor?"

"I don't think anyone in public office could imagine all the issues that would come up until they get into office. Something new every day."

But not everything intrigued me as much as what Juan had to tell me.

❄

24

Clint phoned as I was about to lock the shop's front door. "How's it going, Clint?"

"It's going. Sorry it took me so long to get back to you."

I had phoned mid-afternoon. "No worries. You're a very busy police chief. I wanted to tell you I'm meeting with Gina's husband in a few minutes. It's regarding something he says his wife can't tell me. And he doesn't want anyone to overhear what he has to say."

"*Juan*? What on earth could it be?"

"Ah, so you know him. Good. It's gotta be about Aaron Newel. When I talked to Gina, she admitted she knew a secret about him that wasn't hers to share."

"And how did that happen to come up in conversation? Were you playing cop, questioning her?" He asked in his official voice.

"I wanted to be sure she was okay. You know how she reacted when Chief died. Over the top distressed. And I may have asked her if she'd been involved with him."

"Camryn."

"Anyway, I need to take off, meet with Juan."

"Where at?"

"His fish house, on Green Lake."

"He wants to meet in the middle of the lake in his *fish house*? Well, no one will overhear anything out there. Juan's a good man and has never given me reason to not trust him. But this meeting arrangement he cooked up strikes me as strange," he said.

"I agree. Whatever he tells me, he'll make me swear to not reveal my source. In that case, I'll be your confidential informant, okay?"

"Okay. You know where his house is?"

"He drew me a map, and it's not in the middle of the lake," I said.

"Well the ice is thick enough for a monster truck, and there have been plenty of them on the lake this winter. So when you drive there, you won't have to worry if the ice is safe or not."

"I've noticed all the traffic on the lake," I said.

"I'm covering a shift for one of my cops who's sick, but call me with your report," he said.

"Sure will."

I turned off the shop lights, and they turned back on again. "Honestly, Molly, I'm a little nervous the way it is, and your light tricks aren't helping." They turned off, on, and off again. "You're quite the trickster tonight, aren't you?" A quick on and off and that's how they stayed as I locked the door and headed to my car in the back lot.

I drove to the public landing at Lakeside Park where people launched their boats spring, summer, and fall. And used the access to drive to their fish houses in winter. Some had canvas portables they'd set up to use while they fished and took down when they'd finished. But the majority had permanent wood-constructed houses, large, medium, and small. Some were even equipped with television sets and sleeping bunks.

As a teenager I'd gone fishing with my friends on different lakes, either on open water in boats, or from shore. Or on frozen lakes in holes drilled through the ice with augers. It'd been a fun activity that got us into the great outdoors. I'd admittedly been braver as a teen, but not the daredevil some of my friends were back then.

It had been years since I'd fished. I wasn't afraid to walk on a frozen lake, but when I drove on one, I liked to follow a path made by others. I knew it was safe to drive over holes cut through the ice by fishers, but was still leery. When I walked, I stepped around them. The uncovered holes soon froze over when temperatures dipped below freezing, but still.

Before I got to the edge of the lake, I turned on my interior light and took another look at Juan's drawing. It was maybe the distance of a football field and to the right of the path. With the cloud cover, the moon didn't illumine the ice. At least lamps from the downtown and park areas offered some light on the dark night.

The fish houses weren't clumped together as they sometimes were, like at a hot spot where people caught scores of fish. I drove past ten or twelve houses and didn't spot a single vehicle. As I went by Juan's green house, I saw his truck and continued about thirty feet to the tan house. I parked a little ways away in case the owner showed up after all.

As I climbed from my car on to the ice, the bitter wind across the expanse nearly took my breath away. I hunched over against it and boot skied my way to Juan's house. He opened the door in the middle of my first knock. "Come in out of the cold."

It was toasty inside, a propane heater on full blast in the corner. I unzipped my jacket and sat on a bench. "Juan, no cars around and no one in any nearby houses."

He shrugged. "Unless they walked to them."

"True, but yours is the only one where I saw lights on inside."

"Good to know. What I have to tell you is about a terrible crime, one I can't go to the police about."

A zinging sensation ran through me. "Why not?"

"I just can't. I must remain anonymous. Do you agree to that?"

What crime? "You want me to report what you tell me to the police?"

"Yes. We want Aaron Newel's murder solved, and I can't be seen with any law enforcement officers."

His words made the small space grow hotter. I unzipped my coat. "You *know* who killed Chief Newel?"

Juan folded his hands. "I am ninety-nine-point-nine percent certain I know the guilty one. It shouldn't take the authorities long to find out if it *is* him or not."

My insides trembled. "Why do you think it's that person?"

"Because he is my brother-in-law, and Aaron had a baby with his wife."

It took a few seconds for his words to sink in. He suspects his brother-in-law. "Oh dear Lord, you know the mother of Chief Newel's daughter?"

His eyebrows shot up. "You know about Sylvie?"

I was surprised Gina hadn't told Juan I'd shown her Sylvie's photos, asked if she knew her. That was for another time. "Chief had her photos in his files. His brother Adam found them."

Juan muttered something in Spanish, then repeated my words, "'Oh, dear Lord,' is right," in English.

I wiped sweat off my brow, and felt streams run down my neck. "Sylvie's mother is your sister?"

"She is Gina's sister, Camila."

Gina's sister. It wasn't Gina's secret; it was her sister's. Had Gina known from the start Juan had a prime suspect in mind? "That gives your brother-in-law a possible motive, but why would he kill Chief Newel at this point in time, years after Sylvie's birth? She's about six, right?"

He nodded. "Yes, she is six. The reason is Oscar found out his wife had been secretly planning to leave him and blamed Aaron for wrecking their marriage."

I wiped sweat from my cheeks. "Secretly planning?"

"Camila is afraid of Oscar and didn't know what he'd do if he found out before she could move out. But he somehow found out anyway."

Camila should have contacted an agency that helps people in that situation. "All right. Oscar knew Camila planned to leave him. Did he think she was going to get back together with Chief?"

"I don't know that. What I know is he thought Aaron would have a closer relationship with Sylvie and he would lose his place in her heart. Oscar is jealous and possessive of the girls in his life."

"Girls? Do Camila and Oscar have other children?"

He shook his head. "By girls, I meant Camila and Sylvie. Oscar couldn't have children. Camila wanted to leave back then, not because of that, but because he was so controlling. That's when she got involved with Aaron for that short time." Juan let out a loud "huh."

It startled me and when he saw me jump, said, "Sorry, I didn't mean to raise my voice. Back to Camila and Aaron. It turned into a big mess for them both. Camila was, you could say, devastated when Aaron said he didn't love her. He loved his wife, the one he had just married.

"Then Aaron's wife left him right after she found out about the baby, and he told Camila he'd do the right thing and marry her, but Camila didn't want a loveless marriage. So she stayed with Oscar. And I give Oscar credit for loving Sylvie as much as he does. It sounds like a soap opera, one you'd find on daytime television. But it was real life for them. Like I said, a big mess."

Six or more years of soap opera drama. "A big mess is an understatement. Was Chief paying child support?"

"Yes, in cash. Plus money for Oscar's drug treatment. And for poor little Sylvie's cancer treatments last year."

The medical bills were hers. "*Sylvie's*?"

Juan nodded. "Aaron also took Sylvie to her treatments and cared for her when Camila worked and Oscar was in treatment."

Sylvie had cancer, Oscar had a drug problem, and Aaron Newel was there to help pick up the pieces for Camila when everything else had fallen apart in her life. "I'm trying to wrap my brain around everything you just told me," I said.

"It's a tragic tale. But the good news is, Sylvie is doing very well. She's always been a happy little thing, and to have her healthy again warms our hearts. I can't even tell you how much."

"Does Sylvie know about Chief's death?"

"Not yet. Camila is trying to find a gentle way to tell her and has kept her away from the news. She's homeschooling Sylvie this year, because of all the time she had to miss with her treatments, and to protect her immune system while it rebuilds."

"Understandable."

"And so you know, Sylvie thinks Aaron was her uncle. Her mother planned to tell her the truth when she's older, when she can better understand," he said.

Another secret. "Where's Oscar now?" I asked.

"That's the thing. He hasn't been home since Aaron Newel died, and that's what made us suspicious. When days had passed, I was convinced Oscar was guilty and needed to tell someone. He could be anywhere.

"Their family moved ten miles from Brooks Landing when Sylvie was born. I told Camila to take Sylvie to a metro hotel and wait until she heard from me. And *not* talk to Gina. In case Oscar comes to our place looking for his family. Then Gina wouldn't be lying when she told him she didn't know where Camila and Sylvie were," he said.

"It sounds like you've thought of everything."

He nodded. "When I knew I had to come forward with our suspicions, I tried to think of everything. Even then, sometimes there are surprises—"

The fish house door opened with such force it hit the back wall and bounced against the giant responsible for it.

Juan jumped up. "Oscar!"

Oscar? My teeth chattered together from abject fear. His body filled the only escape route we had from the small shack.

He pointed at Juan. "I followed you. To and from her shop this morning." Then he pointed at me. "I followed you to the park, then walked out here when I figured that's where you were headed. I saw where you parked but waited a while to be sure no one else was around."

"I didn't see you," I muttered.

"What are you doing here, what do you want?" Juan choked out.

"I heard on the news who found Chief Newel's body." Oscar pointed at me again. "It was her. Juan, I knew it was only a matter of time before you talked to someone, or went to the police. Am I right, have you told her you suspect me as the killer?"

Juan remained silent.

"I can tell by the looks on your faces that you have. You don't think I can let you live, do you?" he growled.

"Oscar, two wrongs don't make a right." The same words Elissa had heard her husband say on the phone. The best I could come up with on my presumed death bed.

His eyes zeroed in on me. "Don't worry, it'll be painless, Mayor. The drug will make you fall into a deep sleep so you won't even know when you freeze to death on the ice. You know how people with hypothermia get confused."

It was possible I'd die from fear before that.

He frowned at Juan. "As for you, when you fall asleep, you'll accidentally kick the exhaust pipe for the propane heater, and you won't know when the propane replaces the oxygen and you suffocate."

Either way to die petrified me. What could we do to stop him? He was almost as big as the two of us put together.

Oscar's lips lifted in a mean smirk. "Juan, I think it's only right for you to go first."

"Neither of us are leaving this earth tonight." Juan pointed over Oscar's hunched back. "Look behind you."

I glanced that way and saw nothing, but by some miracle, Oscar fell for it and had to wrestle his wedged body outside the house to turn around. With lightning speed, Juan slammed the door and slid the wooden piece over that locked it from the inside. "Call nine-one-one," he said as Oscar howled outside.

I reached in my right pocket, but my phone wasn't there. I tried the left pocket. Just my keys. *Where was my phone?* I had trouble thinking straight with Oscar yelping and banging on the door. "I can't find it."

Juan grunted, pulled his from a chest pocket, and dialed 911. "No bars, dead zone."

"No!" I said.

The door cracked and split in the middle.

Juan handed me his phone and pointed. "Stand against that wall. I'll open the door fast when he comes at it again. He'll lose his balance and go down. You'll need to run like the wind."

I moved, my back to the wall, close to the door, ready for action. Juan stood across from me, his hand on the wood locking piece. When the next blow came, it didn't go as Oscar had planned. Juan yanked the door open. Oscar yelped as his extended leg, meant for the attack slid inside the house. The rest of his body went down, half in the fish house, half outside on the ice.

Juan grabbed an ice auger and bopped him on the head. Hard. Twice, at least. "Go!" he shouted.

A major obstacle to climb over. "Like over the top of him?"

"Yes! Run to your car, try my phone again, drive for help."

"What about you?"

"I can't let him escape," he yelled.

I had to do what he'd ordered and the only way was across a sleeping Paul Bunyan. I sucked in cold air so fast I prayed I wouldn't pass out. As I crawled my way to his chest, even my knees in his ribs didn't wake him. I slid off Oscar on to the ice. Juan had told me to run like the wind, but I couldn't run as fast as a one-year-old much less the wind. It was a matter of life and death so when another shot of adrenalin kicked in, I made fair time boot skating across the ice to my car. And only fell once.

In the driver's seat, I spotted my phone in the center console. *Are you kidding me?* I plucked it up and saw the same dreaded no bars signal. The closest place I knew there'd be wireless access was outside the public library, a half mile away once I got off the ice. "Thank you, Lord," I uttered when I saw there were no other cars on the path. I drove too fast, but not fast enough.

25

I was at the library in minutes that seemed like forever. My hands shook and my teeth banged together as I selected Clint's number and hit the call button. "We're in big trouble, I mean Juan is, at his fish house with Chief's killer passed out in the doorway," I cried.

"*What!*"

"Where are you, Clint?"

"The PD."

"Take the path out from the public landing at Lakeside. I'll meet you there," I said.

I could tell he was running and breathing hard when he said, "I'll radio for back up on the way."

I dropped the phone in my lap, turned around, and was back at the landing ahead of Clint. Light from inside Juan's fish house shined through the open door and offered enough illumination to see him, auger in hand as he stood guard over Oscar. My newest hero.

Oscar was still on his back, eyes closed. I parked some distance away to give the officers more space and waited in my car for Clint. He arrived in short order, and the sound of sirens in the distance announced more help was on the way. Clint stepped from his car and drew his gun. My heart hammered all the harder as I got out of my car.

"Camryn, back in your vehicle until we have the suspect in custody."

Not the time to argue. I complied but rolled down my window to better see and hear.

Juan took a step back as Clint moved in. Two police cars came down the path and parked behind Clint's. Mark Weston and Jake Dooley, two of Brooks Landing's finest, got out to assist Clint.

Oscar groaned and touched the side of his head. He frowned, his eyes flickered open, blinked, then squeezed shut. He let out a loud, long moan. A beached whale on ice.

Clint asked Juan something I couldn't hear and nodded when Juan answered.

In his outdoor authoritarian voice Clint commanded, "Oscar North, roll over on your stomach and keep your hands visible at all times." When Oscar didn't move, he said, "You heard me, I said roll over." Clint nudged Oscar's shoulder with the toe of his boot.

"Okay, okay." Oscar raised his right hand above his head and pushed with his left elbow, hand up. He grunted and slowly managed to flip over.

"Both hands above your head!" Oscar stretched them out. "Now, get on your knees and keep your arms extended." When Oscar did that, Clint said, "These officers are going to put their hands on the back of your belt to help you stand. I have my gun trained on you, so do *not* do anything unless I tell you to. Do you understand?"

"Yeah." Oscar was so quiet, I barely heard him.

"All right. They'll get into position." Mark and Jake approached Oscar from behind and gripped the back of his belt, under his jacket.

"Mister North, put your right foot on the ice, and stand up on the count of three," Clint said.

On the third count Mark and Jake helped Oscar into an upright position. "The officers will take your jacket off, one arm at a time. Do you have a weapon of any kind on your person; gun, knife, other sharp object?"

"Just my wallet and keys," Oscar said.

"No cell phone?"

"Pants front pocket."

Juan raised his voice. "That's not all. He has some kind of bad drugs he planned to use on the mayor and me."

"Officers, remove his jacket, cuff him, and then search him." Mark and Jake got Oscar's jacket off and dropped it on the ice. Because of his size, they linked two pair of handcuffs together to make it work. I'm glad they knew what they were doing. I wouldn't have had a clue in that situation.

When he was cuffed, Clint said, "Where are the drugs?"

Oscar mumbled and shook his head.

"We can do a strip search out here, but I gotta warn you, your body parts would not appreciate that one little bit."

Oscar made a grunt-like sound. "My jacket pocket."

"Right or left?" Clint said.

"Left."

"Officer Weston, put his jacket in your trunk. We'll deal with the substance evidence after Mister North is in a warm jail cell. Go ahead and pat him down, Officer Dooley."

Jake pulled the wallet and keys from Oscar's sweatpants' back pocket, and cell phone from his front pocket. When Mark returned, Jake handed him the items, and completed the pat search. "Nothing else, Chief."

"All right, secure him in my vehicle and we'll transport him to the county jail where the booking officers will assume custody." Clint looked at Juan. "We'll need your statement, so after you take care of things here, report to the PD, and Officer Dooley will meet you there."

Juan nodded his acknowledgement.

Jake said, "Ten four."

Clint turned to my car, and his eyes caught mine. "You too, Camryn. Report to the PD."

"Yes, Chief," I said.

Clint signaled Mark. "Officer Weston, follow me to the jail, and we'll escort our suspect in together."

With Oscar in the back seat of his car, Clint finally holstered his gun. He had taken no chances in the arrest process. I watched the police cars leave. Juan needed a new door, but shut off what he needed to in the fish house, and climbed in his own car. I shifted into drive and followed him to the Brooks Landing Police Station.

My heart had settled to a steadier pace until I walked to the back entrance of the police station with Juan. Jake held the door open for us. The thought of spilling details of Oscar's attack sent my pulses into overdrive. We followed Jake to an interview room the size of a larger bathroom, with enough space for a small table and four chairs. I glanced at the mirror on the wall, a two-way window for officers to observe from the other side.

Jake pointed at the chairs on other side of the table so we'd face the mirror. "Have a seat, and I'll grab some notebooks and pens."

Juan and I sat down on the same side of the table, exchanged a quick glance, then minded our own business until Jake returned. He slid the writing supplies our way. "Can I get you a bottle of water, something else to drink? We got granola bars if you're hungry."

It was past supper time, but I had zero appetite. "Water'd be good, thanks."

"Same for me. Thank you," Juan said. When Jake left, he turned to me. "I don't know how I'm going to tell Gina. Or her sister Camila."

"Juan, you did the right thing, telling me the truth. After what Oscar tried to do to us, they'll be beyond relieved. You know the saying, 'the truth will set you free.'"

Jake came back, set the bottles in front of us, and a small tape recorder in the middle of the table. "Detective Garrison will be interviewing the suspect in jail and asked that we get your statements regarding the incident. He wants you both to write down every detail that happened at the fish house tonight.

But before you do, I have a few questions I'll record." He turned on the machine. "Why were the two of you at that fish house? Juan, I'll start with you. Please state your name for the record."

Juan took a drink of water and cleared his throat. "Juan Lopez. I had information for Mayor Brooks I didn't want anyone else to hear, so I asked her to come to my fish house."

"Were you able to give that information to her before Oscar North arrived on the scene?"

"Yes."

"And what was it?" Jake said.

As Juan recapped the story, Jake's frown deepened, and his eyebrows raised a few times, especially about Chief Newel's involvement with Oscar's wife, the woman he'd had a child with. Oscar's unexpected arrival at the fish house, what he did and said. But Jake didn't interrupt.

Juan finished with, "And then I struck Oscar with the auger, and the mayor left to phone nine-one-one."

"It sounds like you had good reason to suspect Mister North. Why didn't you go straight to Detective Garrison or to Chief Clint instead of our mayor?" Jake asked.

Juan twirled his thumbs a few times. "I had what I thought were good reasons. As I said, we didn't know where Oscar was, and I feared for our lives—my wife's and mine—if he saw me go to the police. My wife didn't want to believe Oscar would kill Chief Newel, even when I suspected it was him.

"So I decided to tell Mayor Brooks in confidence, so she could tell you authorities, get the investigation going and find Oscar. Maybe even put out a reward for information. My sister-in-law and niece are in a hotel somewhere." Juan smiled. "What a relief they can return home and finally be safe."

Jake nodded. "You can rest assured. Oscar will never breathe free air again." He turned to me. "Camryn, you left Juan at the fish house guarding an unconscious Oscar. You phoned Chief Lonsbury, tell me those details. Start with your name."

"Camryn Brooks. Yes, as Juan said, I didn't have my phone, turns out it was in my car. Juan did, but there was no service on the lake. I drove to the library for a wireless connection, phoned Chief

Lonsbury, and went back to the fish house. He arrived seconds later, you and Officer Weston a couple minutes after that."

"Thank you. Now I'd like both of you to write down what happened from the time you arrived at the fish house, in your own words." He shut off the recorder. Juan and I picked up pens and started on our accounts.

Jake pushed himself up from the table. "I'll be in the office area writing my own report. Let me know when you've finished."

I was almost done when Clint and Mark returned and stopped by the room. "Juan, I'll get the full story on this incident, but in the meantime, all I can say is I can't tell you how relieved I am the two of you weren't hurt," Clint said.

Juan sniffed. "I'm sorry, Chief Lonsbury. I know now I should've gone straight to you with my suspicions about Oscar."

Clint's skin was tight against his cheekbones and he looked the most serious I'd ever seen him. When his eyes captured mine, they were dark. "Mayor, stop by my office when you're done."

Mayor. Serious and formal. "Okay," I managed. A knot looped in my stomach as I wondered what Clint would say. I knew he was angry about the danger Juan and I had faced. It took time and effort to return to my assignment. I finished before Juan and stood. "I'll see you later. I guess I never thanked you for saving my life, so thank you."

He tipped his head. "I haven't apologized for putting you in grave danger. I am very sorry."

My shoulders lifted. "You didn't know Oscar would show up at your fish house. I don't blame you for Oscar's behavior and threats. You need to believe that. The way you subdued him led to his capture. I don't know how we—the city and the police department—can ever show you enough gratitude for that."

Tears formed in Juan's eyes. "There is no need. I had help from above." He raised his eyes heavenward.

I carried my paper to Clint's office where he paced in the small space. When he saw me, he took my paper, laid it on his desk, shut his door, and wrapped his arms around me in a near death grip. I had to tell him, "Clint, I'm having a little trouble breathing."

"Sorry." He pulled back and looked at me with red-rimmed eyes. "I can't stop thinking how close you came to death. How could I have forgiven myself? Why didn't I think to go to Juan's fish house when you met him? I could've parked a short distance away, behind a house, kept watch."

I brushed his lips with mine. "Clint, there was no way to predict the killer would track us down there. Right? You trusted Juan, and so did I. I have to admit I was a little leery meeting him at his fish house, but it was more because I hadn't driven on ice in forever and was never crazy about it in the first place."

Clint's eyebrows creased. "Juan messed up big time by not going straight to Detective Garrison."

"He knows that now but was beyond scared for his family, especially for his sister-in-law and niece. You haven't heard this, so brace yourself. Camila is Gina's sister and Sylvie's mother. Juan confirmed Aaron Newel is Sylvie's father."

Clint's eyebrows lifted halfway to his hairline. "How in the world did Chief get involved with Gina's sister?"

"I don't know all the details, but in a nutshell, Camila was unhappy, got involved with Chief shortly before he married Elissa. Chief loved Elissa, not Camila. But you know how that went when he told Elissa. Chief on paid child support and for Sylvie's medical treatments. Even paid for Oscar's drug treatment. Oscar found out

255

Camila planned to leave him. He was jealous of Chief and did the worst possible thing to him."

Clint shook his head. "The worst I've seen in my career."

"Read Juan's account for more details," I said.

"I will. And I'll talk to him and Gina tomorrow. I'm gonna head over to the jail. Garrison plans to question Oscar North, and I want to hear what he has to say for himself."

"I'll head home if that's all right."

He took me in his arms, more gently, and whispered in my ear. "Of course. Do you want me to call your parents, friends, tell them what happened?" he offered.

"Thanks. I do that when I can."

He kissed my forehead, "Leave out the part about Sylvie and Camila."

"I will, but they'll wonder why Oscar did what he did, why he killed the chief."

"Tell them the detectives will be interviewing Mister North and will uncover his motive. Because we don't know for certain what it was."

"You're right. What Juan told me the courts would call 'hearsay,'" I said.

"They would, yes. And unless Oscar confesses, takes a plea deal, the jury will have to decide beyond a reasonable doubt he is guilty."

"True."

He gave me another gentle kiss. "Is it okay if I stop by later, if it's not too late?"

"Please do. It won't be too late, whatever time it is," I said.

26

I made it home on autopilot and must have looked like a robot when I hung up my coat and stuck my boots in the closet, because I had no memory of doing either, but that's where I found them later.

A hot shower was the first order of business before I told my parents and friends the story. I stood under the spray a long time, soaping and rinsing in hopes the Oscar North confrontation memory would wash down the drain with the suds. Fantasyland, no doubt.

I towel dried and dressed in sweatpants, a long-sleeved cotton shirt, and zippered sweat shirt. Wool socks completed my hunker-down-for-the-evening outfit. My phone jingled in my pocket. Adam Newel.

"Camryn, are you okay? I just got off the phone with Clint and had to call you."

"Adam, what a relief your brother's killer is locked up where he belongs. Waves of shock roll through me once in a while, but they'll pass."

"I can't imagine, given how shocked I feel for you. Come to find out Sylvie's father killed her biological father who was my brother," Adam said.

"So Clint told you about Sylvie's mother and Oscar, who he was?"

"He did, and had to tell me the story twice because it didn't sink in the first time. I keep repeating it to myself, but it doesn't seem real," he said.

"I get that for sure. You've had some big-time whammies in the last week."

"True, and not much has seemed possible. After Clint called, I was ready to head back to Brooks Landing, but my wife thought it'd be better to wait till the weekend, for a couple reasons. Clint said Oscar North has his first court appearance Thursday, and I haven't decided if I should be there, or not."

"I wouldn't know what to do if I were you. I know I won't be," I said.

"Of course not. We can't wait to meet Sylvie but wonder what her reaction might be. Clint says her mother has kept Aaron's death from her so far. Like my wife said, maybe we should let things settle for a few days, wait till the weekend. I'm having a heck of a time making decisions."

"Adam, another thing, Sylvie thinks Aaron was her uncle."

"Secrets and lies," was all he said.

"Try to get some rest tonight and hopefully things will be clearer in the morning."

"That'd be good since I'll be in front of a classroom full of students." He chuckled. "I am beyond grateful Aaron's killer is in jail and you and Juan weren't injured in the process."

"Me too. Thanks, Adam."

"We'll be in touch."

I stared at the phone a minute before I called Mom. She was calmer amidst calamities than Dad. I decided a positive spin on the Oscar events would help them both. "Hi Mom, I have some good news. Chief Newel's killer was captured."

She yipped out a "Yes!"

"A man named Oscar North was arrested and basically confessed at the scene. I think they're questioning him now." At least he'd confessed to Juan and me.

"I guess I don't know him, and that's a good thing. So no one else is in danger then, the other officers, or you?"

"No. I was there when he was arrested, and it's a long story I'll tell you in person tomorrow," I said.

"Well, you've certainly got me wondering. Your father and I will be right over."

"Mom, it's cold and dark."

"We're Minnesotans, we can handle it," she said.

The was no way to change her mind. "Thank you."

A loud knock sounded on my back door. "Cami, It's Erin and me, " Pinky called out.

I opened the door, and they tumbled in, almost knocked me over, and nearly smothered me with their hugs.

"We heard from Mark and Jake that you helped catch Chief Newel's killer. Way to go," Erin said.

"We didn't get all the details, just that there was a big showdown on Green Lake. It scared us half to death wondering what happened. But they said you were all right."

Erin set her bag on the counter. "We brought some wine and beer. The guys will be over too."

"So will my parents."

Erin removed two bottles of wine and a twelve pack of beer. "I hope we have enough."

"It's not like any of us drink *that* much," Pinky said.

My parents gave a quick knock and came in. We moved to make room for them.

They gathered me in a hug as my friends had. "Cami, Cami, Cami," Mom said. Dad didn't say a word, so I knew he was deeply touched by it all.

Tears formed in my eyes. "I know. Everything's okay."

Surrounded by loved ones lifted my spirits. We were safe and warm, and the memory of Oscar's threats would frighten me less and less as time went on. Plus, the brightest spot was Sylvie would meet her uncle and aunt and cousins. They couldn't replace her father, the one who had helped care and provide for her, but they were her family.

We navigated our way to the living room. My parents sat on either side of me on the couch. Dad reached his arm around my shoulder, and Mom took my hand in hers. Their gestures took me back to when I was an orphaned five-year-old and had no clue what would become of me. They'd welcomed me into their home without a moment's hesitation and had been my staunch supporters through the ups and downs ever since.

"What can we get you to drink?" Pinky offered and gave them the choices. Mom and Dad decided on a red blend wine they liked, and I chose a lager beer. Erin and Pinky delivered our drinks then served themselves, a red blend for Erin, a lager for Pinky. They sat in the upholstered chairs.

Pinky waited until we'd taken sips then asked in a lowered voice, "Cami, tell us everything, in your own words."

I took a gulp, set my bottle on the coffee table, and ran through a PG version of what had transpired. Except for any reference to Aaron Newel's daughter Sylvie or her mother. Mom made her sucked in "huh" sound when I told them about Oscar's appearance in the fish house. She clutched my hand till the end of the account.

Pinky crawled over, laid her head on my thigh, and hugged my calf. It gave Erin the idea to do the same. Add to that, Dad's arm was still around me and he had a firm grip on my shoulder.

"What was Oscar North's motive for killing the chief?" Erin said.

"That will all come out in the investigation, I'm sure."

"And why did Juan suspect his brother-in-law in the first place?" Mom asked.

"I can't really say at this point, but he had a good reason that will surface soon enough," I said.

"Next time you get the crazy idea to meet someone who wants to pass on secret information at a fish house in the freezing cold on Green Lake, no less, do *not* do it. Promise," Pinky said.

If I'd had a free hand I would have raised it. "I promise." I wiggled a bit. "Is it okay if I take another sip?"

They all shifted, and I was freed. We chatted, but the four of them returned to the drama on the lake time and again. Finally, Mom noticed my discomfort and said, "Enough. Cami needs to think about something else so she can relax before bed."

"So how about them Vikings?" Dad offered to break the somber mood. It was either a sports team or the weather when we needed to change the subject.

Mom groaned. "The Gophers had a better season."

A knock sounded on the back door, and Mark's voice called out, "It's me and Jake. Can we come in?"

"Of course," I yelled back.

Pinky, Erin, and I headed to the kitchen. Mark and Jake stood by the door in uniform. They tried to smile, but neither could quite pull it off.

"We can't stay, still on duty," Jake said.

Mark raised his eyebrows. "We wanted to drop by, Cami. Nice to see you got good company with you." His eyes lingered on Erin a long moment.

"You're right, four of my besties have made me feel better."

"Clint said to tell you he'll be by when he finishes up at the sheriff's office. Shouldn't be much longer. He got another officer to cover his shift, so he'll be off the rest of the night," Mark said.

Jake gave Mark a nudge. "Hey, don't jinx the chief by making a statement like that." Before Mark answered, Jake got a call on his radio to respond to a burglary complaint, and they both left.

My dad shook his head. "Still hard to believe Mark grew up to be a police officer. He was such a scrawny kid back when."

The blast from the past lightened our moods. He'd been one of our best friends since kindergarten, and he had bulked up since then. We shared some fun memories as we finished our drinks.

"It meant the world to me that you all came over. I've calmed way down, so feel free to take off. Clint will be here soon," I said.

Mom laid her hand on mine. "You'll call if you need us?"

After they left, I semi-lounged on the couch and tucked a comforter around my body. The cold wind whistled outside and took me back to those moments of terror when Oscar broke into the fish house and told Juan and me what he had planned. I shuddered despite the warm house and cozy cover. My phone startled me when it rang some minutes later. I fumbled with the button. "Hi, Clint."

"Camryn, I hate to tell you this, but I'll be at a call a while yet. A long while, it looks like."

It sounded like he was in a hospital emergency area. "Are you okay, are you hurt?"

"I guess you can figure out where I am. No, I'm fine. I'll fill you in later, but it doesn't look like I'll make it over anytime soon. You okay for now?"

"Yep. Lots of company tonight, and I'm pretty worn out, so don't worry—at all—If you can't come over. Take care of what you need to," I said.

"I'll touch base when I can."

Tears welled in my eyes when we disconnected. It seemed that doggone it, Mark had jinxed Clint after all. I pulled the cover even tighter around me, stretched into a reclining position, and fell asleep. Soft raps on the back door woke me up. I had no idea what time, or even what day, it was. Was it an emergency?

I freed myself from the comforter, hurried to the door, and called out, "Yes?"

"Camryn, it's me." Clint.

I unlocked and opened the door. The icy air surrounded him and caught my breath when he stepped inside. "You were sleeping," Clint said.

"I guess I did kind of pass out."

"I should go, let you get needed rest."

I reached over and unzipped his police jacket. "Please stay, for a while at least. You're probably more done in than I am."

He shrugged off his jacket and took off his boots. "Relaxing with you is just what the doctor ordered."

"What can I get you to eat or drink?"

"Nothing. Well, maybe water or a soft drink. No beer while I'm in uniform."

"I suppose." I got him a bottle of water from the fridge and he chugged it down. It made me smile. "Want another?"

Clint huffed out a breath. "No, I'm good. Guess I was thirstier than I realized." He threw the bottle in the recycling bin under the sink then took my hands in his. "I washed up, but didn't take time to go home and shower. I know you're kind of a cleaning machine."

"Yes, I like to keep my house and shop clean, and cleaning is good therapy for me, but I'm not worried about germs you might have on you. They should've all frozen when you were waiting outside my door."

He cracked a smile. "Huh. Valid point."

"I'm not afraid to kiss you, if that's what you were hinting at."

His arms were around me and his lips covered mine in a nanosecond. Excitement flowed through me. When my legs weakened and started to buckle, Clint lifted me, carried me into the living room, and set me down on the couch. He snuggled in next to me, and we held on tight.

"So the hospital visit? It was Oscar North, of all people. Detective Garrison started his interview. Oscar lawyered up from the get-go. Then said he didn't feel well, needed to lie down. He was being escorted to his cell when he keeled over.

"I was behind the deputies, and my first thought was he was faking it, but when I looked closer, I saw his face was red, he was covered with sweat. The ambulance crew arrived in no time. Oscar's such a big guy, a few of us helped lift him on the stretcher.

"Seems he had a heart attack and will need a couple stents. So he's resting not so comfortably with his hands and feet double cuffed to a hospital bed in a room they reserve for special circumstances. They'll keep deputies posted around the clock to watch him like hawks."

It left me numb. "I can't feel bad for Oscar. He's the worst of the worst. A week ago he killed Chief Newel, tried to kill Juan and me tonight."

"Evil all right."

"It's kinda scary he's not in jail." I trembled at that realization.

Clint squeezed my shoulder. "Not to worry, Camryn. He'll be in jail again after his heart procedure."

"What about his first appearance in court? Adam said it'd be on Thursday."

"They tell me he could be released from the hospital right after surgery tomorrow. In that case, they won't have to bring the court proceedings to him. Meantime, deputies will keep him restrained. He won't be going anywhere."

"Okay." My fears might be irrational, but they were real.

"I talked to Adam. He was so relieved his brother's killer was caught. He's hoping to bring his family here to meet Sylvie, maybe this weekend," he said.

"He called me, and he's pumped about that. I hope her mother agrees to it." I pressed my body tighter against his, awed by the comfort his warmth and strength gave me. And fell asleep in his arms.

27

The next two days passed in a blur. Clint had been right—Oscar was released a few hours after four stents were inserted in two arteries and returned to the Buffalo County Jail. They put him in an observation cell to keep a close eye on him. The doctor told him he was lucky he got medical treatment when he did. When Clint told me that, my first snarky thought was, "Lucky for who?"

I had decided against attending Oscar North's first court appearance. Clint called me right after. "The judge set Oscar's bail at two million dollars."

"Wow, that's high."

"About right for the charges against him. A bond would cost him between two and three hundred thousand and there's no way he could post that, according to Gina. I gotta go, talk to you later."

I was at the shop and sank down on the chair behind the counter. I felt emotional and exhausted given everything that had happened the past nine days. Pinky walked in with a mug of something. "I poked my head in a minute ago and when I saw how sad you looked, I figured you could use this." She handed me the mug.

A big dollop of whipped cream with slivers of chocolate and chopped pecans hid what was underneath. "I smell chocolate."

"It's a double chocolate with caramel. It'll help what ails you."

"Thanks, Pink." I took a sip. "Ooh, it's a drink version of turtle candy. You come up with the best combos."

"Right. Why reinvent the wheel?" She studied me. "You're either going to need another turtle drink, or a nap."

"It's all catching up with me, I guess." I told her about Oscar's bail.

"That is *so* good to hear. You don't have to worry about ever facing him again."

"Unless he goes to trial and I have to testify against him." I'd given my friends and family more details about Oscar, his threats against Juan and me.

"Eew, I didn't think about that." She crossed fingers on both hands. "I'm holding on to the hope that won't happen."

"Me too."

Adam and his family arrived in Brooks Landing Friday evening. The outside temperature had risen to a balmy forty degrees. January thaw, a reminder or teaser warmer weather was ahead. After a couple more months of frigid temps, that is.

Clint phoned with the news Gina had convinced Camila that Sylvie should meet Adam and his family. When Camila told Sylvie the sad news about Chief, she added the good news that she had another uncle, aunt, and cousins.

I was okayed to tell my friends and family the larger story about Oscar, Camila, Sylvie, Chief, and Elissa. They all agreed it made the pieces fall into place, why Oscar had killed Aaron Newel, as wrong as that was.

After some discussion between Adam and Gina, they decided Brew Ha-Ha would be a good place to meet, after hours. A neutral spot, not at Chief Newel's house, and not at Camila's or Gina and Juan's.

Pinky was excited her place was chosen and planned special treats. Heart-shaped monster cookies, both mini chocolate and mini vanilla cupcakes, frosted with the opposite flavors, some topped with colored sprinkles. Along with a variety of her most popular muffins and scones. I picked up milk and bottles of water so we wouldn't deplete Pinky's supply.

Clint, Pinky, and I were ready ahead of time and checked the clock every few seconds until Adam and his family arrived. After they'd removed their outer wear, he introduced us to his wife Janie, his seven-year-old daughter Helen, and six-year-old son James. Janie was petite with intense brown eyes. Both kids were as cute as could be. Helen favored her father in looks and James looked more like his mother.

After we exchanged greetings, Adam clapped his hands together. "Well, here we are."

Janie linked her arm in his. "It will be a fine get together." And it was.

Clint opened the front door when he saw Camila, Sylvie, Gina, and Juan outside. Juan and I exchanged a nod. Two survivors. All four stared at Adam and his family for some seconds until Adam and Janie stepped forward. Clint introduced them.

Adam reached for Camila's hand, shook it, and gave her a hug. "I can't tell you how happy I am to meet you."

"Me too," she said.

He released Camila, then took Sylvie's hand and went down on his knee in front of her. "You are a beautiful young lady. It means the world to me to find out you're part of our family." He turned and waved to his children who'd hung in the background. "Kids, come and meet your cousin."

Sylvie's big grin revealed a missing front tooth. Helen was all smiles. "Hi, Sylvie, I'm Helen and this is James." She caught his arm and dragged him in beside her. "He's shy, but he likes you. Right, James?"

He nodded and managed a small smile.

"Sylvie, did you see the treats we get to choose from?" Helen said.

She shook her head.

"Come and see."

Gina and Juan came to the rescue when Sylvie didn't move. "I know they'll be good," Gina said and led the children to the sweets table.

Clint got a phone call and slipped into Curio Finds to talk.

Pinky and I had stayed in the background and stepped in to help serve. I got choked up when the dear little ones eyed the treats and looked up at Pinky and me like we were rock stars.

As the kids decided what to take, I caught Juan's attention and touched my fist to my heart. If not for his quick thinking and bravery beyond belief, neither of us would've been at the party. Or any that followed.

Gina and Juan helped the children with their plates and drinks and guided them to a table. Adam, Janie, and Camila huddled in the back of the room and spoke quietly. Pinky elbowed me, nodded their direction, and whispered, "Aside from the tears streaming down Camila's cheeks, they look like they're having a pretty good time."

I nudged her back and quietly said, "They have lots to talk over, to settle."

"I s'pose. Well, from what I've noticed about Adam, he'll be a good one to help figure things out."

The three left their huddle and joined the rest of us. Clint returned from his call and helped himself to a monster cookie. He held it up as if to toast, smiled, and took a bite. As the new family got more comfortable together, chatter and laughter filled the room.

Adam phoned later that evening. "Thank you again for all your help."

"Happy to do what I could."

"Sylvie's a sweet girl, and when she smiled my heart stopped a moment. She has my mother's smile, and it made me wish she was still here for her grandchildren."

"Yes."

"Wasn't it great the way my kids took to Sylvie? And she took to them? The more they were together, the better they liked each other. And Janie and I had a fruitful conversation with Camila. We'll get to Brooks Landing as much as we can arrange."

"That'll be good for all of you."

"Agreed. I wanted to share what Camila told us. It cleared up a lot of unknowns. Turns out Aaron wasn't in their lives until last summer because he'd wanted to protect Camila and Sylvie and their life as a family with Oscar," Adam said.

"Really?"

"When Sylvie got her cancer diagnosis, it hit Oscar hard. He'd had a drug problem in the past and relapsed, started using again, and ended up in treatment. That's when Camila reached out to Aaron for help. He insisted on paying Sylvie's medical expenses, taking her to her treatments, caring for her when her mother worked. He even paid for Oscar's treatment."

"Wow, that's an awful irony."

"Tell me about it. Camila hadn't told Sylvie Aaron was her father because she thought Oscar was her biological father, and why confuse her. She'd planned to tell her at some point."

"Sylvie knows now, right?"

"Yes, after Oscar was arrested. Sylvie cried and said Aaron was a good man, took good care of her when she was sick. Camila's been through hell, what with Aaron and Oscar and Sylvie's cancer on top of everything else. But the good news is she's healthy again. And with Oscar out of the picture, Camila can focus on her daughter and their future."

"The positive in all this." I thought of the private detective Stormin' had hired. "No one saw Sylvie at Aaron's house?"

"I don't know. Camila said Aaron picked her up and brought her home again, so no one would see Camila drop her off and ask questions. I suppose he drove into his attached garage and shut the door. Maybe when the time's right I'll ask Sylvie about it."

Adam cleared his throat then went on. "Sylvie is Aaron's rightful heir. Camila seemed surprised when I told her that, it hadn't occurred to her. She was so grateful for all that Aaron already gave them. We'll be meeting with an attorney to iron out the details. The proceeds from the sale of Aaron's house and property will go into a trust for Sylvie. Camila wants me to take any personal items Aaron owned, so we'll see how that all shakes down," he said.

"It'll work out, Adam. Your heart's in the right place."

"And before I forget again, when I talked to the priest and funeral director, with everything up in the air, we decided to wait a while for the funeral. Now that his killer's in jail, I'm more ready to make the arrangements."

"That makes sense."

"Hopefully we'll be able to figure out the missing pieces of the puzzle. And if we don't, in the scheme of things, it's not all that important. We've got the best of Aaron in Sylvie, and that's what's important," he said.

A wise and kind man. "I agree one hundred percent. Take care, Adam." *Until we meet again.*

I recognized Clint's knock on my back door a while later. He smelled like fresh air and masculine herbal soap. We locked lips in a long and longing kiss, then Clint whispered in my ear, "What have you got planned for the rest of the evening?"

"I'm open to suggestions."

"Camila, Gina, and Juan would like us to join them for a late supper. At Gina's."

I leaned back. "That's a bit of a surprise."

"They feel responsible at some level for what happened with Oscar, to Chief, and to you. Juan especially wants to have a meal together, his way of apologizing."

"That's nice, but not at all necessary."

"It will make them feel better. They're making chicken and rice enchiladas, along with beef tacos and a nacho tray."

My stomach growled. "You don't know how good that sounds. Real food. First dessert at Pinky's and then a tasty dinner at Juan's and Gina's. I guess it might help give them—all of us, really—some closure." I poked his belly. "And we can fool around later."

He hugged me tighter. "You don't say."

"I got a call from Adam and it helped clear up some things."

"Do tell."

After I finished, he said. "Good to know, all of it."

Juan opened the door for Clint and me. Sylvie stood a step behind him with a sweet, dimpled smile. The Lopez's house smelled like a fine Mexican restaurant with a hint of smoke from burning logs in the fireplace. Inviting. Gina and Camila came in from the kitchen. Juan took our coats, handed mine to Sylvie, and they carried them to another room.

Gina wore a slight frown. "Thanks for coming over, Mayor. And Chief, you too. Now that everything's out in the open, Camila and Juan and I realize it should never have happened that way."

Camila folded her hands and sucked in a breath. "Oscar was a mean man, and I kept that a secret from Aaron. I shouldn't have. I was afraid of Oscar, but never thought he'd kill anyone. Even after Aaron died, I didn't want to believe it was Oscar who did it. When I heard Aaron had been killed, I couldn't think straight. It wasn't until Oscar disappeared that Juan got suspicious, told me that Sylvie and I needed to hide."

Juan and Sylvie returned. Gina shook her head a tad so we'd change the subject.

"I sure had a fun afternoon at Brew Ha-Ha, Sylvie. How about you?" I said.

She smiled and nodded. "I got to meet another uncle and my cousins. Helen's fun and likes to talk. James is quiet." She didn't have a lisp, like she'd had in my dream.

Camila put her hand on Sylvie's shoulder. "And you're somewhere in between the two of them. It'll be nice when they come visit again."

"Mommy, can we go to South Dakota to see them sometime?"

Camila leaned over and kissed the top of Sylvie's head. "We'll do that."

"Supper's ready if you are," Gina said, and my stomach growled again.

We took seats around the table. Gina and Camila set steaming dishes of food in front of us that looked as good as they smelled. Juan asked us to join hands. I sat between Clint and Sylvie. Clint's hand felt like Goliath's compared to dainty Sylvie's. Juan said grace and the feast began.

After we'd finished, I asked to speak to Camila and followed her to a bedroom. "What is it?" she asked.

"I have a couple questions. The detective may have already asked you."

"What are they?"

"You know about the note that was sent to Aaron, with the poison on the envelope?"

"Yes, Detective Garrison told me about that. He asked if I knew where Oscar had gotten that note, and I figured it out. Sylvie was at Aaron's the weekends I worked and Oscar was in treatment.

"I found the note in her backpack, not sure how it got in there, and laid it on the counter to give it back to Aaron. It ended up in a stack with other papers and disappeared. I thought it must've gotten thrown away accidentally and kind of forgot about it. Oscar must've found it when he came home, after he got out of treatment. And . . . " She didn't finish.

I touched her arm. "Thanks for telling me. Take care of yourself and that beautiful daughter of yours."

She nodded slightly.

On the drive back to my house Clint asked what Camila and I had talked about. When I told him he said, "Oscar must've been smarter than he looked, coming up with that scheme."

"I guess. Did Garrison tell you if Oscar showed up on any of the PD's cameras?" I asked.

"No, I asked him that point blank after Oscar was arrested. They'd gone back though a month of footage. Aside from staff, the only other people were those escorted by staff. People with appointments, basically."

"So Oscar must've mailed the letter." At a huge risk.

"Justice will be served, Camryn."

Inside my house, we settled on the couch and Clint took my hands in his. "I wasn't sure how everything was going to shake down when the two families met. It went far better than I dared hope."

"They're all good people. There'll probably be bumps along the way settling Aaron Newel's estate, but they'll work through it. That's what neutral parties, like attorneys, are for."

"How true." Clint pulled me against his chest. "Now, as far as you and I are concerned, didn't you say something earlier about fooling around?"

"Good memory." I reached my arm around his neck, and we came together in a series of toe-curling kisses. And the rest, as they say, is history.